GRADUATION SUMMER
OF
2 GIRLS, 2 CATS

THE MAGIC AND THE MYSTERY CONTINUE

By LAURA BETH

Many more Adventures!

DEDICATION

This book is dedicated to my nephew, Austin, who was one of the strongest warriors of our time and will forever be one of the most **amazing** angels.

TABE OF CONTENTS

ACKNOWLEDGEMENTS

First and foremost, I want to thank GOD for my
wonderful family.
Also, I want to say a big thank you to my cousin, Linda,
who not only praises my work, but helped me review this book
for my silly mistakes.
And, I want to thank my son for sharing my dream with
his classmates on...
"The Great American Dream"!

PREFACE

After traveling and studying abroad for a year, a magical and mystery destiny leads twenty-year-old Lacey to move into her grandparents' home that is right beside of her great-grandparents' old farmhouse. The old farmhouse is where Lacey's grandmother, her great-aunt and their four brothers had all been born and raised. Just before Lacey moves into her grandparents' home, her Great Aunt Daisy is moved to the nursing home where Lacey's grandparents now reside.

Now, the old-farmhouse is supposedly empty, but Lacey notices lights coming on and going off during the wee hours of the night. She invites her thirteen year-old cousin, Jillie, to partner up with her to investigate what is going on at their great-grandparents' home. Jillie is so excited to not only hang out with her cool, older cousin, but to spend time on the farm. Jillie has wonderful memories of her toddler years, when she stayed with her grandparents and her Great Aunt Daisy.

During their investigations, they find a mother cat, Miss Virginia, and her kittens. The girls name their kittens Tye and Tess after their great-grandparents. Not only do they discover that these cats are magical and are a part of their destiny, but they are also reunited with their Uncle Jake. Jake, who has been missing for ten years, discovered a time portal when he was just five-years-old that took him back three hundred years to a time when American Indians lived and survived on this very farm and the lands surrounding it. He has been living on this very land only three hundred years before his family. His life is with the tribe, known as the Cheraw. He not only has become apart of this family and culture, but has a wife and twin boys.

The girls realize that it was the birth of their sweet and innocent cousin, Nadia, which began unraveling the magical and mysterious destiny that had been woven so many centuries before their time.

Not only Jake, but many others from the past and the present help the girls realize their ties and destinies to their family farmland. Lacey and Jillie become an integral part of the magical mystery of this land, as they wait for their young cousin to grow up and join their quest to save their great-grandparents' farmland. Now, Lacey has completed her Environmental Law Degree and Jillie has just graduated from high school. The summer begins as more magic and mystery leads the girls to even more unbelievable, magical and mysterious adventures.

1 COUSINS UNITE

Thanks for picking me up Lacey," Jillie said, as she opened the back car door and heaved her suitcase onto the back seat.

"No problem," Lacey said, smiling at her cousin. "Now, where are those two little angels of ours now?"

Jillie looked around and the cats were nowhere to be found.

"I guess they decided to just disappear and beat us home," Jillie said, as she buckled herself in the front passenger seat and closed the door.

Lacey shook her head and quickly exited the airport to get back to the farm.

"Just why do you think they didn't want you to go on your graduation trip?" Lacey asked. "I cannot imagine that they were just being silly cats. But who knows? Sorry that your trip was ruined, but I'm happy to have you with me. Did you call your parents?"

Jillie shook her head no. "No. I don't think I want to do that just yet. Don't you think we should see what those cats are up to? And how do I explain to them that the cats didn't want me to go?"

"Yeah, you're right and we better get to the farm and see what they're up to now," Lacey said. "You know, Gregory, your brother and all the cousins are coming to help me out this week and will be there with us all summer." Lacey quickly looked over at Jillie as she made an 'oh no' face.

"Oh yeah, what do we tell them?" Jillie asked.

"I don't know, but I am sure we'll think of something like we always do to keep our wonderful secret," Lacey replied.

The girls shared some of their stories they had had with their over protective cats. They laughed and they cried at the stories of Vance Service and the boys on the ski slope.

Jillie gave Lacey more details of her wonderful visits to the mountains and they discussed Miguel and his parents. Jillie pulled out the necklace and showed it her cousin. Lacey filled Jillie in on her graduation visit with Will, Blake and Beautiful Butterfly. She told Jillie of the woods, how she sensed danger and how the cats warned of the strangers on the other side of the woods.

"Do you think the people, who have witnessed our cats' magic, will ever tell what they have seen?" Jillie asked

"Nope, because anyone else would think they are plain crazy," Lacey said, with a quick wink at her cousin. "Jillie, I forgot to tell you something," Lacey said, thinking about her beautiful graduation gifts from Will and Uncle Jake. "Do I have a surprise for you?"

"What? Tell me," Jillie pleaded.

"No, you have to wait until we get back to the farm," Lacey said, with a smirk. "Trust me, it's worth the wait."

"Okay," Jillie answered and she cranked up the radio to listen to a favorite song.

The girls sang along with the song as loud as they could. They were both happy to start a summer of pure fun. As they drove on, Lacey's cell phone rang and vibrated several times, before the girls heard it over the music.

Lacey answered, "Hello".

"Lacey, it's your Uncle Jeremy. Just what does your cat and your cousin's cat look like?"

"Tye is all grey with a cute white star on his forehead. Tess is all white with a grey tipped tail. Why do you ask?" Lacey replied back to her uncle, with a puzzled voice.

Jillie turned down the music and turned her attention to her cousin's conversation.

"Well, Stacey and I have noticed a grey and white cat hanging around our house and it kind of looks like that cat's picture you girls have shown us at the farmhouse. And now, I swear I just saw your two cats with her and they have another little kitten with them," Jeremy went on, until Lacey interrupted.

"What? You think our cats are over at your house with Miss Virginia and another kitten?" Lacey almost yelled out, with excitement and surprise.

Jillie was all ears. "Put him on speaker phone Lacey," Jillie whispered.

"Oh yeah," Lacey whispered and did as Jillie requested.

"Well, it's just too odd Lacey. Where are you? Can you come over here? I know it's a little bit of a hike for you to come all the way across town," Jeremy ended. "We're not scared or anything, but we're just confused why all the cats would be here and it's a little unbelievable that it would be Miss Virginia, Tye and Tess all the way over here.

"No, it's okay. Jillie and I are on our way right now," Lacey said, looking at Jillie shrugging her shoulders

"Jillie?" Jeremy asked. "I thought she was off to Pennsylvania, Paris or something with a P."

"She got kind of sick this morning and opted out of going and called her big cousin to save her. I think her mom and dad are out of town or something," Lacey replied, making it up as she went along. She knew that their Uncle Jeremy was too busy to even really think about it all.

"Oh, sounds good. I'll see you here in about forty-five," Jeremy said and hung up before Lacey could say good-bye.

Lacey clicked her cell phone off and quickly looked at Jillie. "Something is happening little cuz. Uncle Jeremy thinks Miss Virginia, Tess and Tye are hanging out over at his house and they have a little grey and white kitten with them! Miss Virginia must have decided that Nadia needed her protector now. I hope that doesn't mean something bad could happen to our cute, little cousin. She's not even five yet."

"Wow. I wonder if this is why they didn't want me to get on that plane to Paris. Something is definitely in the works. Maybe they just wanted us to see this new little brother or sister of theirs," Jillie said, thinking out loud.

Lacey turned down another road heading towards her uncle's home. The girls were quiet, as they were both deep in thought. Lacey's phone rang and it was Blake.

"Hey Hun, what's up with you?" Lacey asked, with seriousness in her voice.

"Just seeing what's happening with you. Didn't hear from you and thought I should check in to see what is happening over at the farm today. I have to do some things at work, but I promise I will come out in the afternoon and help you with the horses. I don't want Tame Tiger to come and hunt me down for letting him down on horse care.

"Oh my gosh Blake, you're not going to believe what all is happening."

Lacey tried to explain things to Blake, while she was driving. Jillie listened and was so curious when Lacey asked if Blake could be sure and drive by and look in on the place and the horses.

"Horses?" Jillie whispered.

Lacey smiled and held up her finger for her cousin to wait. The surprise was just given away, but it was kind of ruined anyway with the other surprises. Lacey promised Blake that she would call him as soon as they found out anything and they hung up. Blake had promised to drive over to the farm, before heading to his work, to check in on Storm Cloud and Warrior Girl.

Lacey hung up and didn't give Jillie a chance to ask and started telling her about their wonderful horses.

"I am going to have a colt? OMG; it's a dream come true. I have wanted a horse for as long as I can remember. Oh, I cannot wait!"

"You're a true born vet little cuz. Only you would have

14

wanted such a big animal. I am getting used to them, but never in my wildest dreams would I have thought I would have a horse. Warrior Girl is beautiful and Storm Cloud is so handsome. Blake and I love them dearly," Lacey said, as she turned her car into their uncle's driveway.

The girls' uncle came out of the house holding their little cousin, Nadia. "Hey girls; come on in the house. I was just about to feed this little gal. You know how she loves her food."

The girls both laughed and both of them blew out their cheeks. Their little cousin loved her food and everyone else's too. Jillie held out her arms for her little cousin to come to her. Nadia didn't hesitate and practically jumped into Jillie's arms.

"How is my little monster eating machine?" Jillie asked giggling, as Nadia grabbed a hand full of Jillie's long blond hair.

Jeremy led the way and the girls followed him into the kitchen. Jillie placed her little cousin in her booster seat. Nadia was eager for her food. Lacey looked around and didn't see any sign of cats and walked over to the kitchen window and looked outside. There they were all lined up: Tye, Tess, little grey and white kitten and Miss Virginia sitting close to the edge of her uncle's yard near the woods.

"Jillie, come here," Lacey commanded.

Jillie walked over, looked out and looked back at her cousin with big eyes, as if saying "what do we do now".

Their uncle was beside Nadia gently talking with her as she ate her liver pudding that Nadia loved to call liver mush. Jeremy had also reheated her hotdog.

"Where is Aunt Stacey?" Lacey asked.

"Oh she and the boys are out and about. Adam had football practice and Luke loves to watch and get all dirty. I chose to watch Nadia and make sure those cats don't do anything weird."

"Oh Uncle Jeremy, Miss Virginia is a wonderful cat. I think she wants to bring her new kitten to you or little Nadia. Remember at Thanksgiving every year, how the cats just love Nadia. I think she wants little Nadia to have her own cat," Lacey explained.

LAURA BETH

"I don't know about that," Jeremy answered back, as he continued to give Nadia more food to devour.

"Come on Jillie, let's go out and see if we can actually get close to the new kitten," Lacey said.

Lacey and Jillie headed out the door and walked slowly towards their cats, Miss Virginia and the new, little, adorable kitten sitting there so sweetly poised. Its eyes were so different looking than Tye's or Tess'. They were big, round, golden eyes for such a small little kitten.

Miss Virginia got up first and meowed at her kittens. All three obeyed and got up and started walking toward the girls. Tess and Tye guarded their new little brother or sister. The kitten seemed totally calm.

Lacey went down on her knees. Jillie followed her older cousin's lead and kneeled down too. Miss Virginia quickly moved towards the girls and rubbed all around them. The girls both sat down and held out their hands to Miss Virginia. Tess and Tye hurried to get to the girls and the little kitten gracefully moved behind them and waited its turn.

Lacey held out her hand towards the little kitten and it came slowly up to her and sniffed, but didn't go any further. Jillie watched and held out her hand. The kitten moved to sniff Jillie's hand and sat quietly down.

"Uncle Jeremy," Lacey hollered towards the back door. "Bring Nadia out here."

A few minutes later the girls' uncle came out holding Nadia's hand. When Nadia saw the cats, she pulled lose from her dad's hand and ran as fast as she could to reach the cats. Miss Virginia, Tess and Tye all quietly sat back and watched. Lacey and Jillie also quietly sat and smiled, as their little cousin met her protector. Jeremy held his breath not knowing all that there was to know.

Nadia scooped up the tiny grey and white kitten with the big, yellow eyes and hugged it tight. Everyone could hear the kitten purring, as it snuggled its little face into Nadia's neck. Jeremy whipped out his phone and put it on camera mode and snapped this unbelievable picture. Lacey and Jillie looked at one another and exchanged winks.

"Well now, if that isn't something," Jeremy commented and stooped down to join everyone else on the ground.

Miss Virginia made her way over to Jeremy. She softly meowed and rubbed up against him. Jeremy smiled and sat down too and Miss Virginia crawled upon his lap.

"Wow, this cat seems like she knows me or something," Jeremy said, as he smiled and rubbed the cat. "Oh yeah, she is the cat that everyone thinks is a descendant of Great-Grandma Tess' cat. Maybe she does know me. I used to tease that cat whenever it was sitting in the bathroom window. I would come up to the screen, from the outside, and put my face into the screen and just stare at her. She would push back and we would have a contest to see who could push the hardest."

"Well they say that cats have nine lives Uncle Jeremy," Jillie said.

"Yeah and she seems like she really loves Nadia. I mean, she came all the way over here to bring her a kitten," Lacey said, wondering if their uncle would start thinking too much now.

"Yes, it's kind of strange, but 'what-the-hey', my daughter loves that little kitten and that kitten loves my daughter. That is enough for me to be 'in'," Jeremy said, as he smiled looking at this daughter and continued to rub Miss Virginia.

"So, you're going to let her keep it?" Lacey asked. "What is it anyway; a boy or a girl? What do you think you should name her?"

Then, to all of their amazement Nadia answered the question. "She is my cat Tea."

"You mean kitty Nadia," Jeremy said, as he thought about her stuffed animal, Kitty.

"No, my cat Tea," Nadia said again.

"That is cute. You can call her catty," Jeremy said.

Nadia put her little fur ball down and stood up. She placed her small hands on her hips and looked straight at her dad.

"No daddy, she is Tea."

Jillie figured it out. "Uncle Jeremy, Nadia wants to name

her cat Tea."

Nadia jumped up and down. "Tea; my cat is my sweet Tea!"

As Nadia jumped up and down, her tiny necklace caught her cousins' eyes.

"Hey, what is that necklace you're wearing little Nadia?" Lacey asked moving towards her little cousin.

"My 'toof', I mean tooth rock necklace," Nadia said, as she held out a small, black shark's tooth wrapped with a thin, leather rope.

"Oh that is something I found in Jake's things when we were young and he let me hold onto it. He told me not to lose it. Nadia found it in my bedside table drawer and wanted it. She wears it all the time."

The girls both glanced at one another. Lacey sat back and just smiled.

The kitten jumped up into her arms and Nadia responded immediately and caught her perfectly in her arms.

"Wow, my daughter is a smart little thing. Don't you think girls?" Jeremy asked, as he looked towards his nieces and smiled.

The three adults all laughed, but Nadia sat back down looking and talking with her kitten. Tess and Tye joined the little ones and they all seemed to have their own private conversation. Lacey and Jillie noticed, but Jeremy only thought his daughter was too cute. Nadia's older cousins sensed a power stronger than either one had even known. Seeing their little cousin surrounded by these three cats made them see a very strong bond. Nadia looked up and smiled at her older cousins with a look of much knowledge. The girls glanced at one another and then at their uncle, who was just sitting back watching his daughter looking cute.

"So girls, what do we do? Do you think we're supposed to keep this little furry thing? Do you think Miss Virginia here wants to leave Tea with Nadia?" Jeremy asked, holding up the mother and rubbing his nose to hers. "Maybe we'll just keep Miss Virginia here too and make sure we know what to do with this little thing," Jeremy placed Miss Virginia down and her right eye gave that magical sparkle.

Although Jeremy didn't notice the sparkle, Lacey and Jillie saw the magical sparkle come from Miss Virginia's eye. Yes, Nadia had her protector and nothing would separate them now. Nothing would separate these three cousins from joining together for the rest of their lives. It was truly a magical mystery that keeps bringing surprises and adventures their way.

Lacey and Jillie hung out with their uncle and little cousin for another hour. The girls wanted to ask their uncle about his other brother, but didn't want to bring up the sadness. So, they talked about all the things they were going to work on at the farm and invited their uncle to bring little Nadia over as often as it worked for him and Stacy.

"Uncle Jeremy, I would be happy to baby sit little Nadia some this summer. I think she would love coming over to the farm too," Jillie said.

"We'll see if Stacey is okay with it. I hope she is okay with this catty. I know Luke and Adam will be okay with it, but they will probably want their own catties," Jeremy said.

"Mine," Nadia said looking at her dad.

Lacey and Jillie laughed. Lacey looked at her younger cousin and tapped her wrist to let her know it was time for them to leave. Jillie nodded at her in agreement.

"Oh, I better get some cat food," Jeremy said. "Come on little girl. You and daddy are going to take a ride to the pet store for some kitten and cat food. I'll just ask the pet staff for the best food for these two."

Nadia placed her little kitten down beside its mother and was ready to go without any further explanation.

The girls walked with their uncle and baby cousin to Lacey's car. Jeremy and little Nadia said their good-byes to the girls, Tess and Tye. Lacey backed out of her uncle's driveway, as Jeremy put Nadia in her car seat. Lacey beeped her horn and took off.

Miss Virginia and her little one, Tea, sat on the front porch waiting for Jeremy's and little Nadia's return.

Lacey called Blake to ask if he had fed the horses and also fill him in on the new little addition and the shark tooth necklace that now adorned their little cousin's neck. Blake listened and agreed that things were coming together and the girls' destinies were definitely coming to life. He told Lacey he would see her tomorrow sometime, because work had asked him to work fairly late and he was going to take the day off to help her welcome everyone to the farm with a great bonfire and cookout. Since she had Jillie with her, he knew they would love some girl time.

2 FOR FAMILY

Lacey and Jillie took their two protectors and drove home. The cats sat in the back seat purring away and looking out of their own window. The girls chatted about their cute little cousin and her new, unique protector.

"I hope Tea's appearance doesn't mean anything," Lacey said, as she turned off the highway towards the farm. "And that necklace is just a little too weird. I am betting it opens up the time portal."

"Do you think something bad is going to happen and that is why all of this came about now?" Jillie asked with concern.

"I don't know, but I cannot stop thinking about the feeling I got when we were on our ride with Tame Tiger and Beautiful Butterfly," Lacey responded. "Oh, you have to meet the horses. I hope Blake stopped by earlier. Let's not worry about something we cannot control," Lacey said and turned her car into the farmhouse's driveway.

Before the girls could even get out, the cats magically disappeared from the back seat and the girls saw them dashing to the barn.

"They must know the horses are there, huh?" Jillie asked.

"What don't they know?" Lacey asked back, as she

21

wondered if they knew anything was going wrong somewhere and would make a point to ask them. But, she wanted to have some fun with the horses. She and Jillie needed a chance to ride their horses and roam the farm's land.

The girls ran side by side to the barn. Jillie dropped back a bit to let Lacey lead the way to the horses. The cats were already in the barn and perched upon the stall doors greeting the horses. Lacey opened the door to her Warrior Girl and the horse came right out and greeted Jillie with a nudge.

"Hey girl, you must be Warrior Girl and I hear you have my colt on board," Jillie said and hugged the horse's neck.

Warrior Girl whinnied back and moved her head up and down as if answering yes.

Lacey opened up Storm Cloud's door and he leaped out and pranced all around for Jillie to admire him.

"Well sir, you sure are a handsome thing," Jillie said and held out her hand for him to sniff.

Instead, Storm Cloud came up behind her and pushed her gently towards the saddle and reigns.

Lacey burst out into laughter. "They want to take us for a ride. I think they are as excited as we are to have one another."

"Lacey, I don't really know how to put all this on the horse," Jillie said, with a bit of fear in her voice.

"Oh, Tame Tiger showed Blake and me everything. And, they are so smart they will let you know what is not correct. Watch this," Lacey said and grabbed Warrior Girl's saddle.

Lacey's horse came and stood exactly where she needed to be for Lacey to place the saddle blanket and toss the saddle up and across the horse's back. Jillie quietly stood back admiring Lacey with the horses. Lacey saddled Warrior Girl and then Storm Cloud moved up for his turn. He was shaking his head up and down and making horse noises. Lacey talked to him, as she confidently tightened up the bridle.

"Okay Jillie, get on Storm Cloud so that I can adjust your stirrups," Lacey said, motioning for her cousin to step closer and hop onto the horse's back.

Jillie slowly moved closer and Lacey showed her how

to grab the saddle horn and pull herself up and over. Jillie, being a gymnast, did this with ease.

"Oh my gosh, I am really high up," Jillie commented, as she leaned forward and rubbed Storm Cloud's neck.

Lacey didn't say anything until she was finished adjusting Jillie's stirrups and then she hopped up and onto her own horse's back. In a flash, the girls' magical cats were both tiny kittens and propped up on the girls' shoulders. The girls both giggled and rubbed their protectors.

Lacey turned Warrior Girl around and waited for Storm Cloud to follow and bring Jillie beside her.

"Wow, he knows what to do without me even directing him," Jillie said in awe.

"Oh yeah, they are really so well trained that I haven't really had to do much other than clean the stalls, feed and water them," Lacey answered back and took off out of the barn.

Storm Cloud trotted out with Jillie holding onto the reigns and the saddle horn. The horses took the girls and their cats for a nice trot out into the pasture land that was near the big oak tree. The girls just let the horses take them on their own trail and the horses circled the big oak tree a few times making 'neighing' noises like they were talking to one another. The girls looked at one another acknowledging their intelligence.

Once they had circled the oak tree enough, Storm Cloud picked up his pace and took off in a full gallop. Jillie held on for dear life. Lacey told Warrior Girl to get it on and the three of them took off too. The horses took them way down into the pasture land.

Lacey thought about her ride with Tame Tiger, Blake and Beautiful Butterfly and wondered how things were going with what they had found out about people moving near to the village. She looked out over the land and tried to see if anything had the familiarity of three hundred years ago, but it did not.

Lacey motioned for Jillie to hold up and Storm Cloud understood immediately what he needed to do. Lacey slowed Warrior Girl and came up beside Jillie.

"I cannot shake that feeling of worry for Uncle Jake, Will

and the others back in the village, Lacey said with seriousness. "
I fear that something might be happening, but I think Will, Miss
Virginia or Uncle Jake would come and get us if they needed
us."

"Yeah, I think we should just stay put. Let's get back to the
farmhouse and let me get unpacked. Can I just stay with you for
the summer? I don't really want to stay at the other house yet,"
Jillie said, hoping that Lacey would not mind. She was kind of
scared.

"Of course, I just thought you would like your own place. I
would rather you stay with me too," Lacey answered.

Jillie smiled and relaxed. "Come on big cuz, I'll race you
back. Better yet, I'll let Storm Cloud race Warrior Girl. I'll just
hang on for dear life," Jillie said and gave Storm Cloud a light
kick and he took off.

Warrior Girl reared up and took off. Lacey hadn't expected
that and also held on for her life. Tye just calmly sat enjoying
the wind blowing his fur coat against his skin.

When the girls got back to the barn, the horses both halted
right outside the entrance. Both cats jumped down and ran
inside of the barn. Lacey held her hand up for Jillie to stay put.

Seconds seemed like minutes, but to the girls' surprise the
cats came out in their beast forms followed by Beautiful
Butterfly and Beautiful Light. They were both crying and talking
words that Lacey and Jillie could not understand, but knew
something had to be very wrong for these two women to be
here. Lacey and Jillie immediately jumped off their horses.

Lacey looked around to see if anyone was around. She
grabbed the two women's hands. pulled them inside of the barn
and led them deep into the barn to the far area where the
hidden, earthen door was left open. Jillie, the horses and their
protectors all followed.

Lacey let go of Beautiful Butterfly's hand and turned her
attention to her aunt. She placed both of her hands on her
shoulders. She thought for a moment, and in the strange
language she had learned, slowly asked what had happened.
Jillie listened to her cousin speak the language she had heard,

but did not fully understand.

Beautiful Light grabbed a hold of Lacey and cried. She tried to talk slowly both in the strange language and a few words in broken English. Jillie was now standing beside of Lacey listening and knew something was very wrong.

When their aunt stopped talking, Lacey nodded and looked at her cousin. "We have a big problem little cousin. Uncle Jake, Tame Tiger, the chief and many other warriors have been gone since I was there. I knew that there was something wrong, but they wouldn't let Blake and I remain. We have to go try and help.

Lacey looked back at her aunt and asked if she had the arrowhead to get them all back. Her aunt did not and started crying again pulling on her niece's arm toward the earthen door.

"Jillie, we cannot get back without an arrowhead and Tame Tiger forgot to give me that small one I told you about," Lacey said. "Maybe there is another one in the pouch of Uncle Jake's."

Before the girls could turn around and head to the other house to find the pouch of arrowheads, Jillie's necklace started glowing. The three stones were beaming and shining bright. Lacey went 'week in the knees'.

"Jillie, your necklace is glowing," Lacey yelled out.

Jillie looked down at her necklace. Sure enough. the three stones were brightly lit up.

"I think this will open up the portal. No wonder Wise Owl told me to wear it always," Jillie said holding the quartz part of the necklace in her fingers. "What do we do with the horses?"

Lacey looked at them and they were ready to ride. Tye and Tess were pacing in their tiger and panther forms, growling back and forth to one another. Lacey turned her attention to Jillie.

"Little cuz, I think we have to take everyone through the portal. I'll get our aunt and Beautiful Butterfly to go back through the tunnel and meet us at the oak tree. We'll ride the horses down to the oak tree. But first, we need to leave a note for Blake. I don't want to call him, because he'll want us to wait. I don't think we have time to wait. I'll be right back. I'll

25

leave a note on the door for him to find. He'll know what to do," Lacey said, without thinking about Blake not having an arrowhead either. She was too pre-occupied with helping their uncle, Tame Tiger and the others.

Lacey was able to get their aunt and Beautiful Light to go back through the tunnel to the big oak tree. She sent Tye and Tess with them and told them all to wait for Jillie and her to ride the horses down through the pasture. Jillie helped the women back into the tunnel and shut the door behind them. She remounted Storm Cloud and was outside of the barn waiting for Lacey, who had ridden off on Warrior Girl to the farmhouse.

When Lacey reached the farmhouse, she practically fell off her horse and ran to the farmhouse. Of course, she fumbled with the lock and was feeling overwhelmed, but knew she had to do this. Once inside of the house, she found a piece of paper and a pen and wrote a note to Blake, hoping that no one would find it first.

"Blake, Jillie and I are with Will. He needed some help. Remember how we found out about those people. Must be some kind of problem. Jillie and I decided to help out. If we're not back by the time you read this note, then you know where to find us. -Lacey."

Lacey felt that Blake would figure out something was really wrong, but how could she leave such a weird note without 'giving away the farm'. She was scared. She rushed outside, locked the door and securely placed the note on the door handle where Blake would find it. She forgot that her brother and all of her cousins were due to arrive on the farm starting tomorrow morning to help her get some things accomplished. Her brother was on furlough; her cousins were all on summer break from college or high school. She had recruited them all to start a real farm.

She almost leaped up onto Warrior Girl without even using the horn and stirrups and took off back towards the barn. Jillie was there mounted upon Storm Cloud and impatiently waiting. The horse took off in full speed, as soon as Warrior Girl raced through the gate into the pasture. The girls' long, brunette and blond hair blew out from the wind and the girls never looked back. They were going to save their family.

3 COUSINS GATHER AROUND

Blake decided to drive over to the farm early, since he could not reach Lacey on her phone. As he had learned long before now, whenever she and Jillie were together, they were busy doing who knows what. Being that he was 'in the circle' and knowing all that he did, he had learned to give them their space. He drove over expecting to find them busy working around the horses. He couldn't wait to see Storm Cloud.

When Blake pulled into the driveway, he thought it was odd that Lacey had not parked her car under the awning of the granary. He parked so that others could pull in and find a place to park, since he knew Lacey's and Jillie's brothers and cousins would be arriving sooner or later.

He got out of his car as he looked around and noticed total silence. He walked up to the farmhouse and didn't even notice the note, which Lacey had left on the door and now was laying unnoticed on the porch. He tried to open the door, but it was locked. So, he decided to walk down to the barn to see about the horses. When he found both stables empty, he was a bit worried. He thought maybe they were out riding and decided to sit down and wait a bit since he knew how Lacey would be irritated with him if he made a big to-do over nothing. He knew where the spare key to the house was kept. So he went ahead and looked through the house for any signs of the girls or the cats. He felt a little nervous, but he decided to be patient and wait. He fixed himself a pot of coffee.

As he sat reading the paper, he heard a car drive up and he got up to see who might be arriving already. It was Lacey's brother, Greg. Blake went out to greet him and told him that Lacey wasn't around yet. Greg, of course, didn't think anything about it and pulled his duffle bag from the car and followed Blake inside. They chatted and tried catching up. It was so hard for Blake to not just 'spill the beans', but he contained himself, hoping that the girls would walk into the house at any minute.

But before long, all the other cousins soon arrived and were all wondering where their big lunch was that had been promised by Lacey. They were all raiding the kitchen cabinets and the frig for food. Blake was getting worried and kept trying to reach Lacey.

Blake decided to walk outside and just look down towards the pasture land and see if he could spot the girls and the horses. As he stood on the porch looking over the land, Aiken came out and slapped him on the back.

"Where is that cousin of mine, Blake?" Aiken said sounding a bit ticked off. "I am hungry and part of the deal was that we would be fed really well today. I see lots of groceries, but nothing really made."

Aiken wasn't feeling really well and felt like it was because he was so hungry. Aiken looked down and noticed the piece of paper lying on the porch. He bent down, picked it up and read it out loud. "Blake, Jillie and I are with Will. He needed some help. Remember how we found out about those people? Must be some kind of problem going on and Jillie and I decided to help out. If we're not back by the time you read this note, then you know where to find us. -Lacey."

Blake's face drained and became pure white in front of Aiken. He grabbed the note and read it again. He realized that the girls must have really gone back in time. What should he do now? He started muttering to himself until Greg came out to find Blake talking to himself.

"Hey man; what is going on?" Gregory asked with force.

Aiken looked at his cousin and walked over to Blake and

ripped the note out of Blake's hand. "Here, we just found this note."

Gregory read the note. "Hey man, what is up?"

"Um, I don't know how to tell you or if I should tell you. Oh man, Lacey and Jillie are going to be really ticked off at me or they will really love me," Blake replied.

"Jillie?" Greg asked. "I thought she was off to Paris."

"My sister is not in Paris?" Aiken questioned. "Mom and dad are going to be really ticked."

"Oh man Greg, this is just going to sound really weird, but can we gather your cousins so I can tell this only once, because you all are going to have lots of questions," Blake pleaded with fear in his voice.

Greg saw the fear in Blake's face and heard the fear in Blake's voice. "Okay, let's go inside and get the hungry troop to sit down and listen to what you have to say."

The three young men hurried inside and found Andrew, Chase and Adam devouring whatever food they had found. Greg pulled up a chair next to Adam and grabbed a cold, leftover chicken wing.

"Heads up you gluttons, Blake has something really important to tell us all and I don't think we're going to like what he's going to say by the way he's trembling," Greg said, anticipating the worst like the girls were messed up in something really bad. He imagined all the bad things that could be going on here and thought about how he was going to deal with his little sister. It wasn't going to be pretty if he found out she was doing something illegal. "Spit it out Blake!"

Blake cleared his throat and looked at Greg and all the big boys staring him down, but thought about his Lacey and how she may be in real trouble and needed them all. He just let it all out.

As Blake went into the story from the beginning, the cousins all sat in total silence. Greg occasionally looked at Aiken and they exchanged glances of worry over their little sisters. The others were all in shock and didn't know just what to say or think.

It took Blake almost an hour to tell as much as he could and he knew he was leaving so much out, but the boys all got the message that their little sisters or cousins were very important people and they needed to be saved along with their Uncle Jake!

Blake finished up and pulled out a chair. He fell into it with exhaustion and worry.

Greg stood up and looked at all of his cousins. They were all pretty big dudes and all very intelligent. He would have to put together a game plan and now he knew his military training was going to be put to a test, not to mention his medical skills. He was nervous, but he was a leader and he was ready to go into action.

"Okay boys, I mean men; we are going to have to put together some really intelligent plans. First of all Blake, you need to show us everything you know about this house, the tunnels, the barn, the oak tree and the time portal," Greg commanded. "Okay little cousins, we're all here for the summer to get this place in shape. Well, that is what we're doing. No one is to say one thing to anyone outside of this group. Especially, nothing is to be said to our parents. We cannot worry them or drag them into this, because we don't know what this destiny is all about and our knowing may have already caused harm to many people. Not to mention, our Uncle Jake?"

All the cousins stood up in unison. Andrew held out his hand, as if he were in a huddle with his basketball team. The others followed and all hands towered together. "Cousins united", Andrew yelled out. "COUSINS UNITED!" The cousins all pushed their hands down and then back up as one.

"Blake, show us everything you know," Greg directed. "Everyone, we stay together and be very attentive to detail in case the girls left any signs of danger."

The troop of cousins fell into a single line after Blake, then Greg, then Chase, then Adam, then Andrew and Aiken pulling up the rear. Aiken gave Andrew a pat on the shoulder and Andrew followed sending the message all the way to the front that they were ready to go. Blake took the group up the stairs and into the unfinished attic room and talked about Miss Virginia. Aiken remembered the day he saw them and how strange it was that his dad could not see them, but he did. Blake told how they didn't allow him to see them at first and also told about his first experience with the little fur balls and the cousins all laughed making fun of Blake. At least, they had something to laugh about to cut through the fear and the unknown.

Blake found one of the flashlights the girls had left at the top of the hidden stairs and led the way. As they descended down the hidden stairs from the attic room, Greg yelled back for Aiken to shut the trap door behind him and realized they had left the house totally unlocked.

"Wait Blake, we need to make sure the house is locked up," Greg said, as he grabbed Blake's shirt.

Blake looked back and up at Greg. "Don't worry, we'll end up just under the barn in a few minutes and one of us can run back and lock up the house."

"Okay, don't let us forget. We cannot allow people to wander inside and rob the girls of their things or one of our parents to come in and get all worried. At least, they will just think we're all somewhere together seeing all of our cars," Greg responded and motioned to go ahead.

The boys were all really big and getting into the closet and down into the other stairs was a squeeze. All of the boys recognized the closet that belonged to the front bedroom. They whispered back and forth about how hard it was to get through, but were all totally committed to finding out what all was going on and also wanting to find the girls, their uncle and this life three hundred years in the past!

Once they all gathered into the tunnel under the house, Blake opened the hidden door and showed them exactly where they were. "Man, I never would have gone under here," Aiken said. "I was always so scared to come near the opening."

The others all agreed and were in amazement. They all looked all around before Blake closed the hidden door. "Now follow me and we will end up right under the back of the barn."

"We need someone to run back to the house and lock it back up," Greg said.

"I'll do it," Adam said. "Who has the key?"

Blake took it out of his pants pocket and handed it to Adam. Adam put it deep into his cargo shorts pocket and zipped it shut.

"Okay, let's get moving. We need to see all that there is to see and start deciding what we really need to do. My biggest worry is that our parents may come over and start snooping. We'll need to make sure that we all call them and let them know we're here and the girls have us loaded down with our chores," Greg said, as he had already started thinking of all the bases they needed to cover.

Blake continued to lead the way, but now Greg was walking beside of him, since the tunnel was tall and wide enough for the both of them. The others whispered back and forth, talking about their uncle and what they remembered of him. Aiken didn't say much, but was worried about the girls and how he had been so mean to them that night when Lacey was trying to tell them something was happening over at the farmhouse. He made a promise to himself that he would never think they were silly ever again, if he got the chance to even do that.

"Hey man, you okay?" Andrew questioned his older cousin, Aiken. "Don't worry, they will be okay. They are both strong willed, 'mean as a snake' women. They'll not go down without a really bad fight."

Aiken looked at his cousin and smiled. "You're right. Whoever has them, I do feel sorry for those fools."

Aiken and Andrew laughed thinking how sassy they both could be, even if they were petite, little women. They were definitely fighters and both were tough having to put up with all the boys in the family. The others all laughed too and they began sharing stories how the girls were like two little pistols.

Adam thought about his little sister, Nadia, and how he was going to have to really watch out for her too. He thought about her new kitten, Tea, and how awesome it was that his little sister was so important. No wonder that kitten had smacked him whenever he picked on his little sister. He told his older cousins about his experience with Tea and they all laughed hearing how the kitten was protecting little Nadia.

Chase ran up beside Andrew, started talking sports and made small talk until they walked into the open room just under the barn. They all looked around and noticed the table, the chairs, the jugs and now a nice ladder had been placed by their uncle for the girls.

Blake climbed up the ladder and pushed up the hidden, earthen trap door and disappeared from view. They all followed and were all in amazement of being in their great-grandfather's barn.

"I'll be right back", Adam said. I'll go lock up the house." Adam took off running.

"This is so hard to believe," Andrew said.

"All the hidden stairs and tunnels; I wonder if our great-grandparents knew of them?" Chase asked out loud.

"Who knows, but I bet our Great-Aunt Daisy knew of them. I am thinking these tunnels could have been used for other things, like a way of keeping people hidden," Greg said, as he thought about how unbelievable this all was to him.

"Oh yeah, I studied about slavery and just how cruel people were treated. I hope our family helped people to freedom. No person or animal deserves to be treated so cruelly," Andrew remarked.

"Yeah, why can't people just get along?" Chase asked in agreement.

They all chatted back and forth about what they were finding and how history shaped America to what it is today. They waited until Adam got back from locking up the house and also noticed how great the barn looked.

Blake explained more about Will, who they all had met, but not as Tame Tiger. He told them how he had helped Lacey fix up so many things around the farmhouse and mainly the barn for the horses, Storm Cloud and Warrior Girl. The cousins were listening as if they were five years old listening to a great story.

He told them the story how Will had knocked him out with a squeeze of the neck and they all laughed again. Blake made a face at all of them.

"Just you all wait. Will was being 'tame' around all of you to hide his identity. You better not rub him the wrong way or I am quite certain that he'll take you all on and probably win," Blake said with seriousness.

"Yeah, remember when we all played football and how he was knocking all of us off our feet," Chase said.

Adam finally arrived a little out of breath. "Okay, all is locked up. I even put the dishes in the sink, so it didn't look like we all just left in a hurry."

"Good thinking little cuz. We certainly don't want to cause our parents any alarm," Greg added. "Okay Blake, where to now?"

"Let's go back into the tunnel and I'll take you through the other tunnels, which was an awesome cave." Blake thought for a moment. "Well, it actually still is a cave three hundred years in the past. Wait until you all see what all I have seen. I cannot believe that I actually have not wakened from some incredible dream."

Blake went back to the earthen door and motioned for everyone to head back into the tunnel. This time he and Gregory brought up the rear. Before they both went down, Blake pulled Greg back. "We have to work quickly Greg."

"I know, but I don't know enough to really know what we're up against. Let's just go check out this oak tree and see if there are any signs of anything there," Greg said and he moved quickly back into the tunnel with all of his cousins waiting.

Blake followed and pulled down the earthen, hidden door. "Okay, let's get going."

Nothing was said until they got to another opening and another set of steps were neatly placed under another hidden, earthen door. All of the cousins were no longer in amazement, but anxious to move into action. Blake climbed the few steps and pushed up the door and light shown from the outside. As each one of the boys climbed out, they saw the big oak tree that they were all so familiar with all their lives. Aiken went and checked out the deer stand camera and showed his cousins all the deer that were around.

Blake took Greg around the back of the tree and found the crevice, where he knew that Lacey and Jillie would hide things, like their cell phones. And, they found both of the girls' phones there. So, they now knew that they had definitely gone back in time.

"Hey look at all the hoof prints everywhere," Andrew pointed out.

Greg looked around and saw many footprints now. "I see several different types of prints. Look, this is a big cats' print."

"Oh, that must be either Tye's or Tess'. They are rather big when they are in tiger or panther form."

"Are you sure you're not on something Blake?" Adam asked.

"I agree with Adam. This is way too far fetched," Chase said.

Blake explained the arrowhead and showed them the very discreet place that would allow the time portal door to open.

"Well, we cannot open the portal door without a magical arrowhead," Blake said.

"Oh yeah guys, we need a magical arrowhead," Andrew said with sarcasm.

"Just you wait," Blake replied. "You all are not going to be so sarcastic soon and I know just where we're going to get something that will open this portal. Lacey told me that Nadia's kitten has a little shark's tooth dangling from her neck. It's a necklace that Lacey says Uncle Jake had and gave to Uncle Jeremy. Jake told Jeremy to hold onto it."

"Oh, you're right," Adam added. Dad found it and Nadia wanted it. She put it on her Tea's neck like a collar," Adam explained. "Let me call dad and see if we can get that necklace."

"No don't call your dad. It will cause alarm. We'll just have to get over there and get that necklace. You will have to get that necklace," Greg demanded.

But, they didn't have to plan any such time-wasting trip. All the boys heard it at the same time and they all looked up at the same time. Sitting up in the oak tree was Miss Virginia and little Tea, but the roar didn't sound like a nice, old mother cat and a sweet, little innocent kitten.

"Miss Virginia, oh my gosh, am I glad to see you," Blake said with excitement.

Greg and all the others didn't say a word. They weren't sure what to do. In one quick second, the mother cat and kitten took a magical leap and were down on the ground in front of the guys, but when they landed they weren't the mother cat and her little kitten. A large lioness and a big cougar stood before Blake and the troop of cousins.

"Oh my, oh me, God if you're up there please don't-" Andrew was cut off by Blake.

"HOLY TOLEDO!" Adam yelled out.

Chase jumped back. "OMG!"

"Guys, don't be scared, they are here to help us. Look, the necklace is in Tea's mouth," Blake said, as he moved slowly towards Tea and held out his hand.

The big cat moved towards him and dropped the necklace in his hand. "Good girl, good girl Tea," Blake said and slowly moved to rub the big cougar's head. "So nice to meet you."

Tea loudly purred and rubbed up against him and then walked over to Adam and rubbed up against him too. Adam didn't move. He was in shock that this was Tea, who liked to swat at him. Miss Virginia lightly roared and moved towards Greg and circled all through the cousins giving them a chance to reach out and touch her.

"Okay Blake, what do we do with this shark's tooth?" Greg asked.

Miss Virginia went towards Tea and loudly roared out a few times. In front of everyone, Tea became the tiny kitten and vanished into thin air. She had been told to return and guard Nadia. The cousins all looked at one another and watched as Blake moved to the oak tree and put the tip of the shark's tooth on the spot that would open up the time portal and it did.

The portal wavered waiting for them to step inside, but no one moved. Miss Virginia roared and moved toward the portal door. Once she was just about to step into the passage back in time, she stopped and looked back. She waited for someone to make a move.

"Okay, what do we do here?" Aiken yelled out and wiped a lot of sweat from his forehead. Aiken felt a little winded, but he didn't have time to really think about it.

"Maybe we need to go ahead and follow her," Greg said.

"Not all of us. Let's decide who goes and who stays in case something goes wrong," Andrew directed.

"Yeah, good idea Andrew," Greg replies. "Blake, Aiken and I will go on through this whatever you call it. Blake, we can get back without any trouble, correct?"

Blake nodded yes.

"Okay, give us four hours and if we are not back, then make an 'executive decision'," Greg directed.

"Four hours is going to be a long time," Chase added.

"Yeah, no kidding," Adam said.

"We'll find something to do around here," Andrew commented.

"Alright boys, don't know about you, but I am scared," Gregory said and moved forward.

"Hey cuz, we're calling the troops if you're not back here in four hours. So, get going and get your bodies back here," Andrew yelled at his older cousin.

Gregory looked at Andrew, gave him two thumbs up and grabbed his younger cousin, Aiken. Greg pulled Aiken along and gave Blake a push. "Any special way of doing this Blake?"

"First, give Andrew the shark's tooth to get the portal to open if we don't return in four hours. And, I know this may sound weird, but let's hold hands and maybe Miss Virginia will come up in my arms as Tye and Tess do with the girls most of the time. "Here Miss Virginia, can you change and jump back into my free arm?"

Miss Virginia did just as Blake had requested and quickly took a magical jump. Before she landed in Blake's arms, she magically changed back to her cat form. Blake helped her to adjust in his arm. Before he grabbed Gregory's hand, he turned toward Andrew and threw him the small shark's tooth necklace.

"Don't lose it and come and get us if we're not back by 5 pm," Blake said. Blake grabbed Gregory's hand and Gregory grabbed Aiken's hand. Together, the three walked into the portal opening and they were gone in a flash. The portal closed behind them.

Andrew looked at Chase and then he looked at Adam. They all stared at one another trying to comprehend what all was happening.

"Well, let's go do something," Adam demanded. "Come on guys, let's go find something to fix around here and keep ourselves busy. It's just after 1 and we'll try getting things started so it looks "kosher".

"And, just what do you feel like doing?" Andrew questioned. "I mean, I am not sure I can just act like nothing happened. Let's head up to the farmhouse and shoot some hoops."

"Now that is what I call doing something," Chase added. "Let's go."

The three boys all took off running as fast as they could and ended up having a race to the basketball court Lacey had fixed up for them.

"I win," Adam yelled out.

"You did not. It was a tie," Andrew yelled back.

"Come on you two; who cares?" Chase questioned.

"Okay, a ball would be nice, but where would that be?" Andrew asked.

"Well, let's just go look around and see if we can find anything good to know or do. I don't think I can play basketball right now," Chase said and headed back towards the farmhouse.

Andrew and Adam followed behind and quickly caught up and they all started pushing one another and being silly boys.

***

Meanwhile, Gregory, Aiken and Blake were whisked away back into a time long ago. As Blake had remembered, the ride was quick, cold and before they all knew it they were there. It was dark here right now, which was kind of good for them to move around.

"Wow, what a ride that was," Gregory said, as they all stood looking all around.

"Blake, this is our great-grandparents' land?" Aiken asked, trying to see around in the dark. He could see the outline of the oak tree from the moon light. He was feeling weak, but didn't want to say anything and let it go.

"Yep; that is the oak tree about three hundred years ago," Blake replied.

Miss Virginia squirmed out of Blake's arm, jumped down and turned herself back into her lioness form. She roared so loud that all three of them jumped to attention.

"Okay Miss Virginia, we'll follow you," Blake said. "Remember, it's dark and we cannot see like you can in this dark."

"I still cannot believe that cat, I mean that lion understands English and does all this stuff," Gregory said with disbelief and kept on looking all around.

"Let's just follow her. She'll take us to the village. I think I would know the way, but I really don't go back as much as the girls," Blake said. "Besides, it's dark and I don't want to even try to get you there."

"Well Gregory, I guess our little sisters are more important than we would ever imagine. Let's go save our little sisters and their cats," Aiken commented.

"Okay, do you think there is anything else you should be telling us?" Gregory demanded, as they all followed Miss Virginia, who would glance back from time to time.

"Well, I think I told you as much as I could. I have no idea what could be happening right now. I only saw peace and harmony here. But, as I said, I know there were people approaching and I am guessing that they must not have been friendly. I am worried that is what has happened," Blake said and he picked up his pace to catch up with Miss Virginia.

Gregory and Aiken picked up their pace too as they approached the entry to the forest trail that would lead them to the village. Miss Virginia stopped, turned around and lightly roared. The three of them all stopped and had no idea what she wanted. She walked towards them pushed them back. Then, she turned around and took a few steps away from them.

"Do you want us to wait here?" Blake asked.

Miss Virginia lightly roared again and headed into the woods. She wanted to check out the trail before leading them through to the village. She sensed danger, but wanted to get to the girls, Tye and Tess.

Aiken was happy to stop. He was feeling so winded. Gregory and Aiken hid behind a bush and watched carefully all around. They whispered to one another. Blake hid closer to the forest watching for any trouble.

"I'm scared Gregory," Aiken whispered.

"Me too cuz, but we have to find our sisters and our Uncle Jake," Gregory said thinking about the last time he saw his uncle. He would have been about 16-years-old.

"Yeah, I know. Why didn't we bring our hunting rifles or something?" Aiken asked.

"You know, we're only on an exploration mission right now. We have to see what all is going on before we make any moves or start firing weapons," Gregory replied with the knowledge of a military officer.

"Yeah," Aiken started, "I guess you're right. I am so glad you were able to take some leave." Aiken grabbed his older cousin's arm and pulled him in for a hug.

"Okay, don't get carried away. I am not the hero yet. If we cannot figure it all out, we go get the troops. And, I mean troops little cousin. I can have a small army here in no time, but we need to try and keep this secret a secret for our sisters' destinies sake. At least, I am guessing that is what we need to do," Gregory answered thinking a thousand things.

Miss Virginia crept up so quietly that she scared the cousins making them jump. She lightly roared and moved out from the bush waiting for them to follow.

"All clear to go?" Blake questioned, as he moved over to meet up with Miss Virginia.

Miss Virginia loudly roared and began moving. All three young men took off after her and followed her right into the woods. Gregory was alert to everything he passed. Although it was dark, Gregory checked out the lay of the land as he brought up the rear.

Aiken just kept up and made sure he was in the middle between Blake and Gregory. He was scared and he felt ill, but he tried his best not to show it. Blake felt comfortable, but he was worried about his love and her big tyrant, Tye.

As they neared the other side of the forest, it became thicker and the trail became smaller. Blake remembered this and knew they were getting close. Once at the edge of the woods, Miss Virginia stopped and they all came to a stop all around her. They were all trying to look over the land. Blake pointed towards the village and Gregory could hear the small creek gently tumbling along that still existed in his time.

"Miss Virginia is taking it all in. I am sure if she keeps going, we're good to make it to the village. It's not far."

Miss Virginia roared and took off. The three young men took off full speed ahead. Aiken was hurting, as he tried to keep moving. The moonlit village came into view, but not one person was seen from afar. Miss Virginia slowed down and came to a very slow, deliberate movement as if she was stalking something. The three men stayed close to her and didn't separate until they reached the center of the village, where the huge campfire pit sat cold showing that nothing had been lit here for sometime.

Miss Virginia stopped and roared looking at Blake, then Gregory and then Aiken. She looked all around in confusion and started heading towards Jake's teepee.

"Where is she going?" Gregory asked.

"Not sure, but I think she is heading for your uncle's teepee," Blake answered. "Come on, let's follow her. I don't think anyone is here."

The lioness walked right into the teepee and the three men followed. It was too dark for Gregory and Aiken to see how cozy the family lived here. Gregory stumbled over the mats that lay scattered around the large room and saw the twin boys' beds.

"So, we have little cousins here?"

"Yep, they are about nine I think now," Blake answered.

Aiken didn't move from the opening. He was at a total loss for words and he was out of breath. He was amazed, confused and wanting to sit down. Thinking about his uncle helped him forget his problems.

Miss Virginia roared loudly. She was sad, she was mad and she could not understand why she could not summon her children. She knew something was wrong and she wasn't sure what she needed to do. She sat down and loudly moaned.

Blake walked over and stooped down beside of her big head and gently rubbed her. "I know girl, we'll find them. Can you tell me anything?" Blake questioned looking at her. "You now, we cannot really see you to understand your thoughts."

To the three men's surprise, her eyes lit up and they could see them shine. She wasn't sure they could understand her, but she had to try. So, she looked at Blake and thought out that her two little ones must be somehow hurt. But, he didn't understand, but Aiken did.

"I know what she just thought! I understood her. She feels like her children are badly hurt, because she cannot summon them. She's not sure what she should do, but she feels she must leave us and go scan the countryside."

"Okay, let me try," Gregory yelled out walking over so he could see her eyes.

"Miss Virginia, lay it on me," Gregory said and the cat thought out her worries.

Yes, Gregory and Aiken could understand her, but Blake could not. They were the girls' brothers and they were connected to this land too.

"Okay Miss Virginia, here is what I think we should do. We have about two hours, before we need to head back. You go

43

ahead as fast as you can. We'll stay here and look around, as much as possible, to see if there are any clues," Gregory thought, as he spoke.

Miss Virginia came forward and rubbed Gregory so hard that he fell over. He kind of laughed as he pulled himself up and hugged her neck.

"Go, and we'll be around. But, if you're not back in two hours, we head back for lots of help," Gregory said to this ferocious beast.

Miss Virginia roared and took off before the men got out of the teepee. It was as she had vanished into thin air. That is exactly what she did. She could get many places in seconds. She was going to reach that other forest, where those other people were seen last.

"Okay, I want to check out the village for signs of struggle first," Gregory said. "Let's spread out and meet back here in about ten minutes. Do not leave the village. We cannot get separated. We return back home if Miss Virginia doesn't return."

Before the three men could walk the entire village, Miss Virginia appeared out of nowhere and in front of Gregory. She roared and looked directly into Gregory's eyes.

"I found them. They have the entire village held captive. I was able to quietly move around and I also know why my two kittens are not able to come to me. They both have darts in their sides, so they have been put to sleep by something. I know they are alive because I was able to check for breathing. They are in their beast forms, so that tells me that they were taken by surprise by some bad medicine," Miss Virginia thought out as Gregory repeated out loud to Blake and his cousin.

"Miss Virginia, are the men bound or tied up? Are they in a teepee or what?" Gregory asked.

Miss Virginia's eyes lit up and she told the men what she had seen. "All the men are scattered and tied tightly in about groups of three to five, except for your uncle, the Chief and a few others. They are not tied up, but they are talking with the strangers. The women and children are being held in teepees. I

44

don't think anyone has been harmed."

"So, this is another American Indian tribe or is it people like me?" Gregory asked and thinking all about his history lessons.

"No, they are some type of Indian, but I don't know if they are friendly or not. I think your Uncle Jake saw me, but I could only let him see me for a second. I was in the form of a field mouse, so that I could move around quickly. When I saw the men, I became myself and glowed. I think Jake saw me, but he didn't flinch. There are lots of warriors watching them and loudly talking to them.

"Where are my sister and my cousin? Did you see Lacey and Jillie?" Gregory asked feeling scared.

"Yes, they are together and are separated from the group right now. It is probably because they are different looking. I was not able to let them know it was me, because there are too many people inside and outside of the teepee," Miss Virginia thought and turned away to pace around the three men.

"Okay, we're going to have to make a really good plan. Aiken, we have to go back and get our guns and our cousins.

Aiken was happy to go back home.

***

Meanwhile back on the farm, Andrew, Chase and Adam were all messing around, when Andrew's mom drove up in her jeep with Lucky Lad. The three were not sure why she was here and was scared she would start asking questions.

"Hey mom; what are doing here?" Andrew questioned and moved to the side of the jeep where Lucky Lad sat and rubbed him.

"I need to leave Lucky Lad with you. He's been whimpering and very agitated and I have to go help Hank with the boat. I figured you boys can keep him busy and happy here on the farm," Lucy said motioning for Lucky Lad to jump out.

Andrew didn't know what to say, but decided they may just have to use him to help. "Okay mom, whatever. When are you coming back for him?"

"I don't know. I'll call you. Just please remember to feed and water him," Lucy said, as she turned her attention to her two nephews. "Chase and Adam, you both help Andrew remember that okay?"

"Okay Aunt Lucy," Adam said and went up to give her a hug.

Chase followed Adam's lead and gave his aunt a hug. "Don't worry Aunt Lucy, we'll keep Andrew in line and obedient."

"Ha, Ha," Andrew said. "I'll take you down anytime little cuz."

"Okay boys, behave. Where are all the others?" Lucy asked looking around.

"They are all everywhere. We were just getting ready to go get some supplies," Andrew said thinking fast.

"Oh, tell them I am sorry I missed them. Gotta go; be good and take care of my precious, little Lucky Lad," Lucy said and blew them all a kiss after she handed her son a bag of dog food. "Just so I know you have it," Lucy said and she quickly backed out, blew her horn and took off down Levens Street.

"Whew, that was close," Adam said. "Thank goodness your mom didn't want to hang out here and wait on everyone."

"Yeah, help me to remember to feed Lucky Lad guys," Andrew said turning around looking for his mom's dog.

Lucky Lad was off heading down to the pasture. He knew that something was wrong and he needed to look around.

"Look Andrew, Lucky Lad is heading down into the pasture. We better go follow him," Chase said.

"I'm starving. First, let's grab a snack and a drink," Andrew said and he headed into the farmhouse.

Chase and Adam followed and they raided the frig again. They moved in unison as all three of them filled their pockets with goodies and each grabbed a Gatorade. They were ready to go in about five minutes. Of course, they left their mess out without cleaning up after themselves.

"Let's go cousins. What time is it now?" Andrew asked, as he pulled out his phone. "Okay, they have been gone over two hours. Two more and then we need to go find someone to help us."

The three boys headed out the door to find someone pulling into the driveway in a muddy old, black jeep. A dark haired boy got out, stood by his jeep and looked all around. Finally, he waved to the three cousins. Adam still had the key and locked the back door.

"Hey guys. I am a friend of Jillie's. Is she here?" Miguel yelled, as he waited to see if these three guys were going to be friendly or not.

"Yes, this is where she kind of lives, but she's not here," Andrew yelled back. "Who are you?"

"Oh sorry; I am Miguel."

Miguel walked forward and held out his hand. Andrew took the lead, since he was the oldest and shook his hand. Chase and Adam followed suit and introduced themselves.

"Oh, you're Jillie's and Lacey's cousins. I have heard about you and that you were all meeting here to help. I had this crazy feeling that I should come and help too," Miguel added.

Miguel didn't want to tell them really why he was here. He had seen the black wolf recently warning him of danger. Miguel couldn't figure out what the danger was and felt like seeing the wolf so much meant something to do with Lucy, which meant something to do with Lucky Lad or someone close. He had discussed his feelings with his parents and the holy man. They all agreed that he had to come and make sure all was okay. Miguel's life was tightly woven into this family's future, but neither he nor anyone knew just how much.

Not knowing what to say to one another, silence fell upon the four. But not for very long, because Lucky Lad came bounding up from the pasture. He practically bowled Miguel over. After welcoming him with lots of licks and pounces, Lucky Lad began barking at all four of them.

"You know Lucky Lad?" Andrew asked. "Do you know my mom?"

"If you're talking about Lucy, yes I do. She and my parents are dear friends. So, you're Lucy's son? Your mom is a pretty neat lady. Is she here?"

"No, she dropped Lucky Lad off and I am not sure why. But, he's here, you're here-"

"Is something wrong? I came because I have a strong feeling that something may be wrong," Miguel said.

As Miguel started to say something else, Lucky Lad started barking and backing up, as he looked at all four of the young men.

"Lucky Lad wants us to follow him," Miguel said. "I know that something is wrong."

"I don't know, but something is not right," Andrew answered back.

Andrew didn't know how much he could tell Miguel. Andrew motioned for Chase and Adam to follow him. He looked at Miguel and Miguel nodded that he was coming too. They all took off running to keep up with Lucky Lad, who was running to the big oak tree.

When he reached the oak tree, he ran around and around it barking and barking. Then, he stopped, went to the edge of the woods and began howling as if he was calling for someone.

"Lucky! What are you barking at or for or what?" Andrew yelled out.

Miguel placed his hand on Andrew's shoulder. "I think I know what he's doing. He's calling for some help. Are the girls in trouble?"

"We think they might be, but we really don't know. You're going to think this is really weird, but we think they are like three hundred years back in time," Adam blurted out.

"Okay then, is Blake aware of it all?" Miguel asked.

"You know Blake?" Adam asked.

"Yes, I know Will too," Miguel answered. "Trust me; I know what you kind of know."

Lucky continued to howl and bark as he ran back and forth along the side of the woods. The guys all stood watching him run, stop and howl over and over until something totally magical occurred. A black wolf followed by many other wolves came out of the woods and circled Lucky. The black wolf walked up and greeted Lucky Lad with licks and whimpers. Lucky whimpered back and then ferociously barked. All the canines turned their attention to the young men, who all stood a bit frozen in amazement.

The black wolf ran up to Miguel and whimpered.

"Guys, they want to go help the girls. Did Blake and some of your other cousins go with him?" Miguel questioned them all.

"Yes and we have a plan to give them four hours and if they are not back then we get help to help them all," Chase said, beating his other cousins to the punch.

"Okay, then how much time do we have?" Miguel asked.

Chase looked at his watch and read out, "3:30. So, we have one and a half more hours to go."

Okay, let's get to know one another and try and put our heads together. I can tell you that Lucky Lad and the troops here will do just about anything to make sure Lacey and Jillie are saved. Many lives depend upon their survival.

"What? This is just too far out!" Adam said, as he thought about his little sister.

"You cannot question destiny. Nothing can turn back the clock. But, I am sure that we will win this battle," Miguel said, as he thought about all the stories he had been told about how his family line would survive forever. That meant that Lacey, Jillie and Nadia had to survive too. Jillie was far too important to him now and he knew that she had won his heart.

Lucky Lad led the black wolf around between the cousins like he was introducing his own family. Andrew was the first to rub the wild wolf. They were all animal lovers like his mother. Once the black wolf made his way through the humans, he howled and all the other wolves came and moved amongst the young men. They were all experiencing a true, magical moment.

After all the introductions, each one of the cousins had two or three wolves standing close. They had been instructed to protect these humans and protect them they would.

The clock seemed to move so slowly. They all sat waiting

for Gregory, Blake and Aiken to return.

"If anyone was to come this way, they would either call out the infantry or faint," Adam said, as he looked all around at this sight of man side by side with wild wolves surrounding them.

No one answered. They all just nodded their heads waiting for something magical to happen and the others to appear. Lucky Lad stood near where the portal would open.

"Four o'clock," Andrew called out, as he slipped his cell back into his pocket.

***

It was night time and wee hours in the morning, but a big bonfire burned bright, as the strangers danced and howled at their victory. Lacey and Jillie were together in a teepee all alone with these strangers watching them. They slept out of pure exhaustion. All the other women and children were scattered among the different teepees being closely watched, but not harmed.

Running Antelope, also known as Lope, looked all around him and was able to see enough from the glow of the fire. He was tied up to a tree and was the farthest away from anyone. He was determined to get free and go for help. Maybe he could make it back to the portal and go for help. He would just have to find Blake. His father was not far away from him, but he had no idea where his mother might be and he hoped that she was not being harmed in anyway. He vowed that he would take revenge if he should ever free himself.

As one of the enemy walked into view, Running Antelope closed his eyes and made it look like he was sleeping, letting his head hang down. He heard his father's voice and listened. He heard his father asking that the women and children be released. The words that answered back were not understood, but he figured that that was not going to happen.

After he was certain that the enemy must have walked away, he opened his eyes and looked at his father. They stared at one another and Running Antelope felt like he knew that his father was telling him to try and break free and just go. He had no idea that his father was trying to tell him to be patient. Running Antelope felt around him for something to cut himself free.

He moved his fingers around the base of his back to feel for something that he might use to cut through the tough, limber twig branches. He found something that felt like a sharp rock. It pierced through the tip of his middle finger. He held in the pain, as a mighty warrior should always do. As the pain subsided, he began to slowly saw through the branches that held him captive. It seemed like hours before he could break free. It was nearing daylight and Running Antelope decided to stay put and think through a plan. He was so scared, but he knew that he had to make a run for it. He kept his head down so that he would not give himself away. He carefully listened to anything that was said. He didn't understand their language, but realized his father could communicate with them. Running Antelope was so proud of his father and how smart he was. He promised himself he would make his father proud of him too.

When Running Antelope noticed a young man and woman were walking towards him, he was stiff with fear that they would find out he had freed himself. He tried to fix the branches around his wrists. He could tell the woman was carrying something.

The man, about his age, said something to the young woman. The young woman answered back and knelt down very close to him. She unveiled a plate of food. She picked up a piece of deer meat and put it close to Running Antelope's mouth. She smiled and said something. Running Antelope opened his mouth and she allowed him to take the meat into his mouth. The young man stooped down too and stared at Running Antelope's face. Running Antelope tried so hard not to sweat and reveal his secret. The young man said something, but Running Antelope had no idea and shrugged his shoulders. The young man stood up and looked towards Son of Running Deer and pointed. Running Antelope knew at this moment that he was asking him if this was his father. Running Antelope nodded his head yes and said "yes" in his own language. The young man and young woman both smiled at him.

Running Antelope was confused at the kindness. Running Antelope looked towards his father, but the early morning darkness did not allow him to see that his father was no longer tied. Many people were moving about the village and Son of Running Deer had now joined others around the center fire making plans to join the two tribes for survival.

The young stranger spoke again and this time Running Antelope understood. He was matching up his sister to her new husband, Running Antelope!

Running Antelope looked at the young woman and then at her brother. "Over my dead body," Running Antelope muttered and looked away. Then, he turned back around. "So why am I tied up?" Running Antelope asked with confusion and anger.

"To make sure you agree with this match my new brother," the stranger said, as his sister rubbed Running Antelope's arm.

Running Antelope's mind raced and he thought about his girl and he thought about Jillie. He didn't want this woman, even if she was rather beautiful. She was a stranger. He jerked his arm away.

"Well, the answer is no," Running Antelope said and frowned.

The young man grunted and the young woman giggled as she stood up. She smiled down at Running Antelope and said something. Running Antelope looked away until they left. He really had to get out of here now. He had no idea that no one was to be harmed. He wondered about Jake, his own chief and so many others. Where were they all?

Little did Running Antelope know, but Jake had made peace with these people and they were working out an agreement of peace for all. Chief Fierce Tiger was all in favor of having these people joining their families. Running Antelope's father, Son of Running Deer, had also now joined the leaders of the tribes.

Running Antelope briefly dozed off from the exhaustion of trying to stay awake all night. When he woke up, dawn was nearing. He felt that he needed to flee. He knew nothing of the talks that had continued throughout the night. The village had turned quiet while Running Antelope had dozed off. He quietly untied his feet. He looked around and slowly stood up. He looked for any sign of his father, his mother or anyone. He had made up his mind. He was going to go for help and return. Little did he know, but destiny was pulling him away. He had to find help. What if he never returned or he didn't survive. He may never see his family again.

***

Gregory, Blake and Aiken followed Miss Virginia back to the cave to get back to the other cousins. Little did they know that there was going to be a welcoming and hunting committee waiting for them. They moved as quickly as they could and practically fell into the portal opening at the mouth of the cave. Aiken was feeling weak.

***

As Miss Virginia and the three boys appeared near the oak tree, their welcoming committee all came to attention. Blake, who didn't really know anything about the wolves, was a bit in shock now. Of course, Gregory and Aiken also jumped back at the sight of all the new, wild animals. And, to find their three cousins and this other person front and center was another surprise.

Andrew jumped forward, with Lucky Lad by his side, to jolt the three out of their shock and surprise. "Hey guys, the magic just keeps on happening. This here is Miguel, who knows Jillie really well."

Miguel stepped forward and shook Blake's, Gregory's and then Aiken's hands and said, "Heard lots about you all".

Miguel noticed that Aiken's hands felt really clammy, but didn't take the time to ask about his health.

"Oh and don't let me forget Lucky Lad's best friend and his friends," Andrew said with a bit of sarcasm, as he motioned his hand towards the black wolf and the others.

Miguel stepped toward the black wolf and held out his hand. "This, my new friends, is a dear friend of Lucky Lad and your Aunt Lucy. He has brought all of his friends to help."

Miss Virginia walked forward without hesitation and all the wolves seemed to step back and let her walk amongst them. The cousins again saw another amazing moment.

"Well, with what we have all seen and heard today, nothing else should surprise us. So, let's put some plans together and get our sisters back and help our Uncle Jake and his people," Gregory demanded.

The boys all cheered and the wolves and Lucky Lad all howled.

"I have the key to the portal," Andrew yelled.

"Well, it's almost light there now and it's getting dark here thank goodness. Should we return now or later when it's daylight?" Gregory answered.

"I think the wolves would be better moving in at nighttime. Let's make our move now and get set for night fall there," Miguel answered with confidence.

"Okay, let's open the portal door again," Blake commanded.

Andrew held up the tiny shark tooth necklace, which he had taken from his cousin Adam. Gregory held up his hand for it and Andrew tossed it over to his older cousin.

"Lucky Lad, get your friends ready to move through the portal," Andrew called out to his mom's dog.

Lucky Lad yipped a few commands and the wolves all lined up two by two. Miss Virginia joined up with Lucky Lad, as they moved to the front of the line.

As Blake showed Gregory the special spot, Gregory touched the tiny shark's tooth to the mark. The portal door opened and it had a dim light to it as it was glowing from another world.

"Okay everyone, move in closer to the wolves, so they are

somewhat protected," Gregory called out.

All the boys moved to join in with two wolves. Miss Virginia and Lucky Lad waited for Blake to come forward and join them. Gregory hurried to the back of the line and joined in with two furry beasts. Miguel joined up with the Black wolf he had come to know so well and another wolf.

"We're going through," Blake called and walked into the portal opening.

Aiken was dreading going back so soon, but he needed to help find his little sister.

"Is there anything-," Andrew said before he was sucked into the past.

"Okay, Andrew did -." Chase almost screamed out before he was thrust into the past.

"Oh well, I-," Adam didn't get a chance to say anything either before he was pulled back into the past.

No one had any time to back out. They were all on the fastest ride of their lives and it ended almost as quickly as it started. As they all came upon this land so many years before their time, the wolves gathered as if they were waiting for further command.

Andrew, Chase and Adam all looked at one another with big smiles.

"Man, who needs an amusement park?" Adam commented, but the other two didn't have time to respond.

"Okay Miss Virginia, let us know what we need to do," Blake requested.

Miss Virginia roared towards Lucky Lad, who in turn barked out commands to his wolf brothers and sisters. Lucky Lad led the four-legged troop off into the pasture lands. Miss Virginia turned her attention to Gregory and all of his cousins. She quietly roared out her command as her eyes lit up.

Andrew, Chase and Adam all were so surprised when they knew exactly what she was saying. "OMG, we can read her thoughts," Adam belted out.

"Yep, there is a lot going on here little cuz. It's just about all I can do not to call up my fellow air force buddies, but this is our family and our problem. So, let's get moving. Miss Virginia wants the wolves to surround the area, where our sisters, Uncle Jake and the entire village are all being held hostage. We need to be careful and move quietly until dark when we can rush them while they are asleep." Gregory tried to calmly explain, but he was nervous.

"Well, let's get going," Andrew said. "We're wasting the precious time away. I'll never be able to top this day."

"Miss Virginia, lead the way," Blake called out.

As Miss Virginia started moving, all the boys followed close behind her two by two: Blake and Aiken; Andrew and Chase and Adam and his big cousin, Gregory. They moved quickly and quietly all in sync, on a mission, to save family.

Gregory was in deep thought. He was trained for 'something' like this, but not exactly 'something' like this. His mind wondered and thought about his sister, his little cousin and his Uncle Jake.

Adam slipped a bit, but Gregory instinctively reached out and pulled him back to the rhythm of the line.

"Thanks," Adam said.

Miss Virginia slowed down a bit, as they came to the wooded area that led to her wonderful village. She glanced back to make sure everyone was still with her.

"We're good Miss Virginia," Blake said letting her know that he knew what she was thinking.

Miss Virginia gave him a soft yip to answer "okay" and kept on moving.

Soon they came to the part of the path that was very narrow and they had to go into single file. They slowed their pace a bit, which made Aiken happy. He was feeling rather sick.

When they came to the edge of the woods, Miss Virginia stopped and told the boys that they didn't need to go to the village, but they needed to move another way to reach their destination where the hostages were being held.

"I wanted to see this village," Chase said.

"Don't worry, we'll be seeing it once we get our family back," Blake said, as he thought about his Lacey and his friends.

"We don't have any weapons," Andrew thought out loud.

"Oh yes we do," Gregory said, as he dropped his backpack he had brought along not telling anyone. He had left it hidden in the tree, but didn't make a point to tell his cousins. He opened it and he had several pistols, knives, a boomerang, a couple of sling shots and even a bow and arrow that one had to snap together. He was way ahead of everyone the minute he knew there might be trouble. Blake and his cousins were all so caught up in the mystery of the land; they had not noticed when Gregory picked up his backpack before heading down the stairs. Something Gregory had learned in training was that confusion allows people to miss important details.

"Okay, we're all set. Although, we are completely out numbered," Chase commented.

"Not really, remember we have a four legged troop that will totally surround the area and back us up," Blake said.

"Aiken, why are you so quiet?" Andrew questioned, looking at Jillie's big brother.

"Oh, I'm good. I'm just getting myself mentally ready for this battle. You know I have to sit for hours waiting for a deer to cross my path. I have this thing I do to make sure I make it one good shot." Aiken was really not feeling well now, but wasn't going to let anyone know. He had to be strong for his little sister.

"Oh, go ahead and mentally prepare yourself," Andrew said, as he slapped his older cousin's back. "I'm staying close to Gregory."

"Okay boys, we need to go. Miss Virginia is ready to move," Blake tried not to yell.

Gregory handed out the weapons and quickly told his cousins how he expected them to handle them until they needed to use them, if they needed to use them.

Miss Virginia roared and started moving. She continuously circled around the boys, as they all moved in the direction of the camp. She made sure her helpers were all together. As they neared the camp, Miss Virginia slowed her pace and looked around for the wolves. Lucky Lad came up to her and rubbed against her. He saw his Andrew and walked over and gave him a nudge.

"Hey boy, am I glad to see you too," Andrew said, as he rubbed his mom's dear friend. "I'll never take you for granted again and please remind me to feed you lots."

"Okay, Blake and I are going to move closer and check the area out. I want you five to stay put. If anything should happen, stay calm and let Miss Virginia get the troops moving," Gregory explained. "Come on Blake, let's move in and get an idea what we are up against."

Gregory and Blake disappeared. Miss Virginia crept away in the opposite direction and Lucky Lad stayed back with the four younger cousins and Miguel.

What a heck of a summer cousins?" Adam asked. "I'd better be really good to little Nadia. That cat of hers may just want to eat me."

Adam was a bit of a jokester. His cousins laughed and knocked him around a bit.

"Yeah, do you think we need to start bowing down to Lacey, Nadia and your sister, Jillie?" Chase asked.

"Well, I am not bowing down to her, but I know that I am going to be a bit nicer now I know what that cat of hers can turn into," Aiken remarked, as he wiped sweat off of his forehead. He felt so clammy, like he had broken a fever.

Lucky Lad stood at attention and got the boys' attention too. Gregory and Blake were returning in a hurry.

"The village is awake and many are out and about. We see Uncle Jake and the chief walking around with them. He doesn't look like he is being held hostage. We are not sure what to do." Gregory explained.

"We saw Tame Tiger, or Will as you know him, too. He's talking with another young village person. We don't see any of the women, Tye and Tess," Blake added.

"Where is Miss Virginia?" Andrew asked and they all looked around.

"We don't want to jeopardize anything they are agreeing upon. Let's just crawl close up and watch what is really going on. If anything turns bad, then we storm the enemy," Gregory stated and motioned for everyone to go down and crawl on all fours.

The cousins and Miguel quietly and slowly crawled to a place Gregory thought would be a good place to set up their stakeout.

They all settled themselves close to one another and were just watching all the activities of the village. Andrew pulled out some jerky and passed it out. Then he pulled out a water bottle and passed that around too. The others were definitely hungry.

"Hey Andrew, do you have any more water?" Aiken asked. He was feeling really dehydrated now.

Andrew went into his backpack, which he had packed, and dug another water bottle out. "Here. You okay?"

"Thanks bud. I am just really thirsty and I feel a little weak from hunger I think," Aiken answered, hoping that was what it really was.

Blake kept scoping around hoping to see Lacey. As he scanned the area, he saw what he thought was Miss Virginia, in her cat form, creeping around the teepees. He grinned to himself and nudged Gregory, who was on his left. Gregory saw her too and gave Blake a quiet "uh huh".

As the young men all lay side by side as quiet as possible, they didn't even notice others were sneaking up from behind. They were extremely skilled at creeping up on their targets, especially their enemy. Adam was the first one to feel a sharp point in the middle of his back, but froze solid and could not even speak, much less yell.

They were all caught at spear points. Gregory held up a hand in hopes of letting them know he was not there to harm anyone. He was grabbed by the back of his shirt to stand up. He followed the silent command. The other boys were all yanked to their feet and not one peep was said from one of them. They were all in shock and totally scared to death with spears in their backs.

One of the captors spoke something in a strange language that Blake couldn't make out. But Miguel understood many of the old languages. Even though the dialects were different, he recognized the words.

Miguel spoke up and told them they came in peace and were only worried about their families. Gregory, Blake, Aiken, Andrew, Chase and Adam were all amazed and so happy to hear him speak out.

All the cousins relaxed a bit as the spears seemed to be retracted a bit from their backs. One of the warriors spoke out and Miguel interpreted to the rest.

"He is telling me that our families are in no harm. They were taken, but it was not to bring harm, but to join together as they have been running away from the white men and other hostile Indians," Miguel said sounding rather sad and upset.

"Ask them if we can go and join our families and their people," Gregory said.

Miguel repeated what Gregory asked and the one warrior answered quickly back. He also said something else, because the spears all came down.

Miguel spoke again and his new friend grunted out something. "I asked him to introduce us all to one another as friends should do," Miguel explained.

"Great idea," Andrew said.

Andrew stepped forward and placed his hand out and said, "I am Andrew."

Miguel repeated in the strange language, but said Andrew. The warriors tried to repeat and they all laughed.

"Hey, my name isn't funny," Andrew said and smiled.

One warrior slapped Andrew on the shoulder and gruffly said, "AnDu".

Miguel and the others all laughed.

"Okay, go ahead Adam," Gregory said, as he took control.

Each cousin stated their names and then they waited to hear all the warriors' names. The lead warrior said something to Miguel.

"He said he will take us to everyone now. This should be really interesting to your uncle and his family. He doesn't even know me or even his own nephews."

"Oh well, what else should we have done?" Aiken asked and stumbled backward.

Andrew and Miguel stepped quickly to help Aiken steady himself.

"What's up bro?" Andrew asked. You feel really icky, sweaty or something."

Gregory stepped over and took a better notice of his cousin, who was flushed and very clammy.

"I think you're sick man. We need to get you somewhere you can sit down. Miguel, please ask these fine warriors to help us out with Aiken."

Miguel immediately started translating the best he could and two of the warriors came forward, handed off their spears to Andrew and Adam and wrapped Aiken's arms around their necks. The leader blurted out a command and the two warriors whisked Aiken away. They were so strong that Aiken didn't even need to walk. He seemed to be gliding through the air.

The cousins joined the warriors and walked along side of them towards the village's fire.

All communications stopped as they all walked up to the group of men, who were all becoming acquainted. Jake was totally in shock as he looked at Blake with question.

Blake kind of shrugged and said, "We thought you were all in distress and held as prisoners. What did you want me to do, nothing? Lacey left me a strange note and-

"Who are all of these people with you?" Jake demanded.

"Hey Uncle Jake, we are all your nephews, except for Miguel here," Gregory said, as he stepped forward.

"Gregory?" Jake asked and held out his hand.

"Yep, I am in the Air Force now and well I couldn't just sit back and do nothing."

Jake halfway smiled, looked at the other young men and then put his attention to Aiken, who was being propped up by warriors.

"And you are Aiken aren't you? You look just like your dad. What in the world is the matter? You don't look well," Jake said and he began talking to the two warriors holding up his nephew."

Aiken nodded. "Hey Uncle Jake and I feel really bad, but I had to come find my sister and Lacy."

The chief, who was standing beside of their uncle, spoke up and the two men whisked Aiken off to get him some place where he could be tended to for awhile. Gregory and his troop all watched as Aiken was taken away from them.

"Don't worry; he'll be well taken care of here," Jake said trying to not show his concern. "We may not have all the medications that you all know, but we have mother earth's medicines that are just as good."

Jake moved his attention to the nephews that were now standing in front of him. "And you are?" Jake asked, as he pointed at Chase.

"Oh hey Uncle Jake; I am Sally's son, Chase."

Jake nodded his head and smiled.

"And you two are?" Jake asked, as he pointed at Andrew and Adam.

One of the warriors called out, "AnDU" and everyone laughed.

"Andrew, I am Andrew Uncle Jake," Andrew said and smiled.

"And I am Adam, Uncle Jake. I am Jeremy's son. You know your twin brother, who really misses you."

Jake stared at Adam and he could see his brother's eyes in Adam's eyes.

"Yeah well, it's not time to get into all of that."

"Now, who are you?" Jake said looking at Miguel.

Miguel spoke to Jake in a strange language that startled Jake and the others.

Chief Fierce Tiger came forward and put his hands on Miguel's shoulders.

"You live in their time?" The chief asked in his language that was almost the same, but a bit different.

Miguel answered "yes" and went on to explain where he lived and that his people were their descendents.

Jake was so excited, because he realized that it was not all in vain. They would survive the revolution of times.

"Wait, where is my Lacey?" Blake demanded.

"Oh yeah, where is our other cousin too?" Chase asked.

"Oh, they are in a teepee with the other women preparing for a celebration tonight

"Well, what happened to Tye and Tess?" Gregory asked, as he scanned the village in the dark.

"Oh well, they are okay. They were tranquilized, but they will wake up soon too," Jake explained and he went on to explain what all happened and why they had not returned.

"But why didn't you let Lacey and Jillie return to the farm?" Gregory questioned. "We all arrived and found Blake going out of his mind."

"Sorry Jake, but I got scared and thought something was really wrong," Blake said.

"Well, it's only been a little more than a day and I bet the girls totally forgot about all you boys arriving on time. I am sure they will be surprised to see you all here," Jake commented.

"Well, I am a bit beat Uncle Jake," Andrew spoke up and the others agreed.

"Okay," Jake said and spoke to the other leader in the strange language.

"Follow Tame Tiger and he'll take you all to his teepee for a little shut eye," Jake said. "How about if you all stay through the day and at least enjoy a big feast with us all. Aiken needs some time to feel better anyway."

"Hey Blake, Gregory, Andrew, Chase and Adam. What's up?" Tame Tiger said and laughed. "Bet you boys don't want another game of let-me-knock-you-down do you?" Tame Tiger slapped Andrew, Chase and Adam on the back and led them all away.

"Hey Gregory, great to see you brother," Tame Tiger said. "I bet you never dreamed of me as a warrior, huh?"

"Well, I cannot say that that crossed my mind, but after all this how could I not believe anything, huh?" Gregory asked and slapped Tame Tiger on his back too.

The boys all had a good laugh and pushed one another

around.

"Wow." Adam said out loud. "Dad would die if he knew where I was right now."

"You cannot tell everyone little cuz," Blake said. "We'll discuss that later, but let's try and get some sleep if we can."

"I am going to sleep, because we have been up for quite a long time," Chase said.

"We all need to get some sleep and hopefully all of this will make sense later," Gregory said.

Not one person argued and they all crashed, as soon as their heads hit the soft, fur covered mattresses. They were all worn out from worry and exhaustion.

Aiken was surrounded by two medicine men and several women, who were washing him down with cool water. He was very weak. So, he didn't care what anyone did to him. The medicine men were waving something all around him and it smelled like menthol to him and it made him relax and also helped him to breathe easier. One of the women brought a cup filled with broth and motioned for him to drink it. Aiken took some of the broth in his mouth and it tasted so good that he gulped it down. The women talked and smiled, as more broth was fixed for him. Aiken smiled back and whispered "thank-you".

Jake came in and checked in on his nephew, but didn't say anything to him, but spoke with one of the medicine men and they seemed very calm. Jake bent down and patted his nephew on his head and left without say a word.

Andrew and his cousins had all forgotten about Lucky Lad and the wolves, but Miss Virginia didn't. She ran off and led Lucky Lad and the wolves back to the cave to get them back to their time. Lucky Lad stayed back with Miss Virginia. Once the wolves were all safely sent three hundred years into the future, the two creatures ran and jumped all the way back to the new village.

Uncle Jake was surprised to meet Lucky Lad. Miss Virginia thought out whom he was and that he belonged to his sister, Lucy. Lucky Lad loved Jake from the moment they met and the feeling was mutual.

Most of the village men retired for the rest of the day and the women and children came to life. The village fire was stoked with many logs and a huge boar was placed above the flames to smoke and cook. Anyone that came near the fire turned the cooking beast. Pits were dug and all kinds of foods were wrapped in large leaves and covered over smoldering embers to steam for their feast.

No one had noticed Running Antelope was gone. Lacey, Jillie and their cats were finally emerging from their teepee. Tye and Tess were now in their cat forms once they woke from their tranquilization. They were wobbly on their feet and the girls made sure that they found them something to eat and drink. Miss Virginia was with them every step of the way.

When Lacey and Jillie noticed Lucky Lad, they were puzzled and they both looked at one another.

"Here Lucky Lad," Jillie called out. "What are you doing here boy?"

The girls had not learned about their brothers, cousins and Miguel showing up. Miss Virginia came up and looked into their eyes and told them all about last night.

"On my gosh, we forgot with all the excitement. Oh no! What did Uncle Jake do?" Lacey thought out to Miss Virginia.

"Yeah, I cannot believe we forgot about everyone coming and we did leave that note to Blake." Jillie said.

"Oh yeah, the note," Lacey said. "Everything was happening so fast and then we were brought here and we got caught in the mess and it was something we shouldn't have even been involved with and-" Lacey was cut off from finishing when she saw her brother, Blake, Miguel, Andrew, Chase and Adam all walking towards her and Jillie.

"Well, it looks like you have a lot to tell us all girls," Andrew blurted out.

"Hey sis, we're just glad you're okay," Gregory said and hugged his sister.

"I am so sorry Gregory," Lacey choked out. "Are you mad?"

"Of course he's not, sweetie," Blake said and grabbed his Lacey.

Lacey wasn't one for affection for public view and squirmed out of his hold.

Jillie looked around for her brother, but she didn't say much because she saw Miguel and she was speechless.

Miguel smiled at Jillie, but didn't dare hug her in front of her cousins. He wasn't sure where he really stood with Jillie or her family.

"Where is my brother?" Jillie asked.

Lacey looked around now too and was also curious.

"Oh, he's not feeling well and they took him to care for him. He's in someone's teepee," Gregory answered.

"Let's go check on him right now," Jillie said and everyone joined her.

Lacey and Jillie knew exactly where to go.

"Lacey, where are the horses?" Blake asked sounding worried.

"Oh, they are fine and being well cared for by these people that our tribe is joining. They actually have all their horses in a secured area."

"So, where is Uncle Jake?" Gregory asked.

"Oh, I bet he is with his family somewhere. Wait until you all meet our little cousins. They are so cute. And, they are getting big and smart."

Jillie was scanning the area looking for Running Antelope and his girl. She saw his girl helping around the fire. They locked eyes and smiled at one another, but Jillie was still a bit jealous and didn't really say much to her. She saw Beautiful Butterfly too. Beautiful Butterfly was talking and showing off her talent of style. Jillie poked Lacey and pointed her attention towards Beautiful Butterfly. Lacey nodded and smiled.

"She's got talent for sure. I am sure that the designers in our day would be fighting for her designs," Lacey said.

Jillie and Lacey came upon the teepee, where they knew Aiken would be staying.

"Stay out here and let me go in," Jillie said and she pulled the teepee flap back and disappeared.

Inside, the two women were napping not far from Aiken. They both woke up and saw Jillie and smiled, but didn't move to get up. They had been up for quite sometime tending to Jilie's brother. Jillie said "thank-you" in the language they would understand and knelt down beside her brother.

"Aiken, you okay?" Jillie whispered, as she gently touched her brother's forehead.

Aiken opened one eye and then the other. He smiled at his little sister.

"Hey, glad to see you peanut, but I started feeling really bad last night and I think I want to just lay here for a while."

"Okay, you just rest. I'll be back to check on you later," Jillie said smiling.

"Okay little sister. And by the way, I am like really amazed at what you and Lacey have going on. I am proud of you and well, I just want you to know your secret is good with me," Aiken said.

Jillie grabbed his arm and squeezed it. "I'm glad you know. It's been really hard to keep this all to myself. Do you know about Tess?"

"Oh yeah, but I haven't seen her as a black panther, but I have seen Miss Virginia as a lioness and all the wolves were just amazing," Aiken said.

"Wolves, uh what do you mean?" Jillie asked.

"Ask the others, I think I want to get some sleep right now," Aiken answered feeling really exhausted.

"I will for sure. Get some rest. See you later," Jillie said, as she rubbed her brother's head and stood up.

Jillie waved to the two women nearby and left the teepee with her cousins and Miguel all still waiting.

"Aiken needs his rest. Let's leave him be for now," Jillie said.

"Well, what do we do now?" Adam asked.

"I think we should go find our aunt and uncle," Lacey said and looked at her brother and all of her cousins.

"Hey Miguel, I'm sorry that I have ignored you. I cannot

believe that you are here as well." Lacey said.

"Well, call it intuition, call it fate, but I was summoned and we also had many helpers come looking to save you two," Miguel started to explain.

"Who was with you?" Jillie asked.

"OMG little cousin, we had wild wolves travel through the portal of time with us. Lucky Lad apparently has a friend, the black wolf. Well the black wolf brought many friends to come and help save you," Chase explained.

Jillie looked at Miguel and he nodded that it was true. The wolves from the Appalachian Mountains had not only traveled many miles, but also through time to make sure this destiny was not broken.

"I don't know about you boys, but I am starving. Let's go find Uncle Jake and have some breakfast with him and his family. It's kind of a tradition with Jillie and me whenever we're visiting. We have breakfast with them. The porridge is so good." Lacey said.

"Porridge, is that what we have to eat?" Adam questioned.

"Yeah, I don't think I want just porridge," Chase added into the conversation.

"There will be so much food tonight, you will be happy that all you had was porridge and fruit for breakfast," Jillie said. "Follow us. I think I know which Teepee is Uncle Jake's."

4 A BRAND NEW DAY

Lacey and Jillie led the way to where they knew their Uncle Jake and his family would now be together. The tribes had amicably joined forces. They would all be returning to the village where the girls had become so familiar. All of the boys followed along staring at all the activities going on in the village. The strangers greeted them with smiles and hand gestures, as if it didn't seem like anything was wrong with having these strange people from three hundred years in the future visiting their home.

Just as their Uncle Jake's people had accepted him, these wonderful and welcoming people wanted peace and harmony more than anything. They had also heard, from the time they were born, of the destined three to save their lands. Having the girls' family members come to their world made them all feel more secure that they would live on through time.

Andrew, Chase and Adam were dying to go join the teens of the villages and play the stick and ball game they noticed that was taking place.

"Look, it's like they are playing a croquette type game passing some type of leather bound ball," Andrew said hitting his cousin Chase on the shoulder.

Chase grabbed his left shoulder with his right hand. "You don't have to hit me so hard to get my attention and besides I noticed it too. Let's say we join them after we put down this wonderful porridge that I cannot wait to taste,"

Adam and Andrew both laughed as they rubbed their bellies and licked their lips being silly, but stopped dead in their tracks when this rugged looking man came out from a teepee. It was their Uncle Jake, who they had just met hours before, but he was such a stranger.

Silence fell upon Jake as he looked over and admired his brothers' and sisters' children. No one said anything for a moment and then Beautiful Light came out of the teepee followed by the twins, who also stopped and stared at these white men. Lacey and Jillie didn't say a word, but watched as they all stared at one another remembering the day they met their Uncle Jake.

Beautiful Light broke the silence with a nudge to Jake to say something. She spoke very broken English. "You say something, yes?"

"Oh, of course," Jake said and cleared his throat. "Well, let me see if I remember who is who."

"You are Gregory of course."

Gregory nodded and shook his uncle's hand followed by a hug.

"Now, you three were fairly young when I decided to leave and I am sure I am totally a stranger to all of you, right?" Jake questioned, as he looked over Andrew, Chase and Adam.

"I'm Andrew, Uncle Jake. I am Lucy's son and Lucky Lad belongs to me. Well, he belongs to my mom really, but I love him too," Andrew added and held out his hand to shake Jake's.

Jake responded with a shake and grabbed him in for a hug. "Well, well. I do remember you."

"I am Chase, Sally's son," Chase added and held out his hand for a shake.

Jake grabbed him in too and messed up his hair. "How is your mom?"

"She's good."

"So you are Jeremy's son, Adam I believe?" Jake asked looking at Adam.

"I am Jeremy's son Uncle Jake," Adam said.

Jake paused for a few seconds taking in Adam's face and staring deep into his eyes. Jake grabbed him and gave him a big hug. He was getting choked up, but he didn't let it surface.

"And you are the most unexpected, but most welcomed. Miguel, is it?" Jake questioned Miguel.

"I am from the future and I am a direct descendant of this tribe. We now live in the Appalachian Mountains. Your sister, Lucy, is a dear friend of our tribe," Miguel explained.

So the connection is far stronger than we could even know," Jake answered back.

"I want to talk more, but I want to also introduce my family and eat," Jake said and pulled his wife close to his side.

Jake talked in his native tongue, which Lacey, Jillie and Miguel all understood. Lacey looked at her brothers and cousins and translated. The boys were in amazement as they listened to Lacey talk this native language.

"Boy, I guess there are some things I really don't know about my little sister, huh?" Gregory said, as he smiled and put his arm around his petite sister.

"Yeah and it wasn't my choice all of this, but I guess it's meant to be, so Jillie and I have grown somewhat accustomed to it all," Lacey said.

"It definitely wasn't my choice," Jillie said quite loudly. "But, I also have grown used to it all and this is destiny and you cannot fight with destiny from what I have been told."

Miguel moved closer to Jillie and put his arm around her shoulder, which kind of shocked Jillie and also embarrassed her a bit. She looked up at Miguel and gave him a quick smile, but wasn't going to get all locked up in his eyes in front of her uncle and cousins all staring and waiting for her next move.

Jake broke up the uncomfortable moment. "Let's go inside. My wife has made a wonderful breakfast for us all. Find a seat and help yourself."

Once everyone had taken a seat, he spoke in the strange language and his sons moved on either side of him.

"I want to formally introduce my sons to their big cousins.

They are very important to the survival of our lands now and our lands in your time. They will be here when I am gone. They will be here for Nadia. She will be very important to the survival of the land and they will help her whenever she should need them."

Not only did Gregory, Andrew, Chase and Adam listen with fascination, but Lacey and Jillie realized how destiny was set for their little cousin, who had barely began her life.

Jake went around the circle and introduced his sons: Son of Jake 1 and Son of Jake 2, as it translated into English, to their cousins.

"I would like for you all to acknowledge them as Oneson and Twoson. The boys knew their names and they also knew words of English fairly well now. They spoke their cousins' names and made a friendship gesture, which Jillie explained. When they got to Miguel, they exchanged a quick conversation and Jake was also realizing all the lives that were being intertwined.

Jillie continued to ponder the whereabouts of her Lope, but didn't say anything yet. She didn't want to speak of him in front of Miguel. Lacey could tell she was worried and she knew why without asking. They locked eyes and Lacey smiled to comfort her cousin. Jillie slightly smiled back.

"Uncle Jake, do you think us coming here will mess anything up for you all?" Gregory asked.

"I am not sure, but I don't think so. I actually think it's great that you all know and can help the girls with the farm and all that needs to be done. We must keep it in the family forever. This land claimed our family as its protector and we must keep her safe in order to keep our families safe. This is our destiny and I believe it was meant to be as it is happening. I came here, as a very young boy, and the pull for me to stay was strong. As you will find out, these people, my people and your people too were told of three sisters to save the land. A power way beyond our control set this path many, many years ago. We are all a part of this wonderful plan. I hope you all can embrace one another, this land and keep this land safe from harm."

Everyone silently ate the wonderful spread of fresh fruits, wonderful dried fruit and nut rolls and the porridge the girls had come to love. Oneson and Twoson were now sitting in among some of their older cousins.

Jake sat back and looked all around the teepee and smiled as he realized how wonderful his life had turned out. Never in his wildest dreams would he have thought he would ever see his family that he left behind again in such a special way. His life seemed to make sense like never before and he gazed at his wonderful wife and thought how it couldn't get any better. He only wished he could see his parents once again along with his brothers and sisters. Maybe he would, but he was not making that decision. If it was meant to be, destiny would take care of it all.

"Enjoy one another and eat," Jake called out and he began chatting back and forth with all of his nephews.

Lacey and Jillie also sat back and watched all the interaction.

"This is so cool, huh Lacey?" Jillie asked, as she smiled at her older cousin.

"Yep, it is way cool." Lacey replied.

Blake had been so exhausted from all the worry; he had leaned back on his arms and had fallen into a deep sleep again. The girls giggled and pointed his way. Miguel laughed too and gazed at Jillie's beauty.

Jillie noticed Miguel looking at her and she turned her attention away from him. She wanted to find Lope. She leaned over and whispered to Lacey that she was going to go look for her dear friend. Lacey gave her a look of disapproval. Jillie winked, got up and stepped out of the teepee. Lacey looked over at Miguel, who was already in deep discussion with her uncle in their Indian tongue. She tried to follow the conversation but she couldn't keep up.

To all of their surprise, Chief Fierce Tiger, Son of Running Deer and Tame Tiger all came in rather quickly and abruptly. All conversations stopped. Jake jumped up and walked over to the men he had become so close to over the years. The chief spoke directly to Jake in their foreign tongue, but Lacey understood what the topic of conversation was this time. Running Antelope was missing and no one could find him. Son of Running Deer and many of the men had been out looking for him, but found nothing.

Jillie entered into the teepee and was greeted by Tame Tiger.

"Have you seen Running Antelope?" Tame Tiger asked.

"No, I was just looking for him and couldn't find him anywhere," Jillie replied. "Why, what is wrong?"

Lacey got up and came over to Jillie's side. "He's missing and his father is very worried."

Jillie didn't speak. She ran out of the teepee and immediately saw his special girl crying into her mother's shoulder. She hurried over to her and gave her comfort. Their previous rivalry left as quickly as it began. The girls hugged one another and Jillie let Lope's girl cry out her sadness. Jillie guided Lope's girl to come and sit down with her.

Back in the teepee, Jake explained what was going on and everyone listened. Jake's sons went over to their dad's best friend, Running Antelope's father, and hugged him tight. He had been as much of a father to them as their own dad. Running Antelope was like a big brother to them.

Beautiful Light got up, stopped and hugged Son of Running Deer, spoke to Jake and went out to go find Running Antelope's mother and offer her comfort to her.

"Uncle Jake, is there something we can do to help?" Gregory asked, as he stood up and walked over to Tame Tiger.

"Hey Will or Tame Tiger, what's happening my man?" Gregory asked with a big smile on his face.

"Here you call me Tame Tiger," Tame Tiger replied and told Gregory how to really pronounce his name in his Indian tongue.

Gregory tried to pronounce it and botched it up a bit. Everyone laughed for a quick moment, but the seriousness of Running Antelope's disappearance quickly prevailed over the group.

The Chief spoke and everyone listened. Will interpreted to Gregory and his cousins as they all listened. They all stood up out of respect and to listen...

"We are not sure what has happened to our Running Antelope. We have had our men, and men from our new families, out looking for him. It appears he escaped before we could tell him the wonderful news of our tribes joining together as one. Our fear is that he runs into harms way and we never find him again. We would like to go out looking one more time and return by late afternoon."

"Uncle Jake, can we help out?" Gregory asked.

Jake asked his dear friends, Son of Running Deer and Chief Fierce Tiger, and they both nodded in agreement as his dear friend said, "Yes, please we can use all the eyes and ears we can get".

Tame Tiger translated and they all walked out of the teepee to gather more men for the hunt.

Jillie came running up to her uncle. "Uncle Jake, what is happening?"

"We're forming a second search mission right now to go look again for Running Antelope. Miguel and your cousins are all going to assist."

"I am going too," Jillie yelled out. "He's my friend too and I am going."

"I am going too," Lacey called out and whistled for her Tye.

In seconds, Tye, Tess, Miss Virginia and Lucky Lad were all waiting and eager to depart.

"Lucky Lad, you want to come with me?" Andrew asked.

Lucky Lad immediately went to Andrew and jumped up to lick him.

"Good boy. Yes, I love you too. Let's go find this Running Antelope," Andrew said.

The cousins were all split up amongst the tribesmen. Jillie and Tess joined a search party. Lacey and Tye joined another one and Miss Virginia went with Uncle Jake's group. Andrew, Miguel and Lucky Lad joined a few other young men and went off in their given direction.

Chief Fierce Tiger gave everyone the time to return. Many women were crying along with Running Antelope's mother and his special girl. Jillie ran over to Running Antelope's girl and whispered to her that she would move mountains to bring Running Antelope back to her. They embraced and Jillie was off leading her team with her black panther by her side.

Tame Tiger's mother and Beautiful Light took control of the women and put everyone back to work, but Running Antelope's mother. Beautiful Light told her and the young girl to go find peace in their teepee. Oneson and Twoson guided the fragile women to their rest.

Distant cries could be heard for Running Antelope, but the afternoon's efforts did not bring him back home. Running Antelope's disappearance was part of the mystery and the magic of the land. His destiny had called out for him and he answered his calling. His life would not go in vain and his name would live forever more.

5 FORCES ARE JOINED

All of the occurrences were dynamic. The capture of a tribe, the families joined to save so much and now the loss of Running Antelope brought much to celebrate and to grieve.

Once all the search parties returned with no sight of Running Antelope, there was a grave sense of sadness. But, Chief Fierce Tiger and now his co-leader, Chief Charging Bull, walked together discussing what they needed to do to bring their families together once and for all. It would be a celebration. It would first be a celebration to honor Running Antelope and send many protectors, those that walked before them, to be his guide. And, it would be the grandest celebration of all time. A celebration to honor their tribes becoming one as well as a celebration to honor their warrior sisters and brothers, who had been brought back in time to not only connect them forever, but also to save their lands forever.

The chiefs walked to the center of the village, where the main fire was being stoked by some of the older women. They knew that celebrations were the way of healing loss and honoring great events. Chief Fierce Tiger didn't need to make any gestures for silence. He would be the great leader of all these people. His people, old and new, were patiently awaiting his direction. In his native tongue, he began his speech.

Jake, Lacey, Jillie and Miguel all dispersed themselves

amongst their brothers and cousins and Blake to interpret Fierce Tiger's encouraging words...

"My people, we are here for a purpose. A very strong purpose that no one can truly understand, but we know it is all for a great reason." The chief pointed over the crowd and lands his hand in the direction of: Lacey, Jillie, Blake, Gregory, Andrew, Chase, Adam and then Miguel; and he held his hand out to Miguel. Miguel is the proof that their people would survive way into the future. Aiken, who had gotten better with the special care from the medicine men and the women who mothered him, had also joined his family. Jillie was leaning against her big brother.

Everyone stared at these young people for a few moments giving the cousins chills, as they all had thoughts swirling through their minds. Their thoughts were those of being proud, of disbelief, of fear and of happiness. Lacey leaned towards her brother and told him to raise his hand and acknowledge the chief. She did the same and looked towards Jillie and the others to have them also show their sign of friendship and respect. Miguel also followed the lead. The chief smiled, as he raised his hand higher and looked over his people. Hands began to rise towards these young people.

Jake was the last one to raise both of his hands, as he walked between his family he had left behind and his family he joined many years ago. He held up both of his hands for a moment and then brought them together. At this moment, he knew that being the gatekeeper made more sense than ever now. He looked at his wife and smiled and knew that it was all meant to be as it should have been.

Chief Charging Bull also joined in with more words of encouragement...

"Today marks a day that stories will tell forever. We will be sure to tell this story for generations to come."

Miguel thought how he never heard of this tale, but maybe he was not supposed to hear of this part, because it would have never happened as it should. He could not wait to go back and talk with his family to see if his parents and the elders of his tribe had heard this very story. He looked over at Jillie and smiled her way. She was also looking his way and a very strong draw was felt by both of them. Jillie felt uncomfortable, but happy. Miguel knew that his future was right in front of him and he hoped that he was reading her feelings correctly for fear of rejection.

Lacey saw the interaction and felt the electricity. She smiled and looked over at her uncle, who also was very in tune to the attraction. They exchanged smiles and both nodded their approval. Then Jake looked Blake's way and gave Lacey another nod of his head. Lacey smiled and went over to stand by Blake's side. Blake smiled and gave her a gentle hug with his arm.

Their uncle finished with a brief talk and then began a chant that all the people of the tribes began chanting. Lacey and Jillie helped their brothers; cousins and Blake understand and join in the opening celebration. Miguel already knew the words and was already bellowing out the chant.

This marked a great moment in history for these families, both in the past and in the future forever. The food, the festivities and the bonds made were an event of a lifetime. Lacey's and Jillie's brothers and cousins were totally absorbed into this tribe. They were now apart of this destiny. Not to mention, they had all been given wonderful outfits made by Beautiful Butterfly herself. Tame Tiger was in awe of his bride to be. That would be the next big event, their wedding day.

Gregory showed off his weapons, explained his life in the Air Force and many warriors were entranced by his stories. They could not fathom how much the world would be changing. Lacey did the translations for him with help from Tame Tiger.

Aiken talked hunting with Miguel by his side interpreting and they became bonded as friends. Jillie watched from afar, but was still trying to console Lope's family and special girl. Her heart was also broken from the loss of her best friend.

Andrew, Chase and Adam were all competing in the stick and ball game that was almost like soccer, golf and other sports all in one. Their new friends were running circles around them and were laughing as the cousins were given 'a run for their money'. There was no time for interpretation, so they just went with it. Oneson and Twoson were on the sidelines cheering for their bigger cousins. They threw some English words out there that made the cousins laugh and lose their concentration. Andrew ended up grabbing them and showed them how to guard him so that he could score. He showed these athletes a new way of playing the game.

Jake was walking around chatting with many of the new tribesmen, discussing their plans to return to the larger village and how they would work on making it more secure from invaders. The fact that these people had been able to penetrate and take them captive brought worry to his mind. He would have to also discuss some issues with his nephew, Gregory, for advice on what they could do in this time to reinforce their security.

The cats were cats and they romped around with all the village dogs. No other cats were around, which Chase had noticed almost immediately, but didn't think it was important enough to make mention of it. Lucky Lad was also in the mix of animals having fun.

The food was unbelievable, as Lacey and Jillie had already been so lucky to experience time and time again. Their brothers and cousins were 'pigging out' on the wonderful fresh and flavorful dishes made in such simple ways. As the afternoon led into night, the bonfire was built and the party went way into the night, which meant that it was daylight in another time.

"Jillie, we have been gone for several days now. I think we better get back or someone will really start wondering where we all are. I bet someone has been calling one of us. I can only imagine what is going on with the farm. We need to get back and get these guys to work on all the things we need done to really get the farm up and running," Lacey said to her cousin.

Jillie nodded her agreement. "Yep, we need to head back now. Let's go find Uncle Jake."

Jake agreed and walked with the girls to collect the boys, who all needed to get back across time. Once he had them all gathered, along with Tye and Tess, he silenced the crowd.

Chief Fierce Tiger and Chief Charging Bull hugged each and every one of these young adults. Many people came up and also hugged them and said good wishes for their travel and to their futures. The boys were getting choked up, but kept their emotions inside the best that they could.

The hike back to the portal was not going to be easy, since they were all so tired from the adventures and celebrations. Jake decided they should get going, but not to cross over until the night time fell upon their time. That way if people were really looking for them, they wouldn't see where they were appearing and they wouldn't have to 'tell a little white lie' about camping out on the farmland and having some fun. It was all actually the truth, but three hundred years ago!

They all gathered what they had come with and began heading back to the time portal door. Jake and Son of Running Deer, along with Tame Tiger and his best friend, were their escorts back to the portal door. The walk was silent and thoughtful. It was a much longer hike.

Everyone was tired, as it was now close to twenty plus hours for them to have been up. As they walked near the other village, where they all would be living again soon, Jake and Son of Running Deer discussed that they would go back by their village to check on things. Everyone would be returning there to live sooner or later. Much had to be done to enlarge their village area for the additional teepees that would be needed to house the new families.

Jake and Son of Running Deer led the group into the wooded area, where the path narrowed. They discussed more about Running Antelope's disappearance and Jake softly patted his best friend on the shoulder.

Tame Tiger and his friend pulled up the rear, so that Lacey, Jillie and their family were all securely kept safe. Jillie was in the lead behind Son of Running Deer. Miguel was next with Aiken right behind Miguel. Aiken and Miguel had become rather tight and that made Jillie very uncomfortable. Aiken was feeling much better now than he had the day before and was paying more attention to details. Following Aiken was Andrew, Chase and then Adam. Behind Adam, Gregory and Blake chatted back and forth. Lacey had positioned herself in front of Tame Tiger's best friend. The girls were also protecting their brothers, cousins and Miguel. They had been here many times and felt safe, but were always on alert.

Miss Virginia, Tye and Tess were in their beastly forms running through the woods all around the travelers. They would dart in and out, from side to side, making sure everyone was okay. Jillie would make a whistling noise and Tess would appear from nowhere. Lacey was much quieter. She would only have to think out for Tye and he would appear.

Miss Virginia, well, she seemed to be everywhere. She was the most protective of all. She loved this family and would do anything to protect them.

Once they reached the edge of the woods, they all matched up with others and began chatting. The conversations were mainly in English and Tame Tiger would translate things to his best friend, Crazy Horse.

Gregory was now walking with Uncle Jake and Son of Running Deer. "Uncle Jake, do you need us to help you build up your village?"

"Oh no Greg; you all need to help Lacey and Jillie get the farm in order and start farming again. There is much to do and I think Miguel is going to stay around and help get you all started. He has much farming knowledge and he's very connected to us all. He is one of our descendants, so I know we live on and that makes me happy. I wish I could meet the people of the village today, but for some reason I don't think that would be a good idea. Somehow, our people move northwest at some point in time and I don't know if that means we all move or just some of us. Time will have to tell," Jake explained, as he thought hard about the present and the future.

Lacey came trotting up along side of her brother wanting to know what he and their uncle were discussing, "What are all the discussions about?"

"Oh, your brother was asking if we need help with the village expansion, but I explained to him that he needed to help you. I was just about to tell him that you, Will and I have already have outlined what needs to be done to get the farm up and running. I think, with all the help, you'll get plenty done this summer," Jake replied.

The sky was beginning to show signs of dawn.

"By the time we reach the portal, it should be almost dark on the other side," Lacey said.

"Yeah, please be careful. I am not crossing back with you all. It's too dangerous if someone is out looking for you now. Remember, you were all camping out on the farmland and lost track of time, because you were having so much fun," Jake said smiling to himself.

"We did have a great time Uncle Jake," Gregory said.

Blake came up behind Lacey and grabbed her at the shoulders. "You left me behind as usual. I am going to stop coming around if you don't stop leaving me all the time," Blake said, hugging Lacey now.

"I'm sorry Blake; you do always get the raw end of the stick, don't you?" Lacey answered back. "I'll be more considerate of your feelings. I am so glad we don't have to keep this secret from some of the family now. It would be so nice to be able to share this with everyone Uncle Jake."

"Well, let's 'never say never', but let's let the stars direct that fate. Maybe it's in the stars. I don't know. I would love for my brothers, sisters, parents, cousins and everyone to help out, but we don't know this destiny thing. I do hope it was meant for your brother and cousins all to come along as well as Miguel. We cannot worry about it now. It has happened."

Miguel was in deep discussion now with Tame Tiger and Crazy Horse. Even though their dialect was different, they spoke the same language. Miguel's accent had a twang to it and the girls attributed that to being from the mountains. Miguel told his ancestors some of the stories he had heard as a young boy, which confused Tame Tiger a bit. Of course, he had not lived it yet. Or maybe, it was not he that would live to see these things. Tame Tiger said that he would be more in tuned with everything now and when he was leader of the people; he would use this as his guide if needed. Miguel never even realized that Running Antelope, also known to Jillie as Lope, was the same great warrior and chief, Lope, who had joined the people in his village. If he had, history might have changed right here. He was gone from this family, but his life was not in vain. History was winding its destiny every minute.

Jillie was walking with her cousins, Andrew, Chase and Adam. They were all close in age and enjoyed hanging out together. The boys teased their petite cousin how they would never challenge her again, because Tess was way too ferocious for them.

As they mentioned her name, guess who arrived. Tess sat upon Jillie's shoulder as a cute and cuddly white kitten looking at the three cousins. She stretched out her neck to see if the boys would reach to pet her. Andrew did and Tess let out a ferocious roar causing Andrew to fall backwards and the other two to stop dead in their tracks.

Jillie laughed so hard she almost caused Tess to fall off, but her magic didn't allow her to topple off from Jillie's shoulder. "Oh, come on now boys; we are not afraid of my sweet, innocent cat, are we?"

"Totally unfair-. Why did you and Lacey get the magical cats and we didn't get squat?" Chase complained.

"What about me? I have to live with Nadia, who is five with a protective cat, I mean cougar!" Adam added to the conversation.

"Well, I am not complaining. I have Lucky Lad and he's the smartest dog in the world!" Andrew chimed in smiling and realizing that Lucky Lad was not with them. "On my gosh; where is my dog? Mom will be so mad if I have left him behind and how would I tell her he's three hundred years lost!?"

Jillie whispered to Tess to go find Lucky Lad and her little kitten disappeared immediately from their sight.

"Where did she go?" Andrew asked.

"To save your rear end," Jillie said. "She went to get Lucky Lad. I think he was having so much fun with the village dogs, he totally forgot about us and you."

"Thanks cuz. Mom would be so mad. She loves that dog more than me I sometimes think, but then again, he doesn't talk back," Andrew commented, thinking he should really be nicer to his mom. She was a very special person and oh so smart. She was involved in things he had no idea and she never even talked about it.

The group came to the tree and the cave. They all said their good-byes with hugs, hand shakes and wishes of good fortune and care. Uncle Jake gathered them all around him.

"We're all here to help one another. Miss Virginia will be back and forth to check on you all soon and I'll visit once we have our village expanded and secured from intruders. At least I hope we do. Now you all need to get ready and cross back to your time," Jake said.

"Wait, I cannot go yet!" Andrew yelled out. "My mom will be a very upset woman if I have lost her dog."

With that, they all heard loud barking coming closer and they all turned in the direction of Lucky Lad being chased by a black panther. What a sight and they all laughed. Lucky Lad knew exactly who he needed to run up to and knock down. Lucky and his Andrew rolled around happy to see one another.

"That's my boy. You are the best dog and I may just have to take you as my own," Andrew said.

Lucky Lad stopped and looked at Andrew. He barked as if he was scolding him. Everyone laughed again.

"Okay, Okay; I know you are my mom's best friend, but you can be mine too."

"Let's go troop," Gregory commanded. "I think we have lots to do and I think we need to get home, rest and be up by five in the morning to start our exercising and getting in shape."

"What?" Almost every cousin yelled in unison.

Gregory laughed. "Just joking you wimps; I just wanted to see your reactions. I guess I know where you all will be while I am running my five miles in the morning."

"Tame Tiger, our horses? We left them in the fields with your horses. Can you bring them soon? I totally forgot about Warrior Girl and Storm Cloud," Lacey said with worry.

"Yes, I'll come over in a few days during daytime, but night in your time, with them in tow," Tame Tiger said, as he hugged his warrior sister, Lacey, in tight.

"Okay, let's get going Gregory," Lacey said. With Tye safely tucked in her left arm, she took Blake's left hand and walked into the cave's portal opening before she could get more choked up.

"I'll go last," Jillie said, and motioned for her cousins to get going.

Tess assumed her position in Jillie's right arm.

Gregory and Aiken went; then Andrew, Chase and Adam went, leaving Miguel alone with Jillie.

"I'll go with you Jillie," Miguel said and held out his hand for her take.

Jillie stepped forward and placed her left hand in Miguel's right. Together, they said good-bye one more time and walked hand-in- hand to their future.

6 A FARM ALIVE ONCE MORE

The cousins, Blake and Miguel all made it back to the farm and their present lives. Nothing would really be the same for them and the responsibilities that Lacey and Jillie had felt were now shared amongst them all. They were all tired and ready for some sleep. Before they all forgot, Jillie ran to the crevice at the base of the large oak tree and started pulling out cell phones, where they all had left them. There were messages, but not one person wanted to listen to them now. They silently walked back through the pasture as they made their way carefully back to the farmhouse. Gregory led his troop as he looked all around for any sign of trouble ahead. Tye and Tess stayed close to Lucky Lad to keep him quiet. He understood their quiet meows towards him. As the group of tired time travelers neared the barn, they didn't see a soul looking for them.

"Looks like we're okay for now, so let's all get some sleep and we'll review the plans for the farm work tomorrow. It's just ten o'clock, so we should all be ready to 'rise and shine' tomorrow by six AM sharp.

No one disagreed with Gregory. They all just fell in behind the girls, who had taken the lead towards the farmhouse. When they reached the porch, Lacey fumbled for the key that she had hidden in case they needed an extra one. This was a good time to need the extra key. She flipped on the porch light and led the way into the kitchen and then into the family room, where there were two nice sofas for sleeping.

"Blake and Gregory can stay in here. Jillie and I will stay in the front bedroom and the rest of you are upstairs. There are plenty of places to crash."

Their great aunt had restored the upstairs to something like it had been for her four brothers. She had put four single beds up there and some neat memorabilia of their lives from their youth. Lacey had not had the heart to dismantle anything up there yet.

"What about Miguel?" Jillie asked, quickly realizing that he didn't really have a place to call his.

"Oh, he can stay in the living room that is next to our room. That couch actually folds down into a futon bed," Lacey said smiling at Miguel. "You can be our protector tonight."

"I'll gladly take that honor," Miguel said, as he looked over at Jillie.

Jillie blushed, smiled and then walked on into the front bedroom. She didn't want to deal with this uncomfortable feeling right now. She was too tired.

The four younger cousins all headed up the stairs, sounding like a bunch of cows. But almost instantly, there was total silence.

Gregory and Blake said their good nights to Lacey and made themselves comfortable on the couches.

Lacey walked with Miguel to the living room and made sure he had a pillow and a blanket. "Good night Miguel. I'll see you in the morning."

"Unless you see me in your dreams," Miguel said.

Lacey looked at him, but didn't bother to really think about it. She smiled and went back through the house to go to the bathroom and wondered how long it would be until someone came down for the bathroom.

After quietly closing the door to the room she was sharing with Jillie, she could tell that Jillie was out for the night. She quietly crawled beside her cousin. For about one moment, she thought about Miguel in her dreams and drifted off to sleep.

They all slept like rocks. No one actually got up to run to

the restroom before the morning light started waking them up. Gregory was up first of course. He was used to getting little sleep and 'waking up with the chickens'. He got up, put on a large pot of strong coffee and headed to the bathroom to get the first hot shower in days.

"The little luxuries we take for granted everyday," Gregory thought to himself, as he let the hot water rinse off the soap. Before he could turn off the water, a knock came at the door.

"Just one minute," Gregory yelled.

"It's Andrew. I gotta go man."

"Hold it or go outside. This is a farm you know. There is plenty of room and lots of bushes around the yard," Gregory yelled out laughing to himself.

Nothing was said back and he heard the door shut close. Andrew had listened to his direction and Gregory laughed even more, but hurried himself out of the shower and quickly dried off.

As he was walking out of the bathroom, with a towel wrapped around his lower torso, Andrew came in from outside.

"I always liked going outside for some reason. It just seemed cool to me," Andrew said smiling.

"Oh yeah, since you thought you were a dog when you were little," Gregory said, teasing his younger cousin.

"Oh, you remember that?" Andrew asked, as he threw his head back chuckling to himself. Gregory's dad was so worried that Andrew would think he was a dog, because he was born to a house full of dogs. His Uncle Wayne used to bark at him, when he was a little baby. Andrew didn't remember that part, but he was told all about it over the years.

"Come on puppy dog, let's go get your littermates up," Gregory said, as he laughed at his little joke.

"If I was a dog, I would have attacked you already. Go on with yourself and get out of my way," Andrew said and he shoved his older cousin out of the way.

Gregory laughed louder and followed Andrew into the family room, where Blake was still sleeping. "I'll get my sister's dead head up and you go get the others moving. Start with the boys first. If my sister or Jillie get in that bathroom, no one will get in."

Andrew walked into the front living room and Miguel was already up and stretching. He waved to Andrew, but didn't say much. Andrew gave him a nod and went stomping up the staircase to the attic room, where his cousins were all still sound asleep. Even Lucky Lad was still sound asleep at the foot of his bed.

Andrew walked over and gently rubbed his mom's loyal friend. Lucky Lad opened his eyes, but he didn't raise his head. He was still tired and didn't want to move yet. Andrew smiled and whispered, "Don't worry; your food is waiting on you when you're ready." Lucky Lad closed his eyes and was back to sleep.

Andrew went in between his two younger cousins, Adam and Chase. At the same time, he pulled the blankets off of them and yelled, "Wake UP!" The boys both jumped up to attention. Andrew started laughing and moved over to Aiken's bed. Aiken was awake, but watching his cousin bother the others.

"Don't even think about it LITTLE cousin, if you know what is good for you," Aiken said with confidence that Andrew wouldn't mess with him.

Aiken felt like a new person and was so thankful for the care he was given. He hoped that was the end of his sickness.

"Get up then and I won't," Andrew said, as he picked up a small pillow and threw it at Aiken before descending back down the stairs. "It's time to get breakfast if you want some energy before farming starts or whatever that may be."

Adam grabbed his clothes and headed downstairs. Chase sat back down for a moment, rubbed his eyes and then scratched his head. "I have no clue how to farm."

"Neither do I, but we'll just go with the flow little cuz," Aiken replied, as he jumped up, grabbed up his clothes and also headed to the bathroom hoping that it was empty.

The girls had heard the commotion and they had already headed over to the other house using the hidden stairs down to the underground storage area, which led to the outside. There were two bathrooms there and they could have a few moments of peace.

The boys all thought they were still asleep and no one wanted to bother them yet. Gregory had decided to get breakfast going for the troop. He had bacon and sausage cooking and coffee ready to pour. He had given Andrew the chore of scrambling enough eggs to feed everyone.

When Adam walked in from the bathroom, he was given the duty of making toast. Aiken was next out of the bathroom and he was given the chore of finding the plates, cups and glasses. Finally Chase was done getting ready and he was directed to get silverware and napkins out. Blake and Miguel had gone out to the shed, next to the house, and were inventorying the supplies: hammers, nails, hoes, rakes, etc. Miguel knew enough of what was needed to farm and make repairs. Blake was anxious to learn. He would be living on this farm for the rest of his life, if his plans went the way he hoped. He wanted to carry his weight and make a difference.

The girls walked around the well house, where they found Blake and Miguel in the shed. They walked in to greet them good morning and surprised the two, who thought they were still sound asleep.

"Well good morning boys, I mean men," Lacey said with a huge smile on her face. She walked over to Blake and gave him a gentle good morning kiss.

"Hey sweetheart," Blake said with an even bigger smile.

"Hey Miguel," Jillie said next.

"Hey my little medicine woman," Miguel said with a wink.

Jillie blushed and smiled at him.

"We thought you two were still sound asleep in the house," Blake said.

"Well, how could anyone sleep with all the commotion going on with Andrew stomping up and down the staircase? We made a quick dash to the other house and had our own bathrooms," Lacey replied.

"Wow, I keep forgetting about all the hidden stairs and the escape to the outside," Blake said. "I should have thought of that myself and ventured over to the other house this morning instead of waiting on the bathroom."

"Hey guys, food is ready," Chase yelled, as he poked his head out from the farmhouse porch. Chases didn't bother waiting to hold the door open. He was starving.

Lacey, Jillie, Blake and Miguel headed into the farmhouse for a wonderful breakfast organized and prepared by Gregory. Andrew was on the porch tending to Lucky Lad; he had finally decided to come down and eat. Tye and Tess were quietly watching Lucky Lad eat, when the girls, Blake and Miguel walked into the porch.

"Oh Andrew, don't forget our cats now," Lacey said. "Their food is right there in the cabinet."

"Hey don't get the idea that I am the animal feeder," Andrew complained, but headed toward the cabinet and retrieved the cats' food to pour some food in two bowls.

"Just leave the door ajar and they all can let themselves outside to go to the potty," Jillie added, as she disappeared to the dining room behind Lacey.

"You're not ordering me around," Andrew yelled back. Before he joined his cousins for breakfast, he filled three bowls with fresh water and fixed the door to the outside as he had been instructed.

The others were all surprised to see the girls up and dressed and ready to begin the day.

"Gregory, you have definitely learned something in the Air Force," Lacey said to her big brother. She grabbed a plate already fixed with everything and headed to the big dining room, where the boys had everything set out. They had even used the antique buffet, where they had set out juice, milk, creamer and condiments.

"Wow, this is great," Jillie said, as she walked in the dining room with her plate. The boys left the two end chairs open for the girls and had moved chairs around so that all nine of them could fit around the table. Andrew was the last one to join them and he was mumbling to himself.

The girls laughed at their cousin. "Too much work for the spoiled one?" Jillie kidded her cousin.

Andrew huffed and then gave a big smile. "If any trouble comes our way, I bet I will be the one they all save first," Andrew said. "I'll feed them every morning as long as I know they will take care of me too."

Everyone laughed and then dug into their wonderful breakfast. They ate, they talked and they planned out their day. They didn't revisit their entire experience of the last couple of days, because they didn't need to talk about it. They all understood how important this farm was, is and always will be to so many lives. They all wanted to get it up and running, so that it could almost pay for itself and have jobs to offer to any family member who wanted to help out. As Lacey had promised, it was the families' farm and she planned on keeping her word.

Jake had helped them out a lot and had made a list of the things that really needed to be considered and hopefully accomplished during the summer months: plough up, plant and harvest two huge fields. One field, which was the same field where their great-grandfather had harvested pumpkins, corn, water melons, squashes and eggplants, was going to be just that. The other would be smaller, but closer to the house and it would be the garden for: peas, beans of different kinds, beets, potatoes, okra, lettuce, cabbage and whatever else they decided they wanted to try.

A fence was needed to start surrounding the property line. Partial fences were halfway standing, but so much needed repair. The one thing they didn't have to worry about was the barn. Tame Tiger had taken care of most of its repairs and it was awesome.

As they were finishing up their breakfast and the list, Gregory asked who wanted what tasks. Miguel would be over the two fields' plowing and planting. He would teach Andrew and Chase to plough the fields with the tractors, while Gregory, Blake, Aiken and Adam began working on the fencing.

Lacey and Jillie began their jobs by cleaning up, preparing lots of sandwiches and putting on a huge pot of spaghetti sauce to simmer all day. These boys would need lots of carbohydrates for energy. They decided to plan out a week's worth of menus and head to the store to get what they would need to keep these guys working. Jillie wanted to buy up some herbs, which she now knew could be used for different things.

"Seeds, we need to get seeds don't we?" Jillie asked.

"There are lots of seeds in the granary all nice and tucked away in tin cans," Lacey replied. "That is another place where Tame Tiger had spent some time and it is amazing what all he did for us."

Jillie smiled as she thought about him and then her smile went away as she thought about her Lope. Lacey noticed the look on her face and knew exactly what she was thinking.

"I know it's hard to think that Lope may be really gone, but maybe it is something that was supposed to happen too," Lacey said sounding like a true warrior and a leader.

"Yeah, I guess. I just felt so sorry for his family and his girl," Jillie replied back. I am going to think it was all for a reason and I hope that one day I get to see the reason."

"I hope we both get to witness that Jillie," Lacey said and put her hand on her cousin's back and gave her a slight hug.

"Thanks Lacey. That's enough. I am ready to move forward and put the past behind me," Jillie said and left the room with tears in her eyes to fetch her pocketbook.

Lacey let her go and also went to get her purse in the same room, but didn't say anything further about it at all. The girls left in silence to the grocery store. Lacey drove and turned on some up beat music to try and change the mood. Jillie sensed what her cousin was trying to do and realized that it wouldn't do any good to pout and started talking about their day's work.

"I guess we're going to end up being the cooks and cleaners, huh?" Jillie asked, as she thought about what they really needed to do.

"I think you guessed right, but we cannot do all this ourselves. So, if we have to cook all summer, then so be it. Think about our great-grandmother, who I hear cooked three huge meals everyday and also did other chores like gather eggs, make butter and cottage cheese, make sausage, make pies and cakes and also sew most of her children's clothes. So, I am not going to complain one bit and I don't think you should either," Lacey answered, as she glanced over at her cousin.

They rushed through the grocery store spending about two hundred dollars, but felt like they did really good. Jillie's mood was so much lighter on the way back home and they began talking about the farm and how much they wanted to do. They arrived back to the farm with tractors moving, hammers banging and the animals running around over seeing all the work. Lucky Lad came running and grabbed a bag from Jillie's hold and took off to the house. The girls laughed so hard. Soon, the cats turned into their beast forms and also helped carry the plastic bags into the house. No one would have believed it and the girls only hoped that no one passing by noticed. They didn't have the heart to scold their protectors and let it ride.

Jillie offered to start the sandwiches, while Lacey put the groceries away. The cats turned back into their small feline forms and joined Lucky Lad out of the way taking a rest. They watched their girls, as if they were making sure they were doing it all the right way. Every once in a while, Jillie would go over and toss a small bite of deli meat to the threesome. They loved it and took their turns.

Just as the girls were putting the last bit of groceries away, the men folk came bounding inside with hunger. They were all lined up and taking their turn in the bathroom. One by one, they walked into the dining room and filled their plates with sandwiches, chips and cookies. The girls had also put a bowl of fruit on the buffet to adorn the table, where they had the homemade lemonade already poured out. It was their great-grandmother's recipe and made in the same large five gallon jar that she actually had used. Lots of lemons, lots of sugar and served super cold!

"Boy, this lemonade is the best," Adam called out, as he went for his second glass.

All the cousins agreed and they were all begging for more. Lacey and Jillie were all grins.

95

"Well, if they are able to really see us all here, I bet they are so happy to see so much hustle and bustle around this place again," Lacey said. "I can tell you, this preparing and cooking for so many is a job all itself and our great-grandmother did so much more."

"I think we should raise our glasses to our great-grandparents, our parents and all those farmers in this world," Aiken said, as he raised his glass.

"Here, here," Gregory followed.

Everyone raised their glass and held it there until Jillie said, "To all of you that walked this land before us."

The glasses clanked together and they all guzzled down their cold, refreshing lemonades. It was a day to remember. It was the day the farm began a new life that would live on forever and allow all those that passed on to walk and enjoy it forever.

"Oh, I didn't feed the animals," Andrew said.

"They only need to eat twice per day and we gave them plenty of deli meats earlier. Just feed them after we eat dinner," Jillie said. "You're taking your job very seriously there, Andrew."

"Well, someone has to remember to take care of them," Andrew said, as he looked over at the three animals lying very content all snuggled together napping. They were just being the perfect pets.

As they were finishing up their lunch, they heard a car drive up. Lucky Lad took off with a flying leap. He knew the sound of the jeep.

"Hey, it's my mom. I thought she wasn't going to be back for a while," Andrew said and headed out to greet his mom.

Lucy was hugging her big, loyal dog with one hand and had something else snuggled in her other arm. Andrew called for Lucky Lad to calm down.

As the others came outside to great Andrew's mom too, they all noticed the something in her arms. She was holding a black and white cat.

"Hey sweetie," Lucy directed to her son. "How's it going?"

"We're fine mom. What have you got there?" Andrew questioned with a look of disbelief. "Not another animal mom?"

"Well, don't ask me why, but this sassy thing hasn't left me alone since about a day or so after I dropped Lucky Lad off to you. He came up to me in a parking lot and when I came out from shopping, he was still there. I couldn't go off and leave him, so I offered him to jump in and he did. So, we have a new animal for the farm," Lucy explained.

The cat jumped down and instantly ran over to Lucky Lad and walked in and out and around his legs. Lucky Lad bent his head down and the two of them greeted one another with smells and licks.

"Well now, that is not something I expected. It's as if they know one another, but from where?" Andrew asked.

"Well, you never know about things. Life is full of surprises all the time," Lacey said, as she stared at this cat.

"Yeah, something is definitely familiar with that cat," Jillie said.

"I thought so too," Lucy said. "Oh well, do you guys mind taking him in too for a while?" Lucy asked. "How are things going around here? Getting lots done?"

"Well, we took the first few days to kind of just hang out and get to know the lay of the land," Gregory put in really quick.

Everyone nodded and agreed. Lucy looked at them all with a kind of puzzled look, but was so tickled at how they seemed so happy to be here.

"Well, do you think you could give your old aunt a glass of lemonade?" Lucy asked.

"Sure thing, come on in Aunt Lucy." Lacey said and they walked inside together.

"Lucky Lad, do you know this cat?" Andrew whispered, as he came close to his dog and the cat.

The cat came and rubbed all around Andrew and then walked amongst all the cousins, Blake and then Miguel. He seemed to linger around Miguel the longest and kept meowing.

"Something seems really strange, like this cat knows me,"

Miguel said, as he bent down to pick up the cat.

The cat seemed to snuggle right into Miguel's neck, as he gently rubbed his new feline friend.

"Well Mr. Miguel, it looks like you have a new friend," Andrew commented. "And guess what, he is your responsibility. I am not going to be in charge of all the animals."

"Gladly," Miguel said and walked away with the cat happily snuggled in his arms.

Inside, Lacey and Lucy were chatting, while Lacey was picking up from lunch. Lucy helped herself to some deli meats and cheeses. Jillie came back inside and joined her aunt and cousin. She helped Lacey with the last bit of clean up.

"Hey, I want to see the horses I hear you have now," Lucy said.

The girls both froze in their steps. Lacey was thinking of what to say, when Gregory walked into the kitchen,

"Aunt Lucy wants to see the horses, Greg," Lacey said, as she looked at her brother with big eyes.

"Oh, sorry Aunt Lucy, I turned them out to pasture earlier this morning. I'll go round them up if you want me to," Gregory said with confidence.

"Oh don't bother; I need to get on my way. I'll see them when I come back for Lucky Lad and I guess I'll take the cat," Lucy said.

"Oh, I think that cat has found his new owner. I do believe he has claimed Miguel as his," Jillie said.

"Yep, that cat seems like he knows Miguel. And well, I think he wants him too," Gregory added. "I am heading back to the fields to get some more fencing up and I better make sure the horses haven't gotten away from the land, huh sis?"

"Oh yes, you better do that," Lacey said.

Lucy looked at them and thought they were acting odd, but it was probably just her and the communication gap between generations.

"K-then, I am off," Lucy said, as she hugged her nieces and nephew and headed out the door behind Gregory to say good-bye to the rest, but they were all scattered.

Lucy saw her son on a tractor heading down the field. She honked her horn and he turned around and waved. She left with a wonderful feeling about her grandparents' farmland.

"Jillie, when do you think Tame Tiger will remember to bring the horses?" Lacey asked wondering about them. "I miss them."

"Me too; maybe we should go back and get them," Jillie said.

"If he doesn't bring them back tomorrow, then we'll go get them right after dark tomorrow when it will be light there. We can travel much quicker," Lacey said, as she made a mental note to herself to remember the horses tomorrow. They still were not quite used to having them, but they wanted them.

"Okay, let's go see if we can be of any help around this place. Let's see if Chase has a garden ready to be planted," Jillie said, as she and Lacey left the house to find their cousins.

Miguel was riding on the tractor behind Chase, as he was pointing out things for him to notice. The new arrival was riding on the tractor as well. The girls were amazed and they looked for the other three animals. There they were, all quietly sitting at the edge of this new garden watching the tractor go up and down making rows and rows for the seeds to be planted.

"Lacey, let's go walk the field and look for arrowheads like our Uncle Jake used to do," Jillie said.

"What a great idea Jillie," Lacey replied and they both jumped up and ran to start walking the turned up earth to look for treasures like their uncle had found.

Tye, Tess and Lucky Lad came bounding across the field and followed behind the girls. Chase noticed the girls walking and looking around. Chase smiled at his cousins as he put his thumb up to let them know that he knew what they were doing. He was happy to be a part of this great land and its secrets of life.

Miguel said something to Chase and Chase slowed the tractor down enough for Miguel to jump down. And down came the cat too. The new cat followed right beside of Miguel, who was walking to catch up with Jillie.

"Hey what are you and Lacey doing?" Miguel asked.

"Looking for arrowheads like the ones Uncle Jake found years ago," Jillie said. "It appears you have a new friend. What are you going to call him?"

"Well, I don't know if he's mine to name." Miguel commented.

"I don't think Aunt Lucy would mind if you wanted to keep him. She just wants him to have a home," Jillie said, as she squatted down to look at a stone, but got up without it.

"Not an arrowhead-" Jillie started, but got cut off by Lacey yelling about her find.

"Look, look, I have found something. Oh my gosh; it's something that I am pretty sure Tame Tiger made. Look, look!" Lacey yelled, as she came running at Jillie and Miguel.

Lacey held out the large, carved arrowhead with a certain insignia etched into it. "This is how Tame Tiger acknowledges himself. See it's a tiger's paw with a happy face. He made this long ago and now I have found it. It's almost impossible to think that he is living right now three hundred years ago. He probably killed something with this arrowhead. I'll have to show it to him when he brings the horses back." Lacey took her shirt and rubbed the stone clean. She admired her find and gently slid it into her right, front pants pocket.

Lucky Lad, the new black and white cat and the two magical cats were all running all around. Lucky Lad barked as the three cats meowed and hissed. It seemed as if they were playing a game of chase.

"I swear I think something is up with that cat," Lacey said.

"What do you mean Lacey?" Jillie asked.

"Well, I think there is more to that cat than meets the eyes. He is way too comfortable around all of us," Lacey answered.

"You know, I feel the same way. I feel like I know him, but I have never seen him," Miguel added.

"Oh well, he seems to be a really good pet, so are you going to claim him Miguel?" Jillie asked, as she glanced up at Miguel's deep, brown eyes.

"Oh yeah, I want him for sure. I think he is special too and maybe we'll find out one of these days. I think we should get some things planted in this here garden or your brothers and cousins will be furious," Miguel said, as he smiled directly to Jillie.

Lacey noticed the two of them making eyes at one another and decided that 'three is a crowd'. "I am going to go find Blake and see if he needs my help."

Miguel and Jillie didn't really hear her, but they both nodded and smiled at one another.

"Let's go grab some seeds to get this garden growing," Miguel said, as he kept smiling at Jillie.

Lacey left smiling too and went to find her sweetheart.

"What should we plant here?" Jillie asked.

"Well, you want to plant those things that you would like to have close at hand like: green beans, squash, butter beans, okra, cucumbers, lettuce, kale, egg plant, potatoes, and sweet potatoes. But, we'll plant the potatoes, sweet potatoes and corn in another garden so that we can plant lots of vegetables. Let's go get all the ones we want to do here and we'll do two rows per vegetable," Miguel explained.

"Okay, we have all the seeds in the granary in tin cans to keep them dry. Let's go grab some and a couple of hoes to move the dirt back over the seeds," Jillie said.

Miguel and Jillie closely walked to the granary with the animals all in tow running all around them. The black and white cat kept coming up and rubbing up against Jillie and then Miguel.

"I feel something strange about that cat too Miguel," Jillie said. "It's a good feeling, but strange."

"Nothing will surprise me after all that we have seen and experienced now," Miguel said. "I think he was meant to be, so let's just enjoy him." Miguel opened the door to the granary, walked up the step and then turned to hold his hand out for Jillie.

Jillie accepted and allowed Miguel to pull her up. The sparks were igniting between them, as they were meant to be. Neither noticed the glow coming from underneath Jillie's dark shirt. Miguel knew she would be his future and now she was beginning to understand it all too. Lope was no longer in her thoughts, but always in her heart. Little did she know, but Lope was making his own history and history that would touch Jillie's life many more times in the future.

"You get the seeds and I'll get the hoes. Let's try and get this garden planted by tonight," Miguel directed.

"Yes sir. I agree," Jillie said and smiled with her eyes beaming.

This moment began their future of working side by side.

***

Meanwhile, Lacey had gone to find Blake, who was helping Aiken with some fence repairs.

"Hey, where are Gregory and Aiken?" Lacey asked.

"Oh they are further down in the pasture checking out where more repairs are needed. You are welcome to help us out if you would like Lacey girl," Blake replied back to his girlfriend.

"Adam thanks so much for coming and helping us out," Lacey said to her younger cousin.

"What and miss all the fun? I am having a blast. This is too surreal," Adam said and gave his cousin a big smile and a wink.

"Okay, what can I do?" Lacey asked and she pulled out some working gloves to help save her hands from wear and tear.

"How about holding up the post, while Adam and I tighten up the barbwire and nail it to the post? We could work a lot faster with another set of hands," Blake said and he leaned over and gave Lacey a light peck on her cheek.

"I didn't get one of those for helping you," Adam said kidding Blake and turning his face so that his cheek was there for a peck.

Lacey leaned in and gave her cousin a little peck on his cheek. "There you go little cousin. Now get to work," Lacey said and laughed.

The three worked in harmony chatting it up. Lacey asked Adam to catch her up on his life and Adam asked Lacey all about her adventures back and forth in time. Blake added some great stories and even the one of how jealous he was of Will, really known as Tame Tiger. Lacey giggled and thought back when Tame Tiger knocked Blake out with the squeeze of the neck.

"I know what you're thinking about and I now know how to do that little maneuver, so don't mess with me little woman," Blake said and winked.

Adam laughed along with them.

"Do you think my little sister will be okay? I mean she is so young. Will she have a normal life?" Adam asked.

"She'll be fine, but a normal life is doubtful. How does one have a normal life with a protective cat that can change into a cougar?" Lacey replied. "Don't worry about her. Tea will not allow anything to happen to her.'

"Yeah, I bet and I just hope I don't get eaten along the way," Adam said, as he thought about a cougar pacing around the house.

"You should feel really lucky, because you're in the circle and she will be there for you and Luke too. Trust me, our feline friends are wonderful. Sometimes they do get a bit sassy or rebellious, but for the most part they are awesome," Lacey said.

"Not to mention that they can be tyrants if they don't like you," Blake snapped out.

"Oh Blake, get over it. He was just protecting me and he was just a kitten in training," Lacey said and started laughing uncontrollably.

"What? Tell me what happened to you Blake?" Adam begged.

"I told you guys, the little demon hid inside a coffee mug waiting for me to pick it up and it scared me so that I dropped the glass coffee pot with hot coffee in it. Yeah, all over Lacey's kitchen," Blake said, as he remembered the event and started laughing too. "I guess it is a bit funny now, but it wasn't at the time. Especially when the two of them started hissing and growling at me, I was a bit scared."

"Hey, they didn't turn into their beastly forms," Lacey added laughing.

Blake looked at Lacey. "I think that would have done me in for good."

Adam laughed and laughed and then he stopped. "Tea better not do things like that to me or I will-" Adam stopped, as he thought about it all.

"You will do nothing," Lacey commanded. "That little creature turns into a great big cougar my dear and she will do anything to protect her Nadia. Anything, you hear?"

"Okay, okay, but I am just keeping my distance and letting that nice, little kitty come to me," Adam said and resumed his work.

Blake and Lacey smiled at one another and then they both winked at Adam, who rolled his eyes. The three of them kept on working side by side and moved further and further down into the pasture, where they finally saw the Gregory and Aiken.

***

Gregory and Aiken, the hunters of the family, happened to stop near the oak tree and the deer stand, where they were viewing the footage of the animals.

"Oh my gosh Gregory, look what was captured!" Aiken said, as they watched the event of the wolves all showing up.

"I think we better delete this footage before our dads see this or Uncle Nash. We'll have hunters, from all over, wanting to come here and exterminate them," Gregory said, as he began deleting the film's captured moments.

As the two young men stood together taking care of something that could lead to total disaster, the time portal opened up. Neither one of them flinched or jumped as they just stood there waiting to see who was coming for a visit.

It was Tame Tiger and he immediately saw them too. He smiled real big and said, "HOW" and started laughing. Tame Tiger had a great sense of humor.

Gregory and Aiken both put their hands up and said

"HOW" back. They all three laughed as they slapped one another quite hard across the shoulders to show each other their muscles.

The portal closed.

"I wanted to bring Warrior Girl and Storm Cloud back to the girls, before they think we want to keep them. They need them here for more protection," Tame Tiger stated.

"It's clear; it's just us, who know all about the big secret. We're all working on the farm, planting two huge gardens, mending the fences and trying to be normal. You know, all that normal stuff," Gregory said.

"OK. I will go back and bring them forward with me. I'll be right back," Tame Tiger said and he went to the oak tree and placed an arrowhead to open the portal door again. He ran so fast and jumped into the portal that Gregory and Aiken were impressed.

"Obviously, he is not scared of that opening, but I am not a big fan of jumping through time," Aiken remarked.

"Me neither brother, but it is an adventure we'll never forget. I hope we only have to return for the annual Harvest festivities that we hear are so great," Gregory replied. "Come on, let's finish up with this tape and finish looking for broken fence. We'll need to keep the horses inside this farmland. Not to mention other animals the girls bring here to get this farm going."

Aiken nodded, as he took the camera and finished erasing the tape. Gregory walked over to the edge of the woods and began inspecting the fence that had been there for close to a hundred years now. His great-grandfather had fenced his entire farmland probably around the 1920's.

In just minutes, Tame Tiger appeared again with the horses and his beautiful bride to be. She had made wonderful clothes for all of Lacey's and Jillie's brothers and cousins. The bundles were tied onto Storm Cloud, who was ready to see Lacey, Jillie and Blake. Storm Cloud knew Blake was his owner and wanted to find him. He neighed to Tame Tiger and he nodded.

"Where is Blake?" Tame Tiger asked. "Storm Cloud wants

to see him."

But, it didn't take long for the horses to spot Lacey, Blake and Adam. Tame Tiger took the bundles off of his back just in time for him to charge off in full speed.

Blake saw him coming and was running for him too. They were a pair now and Blake was 'in the circle' forever now.

Warrior Girl, who was with foul, gently galloped to see Lacey and the greetings were another mysterious miracle. These two animals, brought from the past, brought another link to tie this land together from the past to the present to the future. Destiny was working as planned.

Gregory and Aiken admired the wonderful, handmade leather outfits.

"You will need these for the Fall Harvest festivities. It's pretty cold and Beautiful Butterfly wanted to make sure you all felt at home and also be warm. She is going to make the best Chief's wife. I will be a great leader with her by my side, just as your great-grandfather worked this farm with his lovely Tess by his side. They were great leaders of this family."

Gregory and Aiken smiled, as they admired the garments and thought about this land and their heritage.

"We're so honored," Gregory said and he held out his hand to hook Tame Tiger's.

Aiken did the same and then both men gently kissed Beautiful Butterfly on her cheeks.

"Let us say hello to Lacey and Blake and then we must go. There is much to do on our farm too this summer."

Lacey, Blake and Adam were already heading down with the horses following closely behind them and voicing their excitement to see their people. Adam fell back in between the horses and was enjoying their nudges of love.

Lacey immediately hugged Beautiful Butterfly and noticed the handsome outfits. They chatted in one another's language trying to have a conversation. They had come a long way. Tame Tiger smiled at these two remarkable women.

Blake gave Tame Tiger a hard smack on his shoulder and then received his. They hugged and both laughed together.

They were now brothers forever and shared many responsibilities to keep this land safe. Although Blake was not bound by blood, he was bound by his loyalty to Lacey and to winning Tame Tiger's respect and friendship. Blake had already accepted the responsibility of making sure Lacey would be safe and he would work by her side to keep this land safe for many lives that depended on them all.

Tame Tiger didn't leave Adam out of the welcomes and slapped him not so hard on his shoulder. He didn't want to totally scare the younger men yet. He was a passionate leader and he knew that to lead by fear would never work, but to lead by kindness would make him strong and he would have his warriors to always defend him and their village.

Adam gave a good smack back and smiled. "Nice to see you again Tame Tiger."

"Same here, my young warrior; take care of your little sister for us all. She is a big part of this land and will be so important to our families' survival forevermore," Tame Tiger said, as he looked deep into Adam's eyes.

Adam got the seriousness of his look and he nodded that he understood what he was saying, but he really didn't. "I'll be there for her when she needs me."

"Good," Tame Tiger said and slapped him again on his other shoulder.

Tame Tiger held out his hand to his wonderful woman and she put her hand in his. They smiled and said their good-byes one more time. He handed the arrowhead to Adam to open the portal and waited for the stone to be returned.

"Tame Tiger, wait!" Lacey yelled out, as she dug her hand into her right pants pocket and pulled out the stone she found just earlier today. "I found this today, when Chase was plowing up a garden near the farmhouse." Lacey handed the arrowhead stone over to Tame Tiger.

"I lost that today when we were hunting. I didn't strap it onto my stick good enough and it fell off. I should have done a better job," Tame Tiger said, as he examined the rock and looked at everyone. "I am not sure I should take it back, because I am fearful that it may change things. Your uncle tells me we have to be conscious of the things we give back and forth. You should keep this now, not only to remember me in case this door should ever stop opening, but also to keep things as they should be."

"I will cherish it my entire life and it will be handed down to my children," Lacey said.

Blake looked at her and smiled with the thought of Lacey's children, as they would be his too. Lacey smiled back and felt content as never before.

"Okay, time for us to get back to our lives," Tame Tiger said and pulled Beautiful Butterfly along to the portal door.

Before they stepped away from their sight, he turned back and said, "Until the Fall Harvest, unless we should need one another. Be safe and be strong my dear family."

Lacey had tears in her eyes, but quickly wiped them dry. "I think it's time to get back and start preparing dinner now. Someone needs to go let Andrew know he needs to start heading back up to the house soon."

"I'll go get him," Adam said. Can I ride Storm Cloud, Blake?"

"Of course, he's a gift to us all, but he's mine to own and love," Blake said and he walked over and gave his wonderful gift a big hug.

Adam jumped upon Storm Cloud's back and took off across the pastures, down to the big field Andrew was turning over for seeds to be planted tomorrow.

"Wow, he's a natural rider," Lacey said.

They all agreed and they walked silently back up to the farmhouse with Warrior Girl nudging her Lacey.

***

When they reached the pasture land close to the main house, Chase was now plowing another garden to the left side of the barn. Jillie and Miguel were in the first garden still planting seeds and 'chatting it up' and laughing.

Blake knocked Lacey and they both looked at one another with a look of 'how cute'. Aiken noticed too, but he had spent enough time with this strange guy to know that he was a major part of their family destiny and decided to let it go. He wasn't in control anyway.

Jillie saw her brother, Gregory, Lacey and Blake approaching with Warrior Girl. She rushed over to the horse and gave her a big hug and then rubbed her belly. "Hey little one, I cannot wait to see you."

"So, I guess Tame Tiger came over with them?" Jillie asked.

"And Beautiful Butterfly with all these wonderful outfits for the all the boys for the Fall Harvest and there is one for you too, Miguel," Lacey said, as she pulled out Miguel's handsome outfit.

Miguel was shocked and excited. He had something that his ancestors had made especially for him. His parents would be so happy and know that the stories were really true and he was going to be a major part of their family's destiny.

"Let's go get some dinner everyone. Wave at Chase and tell him to come on to the house," Lacey directed.

"I'll go get him," Miguel said and took off running to get Chase's attention. He had his head phones on and singing out loud as loud as he could. Miguel laughed, as he got closer and heard Chase singing his heart out.

"I'll take Warrior Girl to the barn and get the saddle and blanket off of her," Blake said and walked away with Warrior Girl beside of him.

When Chase finally saw Miguel laughing and waving, he turned off his music and drove the tractor up to him and shut it off.

"Come on, 'I'm so sexy' tractor driver," Miguel said. "It's getting close to dinner time."

"Great because I am starving," Chase said, as he turned off the tractor and jumped down.

The two young men headed straight for the farmhouse.

***

Storm Cloud galloped, with Adam riding to the large field,

where Andrew was plowing up the old garden, which was exactly like that of their great-grandfather. He wasn't alone, because Tye, Tess, the new cat and Lucky Lad had all wandered down to run all around the garden watching and guarding Andrew. Every once in a while, Tye or Tess would appear on Andrew's shoulder, as if they were checking on him. The first time Tye appeared he about wrecked the tractor. But afterwards, he welcomed the love.

Andrew noticed Adam and Storm Cloud coming from the hilltop. He slowed down and waited for them to come to him.

"Hey, it's about dinner time cuz," Adam yelled over the tractor's noise.

Andrew gave a thumbs-up and turned the tractor towards the road through the pasture with Adam and Storm Cloud trotting nearby. All the animals were running and jumping all around them. The boys were smiling and looking forward to dinner.

As they neared the house, Adam slid off of Storm Cloud and led him to the barn, where he took off the saddle and blanket. Warrior Girl was already in her stall resting. The horses whinnied at one another and Storm Cloud gladly went into his stall. He was hungry and thirsty. Adam made sure he had feed and fresh water, which Blake had already set out for his horse.

"Okay boy, we'll go out again tomorrow and get some exercise," Adam said and rubbed Storm Cloud one more time before he closed the stall door. "Warrior Girl, get some rest and take care of that little one on board. Maybe, I can have one of your fouls in the future."

Both horses whinnied in response, making Adam laugh. "Maybe they understood me," Adam thought and hurried up to the farmhouse for some food.

***

Everyone enjoyed their dinner and talked non-stop about their work, the work still to be done and how much they loved this place.

"Hey, I want a foul one day," Adam said. "I love Storm Cloud and I want a horse of my own."

"Adam, I could really use some help with the horses, so you are welcome to come over as much as possible and help me," Lacey said.

"I am going to ask if I can stay here all summer. Are you okay with that Lacey?" Adam asked.

"Sure, the more the merrier and the more we get done. Just make sure your dad and mom are okay with it," Lacey said.

"That would be awesome Adam," Blake said. "Lacey and I have to work our jobs too, so this would be really helpful."

"I'm in too," Andrew said. "I know my mom would love for me to work."

"Me too," Aiken said. "I'll need to work some for money, but I'll be here whenever I don't have to be at my summer job."

"Me three," Chase yelled out. "I love riding the tractor."

"And singing," Miguel said and laughed. "Chase was singing his heart out to be heard over the tractor."

"Just tell them how good I sounded," Chase added and gave Miguel a look of 'I am great'.

Everyone chuckled.

"I guess I better let mom and dad know that I didn't go to Paris now," Jillie added and looked at her brother with a 'will you help me tell the story' look.

"Don't worry, we'll go home together. I'll let them know that you decided you didn't want to go and called me to pick you up and we just headed out here to help out," Aiken said and winked at his little sister.

"Sorry sis, I cannot stay all summer, but I'll be here everyday of my leave, unless dad and mom need me for something. Oh, I have to plan my wedding too just a little bit or someone will be a bit upset," Gregory said. "I have a great idea. Why don't Bridget and I get married here? Once we get this place all fixed up, I bet it would be awesome. I am going to ask dad to ask Uncle Nash and grandma what they think."

"I love that idea and you don't have to ask anyone, because

remember I run this place now," Lacey said. "If you want it, this is your venue big brother."

"I'll call Bridget right now and say hello. She doesn't get leave until a few weeks before our wedding," Gregory said.

"Okay, let's finish up and get back to work everyone," Jillie shouted out. "We have lots to do and there is still some daylight left. I have to get to college at the end of the summer you know, so I can be a vet for this farm of ours."

Miguel smiled and winked at Jillie. Jillie smiled back, got up and took her plate to the kitchen.

And so, the summer began and the farm became alive once again. Great Uncle Nash came by almost everyday to inspect what all the children were doing. Some of their many cousins came by and offered help all throughout the summer. It was great. The girls got to know so many cousins that they really didn't really know. Even their parents came on the weekends and joined in on the fun.

They even brought out their grandparents and their Great-Aunt Daisy to watch the farm grow full of plants and life. They added some miniature goats, some chickens and a few milk cows. They decided that they would take one or two deer per year to supply meat for anyone that would like some. Of course, Uncle Kent loved the honor of hunting the meat. He wouldn't allow Aiken to have the honor.

The gardens sprung to life and lots of vegetables were harvested throughout the summer. Lacey's mom had helped her learn all about preserving and canning their foods. They also learned some great tips from their Uncle Jake and dug up big pits near the spring, where the ground was very cold and stored some things deep into the ground.

Then, of course, there was the cellar where this had all began. The girls used the room, at the end of the tunnel, to store lots of great food. The tunnel was very cool in the summer and very cold in the winter. It was like having an underground freezer. Of course, they couldn't tell anyone about these tunnels. It was still a secret to keep the farm safe.

Sometimes, Lacey felt like she would see their great-grandfather walking across the field and she would hear someone humming in the kitchen during the wee hours of the night. She figured this was their Great-Grandmother Tess, who she was told loved to sing and hum. Jillie never saw or heard these things, but felt like they probably were visiting their beloved grounds and home. Things seemed at peace, at least for a while.

7 MORE MAGIC AND MORE MYSTERY

The summer quickly passed with so much work going on everyday. Family gatherings began happening on Sundays, when lots of family members began coming over in the afternoons to visit and bring food. They ended up having pot luck lunches almost every Sunday and anyone who could come would come.

Little Nadia would come and all the cats, along with Lucky Lad, would surround her almost the entire time. They knew this little one was so important and nothing or no one was able to bring harm her way.

Gregory had to leave at the beginning of August. All the other cousins stayed right here all summer and helped out gardening, mowing, repairing and enjoying the land their great-grandparents had secured for them all to have.

On one particular Sunday in early August, many family members came over to enjoy the afternoon on the farm. As they were all sitting out on the front lawn, a car slowed down and pulled into the driveway. No one recognized the car or the people in the car, except for Jillie, Miguel, Kent, Karla and Lucy. It was Miguel's parents, Dancing Star and Brave Wolf, from the North Carolina mountain village. Miguel was very surprised to see them.

Miguel and Jillie walked over to greet them and

immediately saw the seriousness in their eyes.

"Dad? Mom? What is happening? For you to show up here makes me uncomfortable," Miguel said quickly looking back to see if anyone else had decided to follow them.

"Visions are seen. Something is not right. We had to come and warn you from our village wise man. Strange visitors are seen," Miguel's father said with much seriousness.

"Come and say hello, because you cannot just show up and leave," Jillie said.

"Yes, we will say hello and then we must get back," Miguel's mom said and she hugged her son. "I am so proud of you. You too, Jillie my dear; you both have grown up immensely and you're both have taken on great responsibilities." Dancing Star gave Jillie a big hug too.

"Aunt Lucy will be so happy to see you both," Jillie said and they all walked in unison to the front yard.

Lucy was shocked to see them, but so happy to see them. They only drove motorcycles, jeeps or road horses. She hugged them and then allowed Kent and Karla to join in and say hello. Kent was his usual untrusting self and didn't really go out of his way to be friendly. Karla gently pushed him and made a face to her husband to be nice.

"Hey there," Karla said and hugged Miguel's parents, as they had been very sweet and kind to her daughter. Now she had gotten to know Miguel and saw that her daughter was quite smitten with him.

Kent was not happy, but he wasn't allowed to express his opinion without talking with Karla first. Kent smiled and shook Miguel's parents' hands and went back to join his brother-in-laws to complain a little bit more. Wayne and Jeremy laughed at Kent and Wayne gave him a 'lighten up' wink.

No one noticed the seriousness that came with Miguel's parents. They were all having too much fun. Lacey didn't even notice something was wrong and Jillie decided not to say anything until everyone was gone.

Lucy took her friends around and introduced them to her parents, her aunt and cousins, who had also grown up here during their youth. They were all very kind and welcoming.

After about an hour, Dancing Star and Brave Wolf told Lucy they needed to get back to their village and excused themselves to talk with Miguel. Lucy still didn't pick up on any problem and went on to join her sisters and family clean up after their huge spread.

Brave Wolf took Miguel and Jillie with them to the car and made sure no one was close by to hear. "Listen Miguel and Jillie, visions show that someone or some people will come here and make trouble, but also there will be trouble with our people on this very land many moons before now. It's like things are going to happen simultaneously to keep you from helping one another out. Get with Lacey, Blake and your cousins and make a plan very soon. You cannot go back and warn our families, because it could change the course of history and all of our lives. This may be the reason we end up in the North Carolina Mountains, so please remember, do not go back. Once you have won the battle here, the battle there will be over too," Brave Wolf quickly explained. "I cannot help you, son. This is a battle for this family, but you can help. So stay here and be careful."

"Don't worry, dad. I can take care of myself and this family. They are my family too and he looked at Jillie and rubbed her scared face. "It will be okay."

Miguel hugged his parents and then Jillie hugged them too.

"We love you, Jillie, like our own daughter," Dancing Star said, as she hugged her in tight.

"I love you too. We'll be okay. The cats will be here and remember we have great connections," Jillie said, as she thought about Vance Service and her friend, Dan, whom she had met at the ski resort not so long ago. She and Lacey knew that they had to make friends along the way to help them out.

"Come on Jillie. Let's go help get things cleaned up, get your family on their way and sit down with Lacey, Blake and the others to be ready," Miguel said, as he shut his mother's car door.

His parents waved as they backed up and pulled out onto

the Levens Street to head back to the mountains. When they went to join the others, the black and white cat appeared out of nowhere and rubbed in between both of them. They bent down and rubbed him. He not only purred, but he also growled the sound of a wolf and then stopped.

Miguel looked at Jillie and they both knew at that instant, this was their black wolf, which had changed to be able to be near both of them.

"Okay, your secret is out my friend. We need to name you something, because you're not just 'the cat', as we all have been calling you, or 'the black wolf'. I am naming you Kai, like the Kai Ken or tiger dog," Miguel said.

Jillie and Miguel both hugged Kai and then they rushed to help clean up. Kai was off to find his other furry friends. Jillie was able to whisper that they needed to get everyone off the farm so they could talk. Lacey knew not to ask questions and just made sure everyone got off the farm as quickly as possible. But as she was hurrying around, Nadia's cat, Tea, was meowing very loudly and circling around little Nadia, who didn't look so good. All the animals came running to circle their little Nadia.

"Hey Uncle Jeremy, Aunt Stacey, I think little Nadia is tired. She doesn't look so good and Tea looks like she is trying to get someone's attention," Lacey said, as she walked over to Nadia and bent down to sit beside her on the ground. The animals all sat down watching and listening, which Ginger thought was so very odd and interesting.

"Look Wayne, look at the animals all sitting quietly looking on over there. Don't you think that is so strange, but very interesting," Ginger said to her husband. "I am telling you something strange is happening around here, but our daughter is so 'tight lipped'. I do know our daughter better than she thinks I do."

Wayne looked over and nodded his head. "Yep, mighty strange, but they're animals and they all love little Nadia for sure. She does look like she is hurt."

Jeremy and Stacey rushed over and bent down too, as Tea stayed close to guard her Nadia.

117

"My arm hurts," Nadia whimpered, as she raised her little arm and showed her parents and Lacey her bruised arm.

"Oh my gosh Stacey, look at this," Jeremy cried out. "Get Luke and Adam, we're going home. Tomorrow we're taking her to the doctor. Maybe it's broken."

"I'll get them," Lacey said and was off in a second.

All the animals took off with Lacey and were following right behind her, as she was yelling out for Adam and Luke. The boys came running. Lacey told them to get their things together and told them about Nadia's little arm.

Adam grabbed Lacey's arm. "Is something really wrong?"

"I don't know, but Tea is definitely upset," Lacey said. "Take Luke and help your mom and dad as much as you can. I have a bad feeling."

"It's done. I'll call you later and let you know if anything else happens," Adam said and hugged his older, but smaller cousin.

Adam grabbed his little brother's hand, helped him gather all of his toys and helped him to the car, where Jeremy was already strapping Nadia in her car seat. Of course, Tea was right there with her paw gently on Nadia's little leg. Once Jeremy was in the driver's seat, they headed home. Teresa and Ted waved and blew kisses to their son and were both worried. Aunt Daisy was not really in tuned with everything and just smiled at them.

The hardest to get on their way were all of their parents and Ginger kept on commenting about the animals to Lacey, but she just ignored her mom. Finally Wayne got his wife to drop it and they were the last to leave with their grandparents and their great-aunt to take them back to the nursing home.

Lacey and Blake said their good-byes and rushed back inside the farmhouse to find all the cousins having coffee while they waited on them.

"Here Lacey," Jillie said, as she handed Lacey a coffee. "Just as you like it too. Blake, this one is yours." Lacey and Blake both nodded their thanks and they all sat down.

"So Miguel and Jillie, what is up?" Lacey asked.

"Well, we don't exactly know," Miguel began. "My parents say that the wise man has had visions of strangers both here and back in time with our forefathers. They warned us not to go back and neither family can help one another. We need to be aware of strangers and then we have to take care of business here, while your Uncle Jake and our people take of business there."

"So, what do we do? Sit around and just wait for trouble?" Andrew questioned.

"No, but we need to be ready with warnings around the farm and a plan to take care of any bad business. The one thing we have on our side is that we have ways of hiding that no one could find us, if we needed to be that safe," Lacey explained.

"We move on like usual with our chores, but we're on alert from today until -," Miguel replied.

So the seven of them stayed up drawing up plans of defense in case of any type of physical attacks, but it wasn't that kind of attack they had to worry about. They would soon find out what they were up against. Miss Virginia had shown up earlier and now they knew why. The mother cat left to return to her other family three hundred years in the past.

***

On this very day, more than three hundred years in the past, Uncle Jake was out scouting along with Tame Tiger, Son of Running Deer and other scout warriors. They began traveling further and further away from their village to make sure they were not caught by surprise. They had set up scouting groups to go out in intervals. As one group would come in for a week, another one would head out for a week to scout the lands for possible threats upon their village. Jake knew that at some point his people would vanish from this land because how else did his grand-father acquire the farm? Yet he knew that destiny was destiny. And, it was all for a reason.

Jake began leaving little 'gifts' to his nieces and nephews to find and to remember him by if by chance the portal door closed forever. His mind was in deep thought as he was brought back to reality by sounds of many horses running their way. Tame Tiger made a motion for them to move and hide. Everyone followed their future leader.

They all relaxed and showed signs of relief when they witnessed about a hundred wild horses running across the plains. But not far behind them was a troop of soldiers. Jake noticed their uniforms to be that of the British and whispered something to Tame Tiger and how America wasn't going to be free from England until 1776. This of course would have meant nothing to Tame Tiger, but he had learned so much when he spent time far into the future.

Tame Tiger whispered to Jake, "What do we do with them?"

"Let's just watch them a bit and see if they turn around soon. I cannot believe they are even here yet. It's going to be years before we break lose from England, if I have the year correct here. But, we have to realize that more white men will be coming and we have to start planning for our future and our survival," Jake explained. Jake was worried about his precious family here in this time.

"We will follow behind these men and see where they travel," Tame Tiger said.

Jake nodded his approval. He wanted to know too. They all quietly waited for the British soldiers to give up on catching the wild horses. Once they began heading back in the direction, from which they had come, the scouting team broke up and moved out to follow this group of soldiers on the left, the right and behind. Tame Tiger headed up the group to the right, Jake headed up the group to the left and Crazy Horse, Tame Tiger's best friend, headed up the rear. They were all making sure these soldiers headed away from the direction of the village.

The soldiers' leader held up his hand for his troop to hold up. They all came to a stop and the leader was talking and looking around. He must have sensed something or someone near. Tame Tiger and his team sat quietly, Jake and his team did the same, but Crazy Horse and his team had not seen that these soldiers had stopped. Tame Tiger heard the horses and he sent out a warning cry that sounded like a screech owl. This made the soldiers become more alert of their surroundings and they all moved into a circle facing outward to be able to scope all the area.

Crazy Horse heard the warning and he brought his horse to a dead stop holding up his hand for his team to hold up. They didn't move and waited to make sure they didn't need to get out of sight.

Tame Tiger held his breath, as he watched the soldiers look all around, but they didn't see anyone. After about five minutes, the leader of the soldiers motioned them to move on and they all started out again. Now the English soldiers were moving a lot faster. They must have been spooked.

Tame Tiger gave out another message of all clear for them to come together. He wanted to stay around this area to make sure no more soldiers came this way. They would make a camp in a wooded area to hide themselves. No fire would be built, so they would not have a hot dinner, but only dried beef, dried fruit and nuts. They had rolled up food snacks that were put together with a bit of honey.

8 THE BATTLES AHEAD

The last few weeks of summer were darkened by the illness that came upon little Nadia. She was diagnosed with Leukemia, a blood cancer and because of all the advancements in medicines her prognosis was in her favor. Now all the cousins' focus turned from worrying about the farm to their little cousin. Everyday, they either called or one or two of them visited her if they were allowed. Lacey got word to her uncle about The Leukemia & Lymphoma Society for information that would help them all understand this diagnosis. Lacey and Jillie took the time to help their aunt and their uncle gather all the information they could.

Lacey, Jillie and their cousins also started raising money to donate to this organization in honor of their cousin. They also learned about all the campaigns which are organized for people to participate and raise money to help fund research for cures of blood cancers. Lacey and Jillie decided to form their own team and started raising money to benefit one of the campaigns that is called 'Light the Night' Walk.

The summer ended and everyone had to return to their homes or college to continue with their studies. Lacey and Jillie were so upset to see everyone leave, but knew that they would all be together for 'the walk' in the fall. Miguel also had to leave to finish up his senior year and his studies of horticulture, forestry and land conservation. Along with him went his new best friend, Kai, the cat aka the black wolf.

Jillie had to leave for college to begin her studies at NC State for her veterinarian degree. At least her brother would be there for comfort.

"I don't think I should go," Jillie said to Lacey the night before she was to leave for college.

"Oh no; you are not giving up your dream and we need you to have that degree. This farm will depend on your skills. I will be fine. Blake, my dad and some of our relatives will all be around to help me now. Little Nadia is doing well and with our new mission, we're going to make a difference," Lacey said. "Now, let's spend the last night relaxing and laughing over memories."

And that is what the girls did. They talked about the first day on the farm together, how they found the cats, met their uncle and the travel back to the past and so many other unbelievable moments. They talked about Lope and Jillie's eyes filled with tears, as she remembered her best friend. Lacey allowed her to be sad, but moved on and talked about happier times. But, they ended their last few words talking about Nadia and knew a big part of their lives would be fundraising to help find a cure.

The girls finally called it a night with big hugs and tears. Jillie held onto a secret and was so happy for her big cousin. They both tossed and turned.

Lacey didn't know, but Blake was going to ask her to marry him soon, but he was waiting for the right moment. It always seemed that it was never the right moment. But, now that everyone was going to be gone and it would be the two of them alone, he was going to plan a wonderful day, evening or something. Jillie, Miguel, Gregory and all the cousins knew, but he had made sure that they all kept his secret. All the boys had wanted it to happen with them around, but Blake was more romantic than that and was a bit selfish, He didn't want to share their special moment.

123

The next morning came quickly and the girls were up together, ate breakfast together and ran down to the barn to tend to the horses. Jillie's car was already packed and she ran to the house to wash up before she would hit the road for college.

Jillie came out with Tess in her arms and Tye, in his kitten form, on her shoulder. Lacey smiled, as she looked at Jillie with their precious animals.

"Okay, but I'll only be a little over an hour away and I can be here in no time. I am going to leave Tess here, since we know that she can show up any moment if I should need her. I think you need her and Tye will be so happy. I miss seeing Miss Virginia. She hasn't been back in a while now. I guess she is taking care of our other family. I hope they are okay. Do you think we'll be able to go back for the Fall Harvest this year?" Jillie asked.

"I hope so and don't you worry about this farm. We'll be fine. Get in your car and go get that vet degree," Lacey directed her cousin and gave Jillie a big hug.

"I haven't even seen Uncle Jake and everyone since the beginning of the summer. We don't even know about Lope or anything. How can I study? This is going to be a very long venture," Jillie said.

"I know. I am worried about Uncle Jake and everyone too. But, let's just move forward and wait to hear from them. I don't want to do something to change all of our lives. Uncle Jake will get with me -," Lacy was cut off by noise coming from the barn.

Lacey and Jillie both stopped their conversation and looked in the direction of the barn. To their surprise their Uncle Jake, Tame Tiger and Crazy Horse appeared. Seeing Crazy Horse was strange and the girls looked at one another as they shrugged their shoulders. The men were all smiles too. The girls ran to meet them.

"Uncle Jake," Jillie yelled.

"Well hello men," Lacey said. "Where have you all been? We have been so worried."

Jake smiled and Tame Tiger was smiling even bigger.

The girls hugged each man one at a time. Crazy Horse was in awe of his surroundings and immediately walked over to Jillie's little car.

Miss Virginia came along too. Tye and Tess came out of nowhere, as usual, and began romping around with their mother. The reunion was always adorable.

Jake and Tame Tiger both laughed at the cats and at Crazy Horse's reaction to a car. Tame Tiger remembered how he thought they were some kind of monster. He couldn't wait to show his best friend that you ride in them, but not today.

"I was just getting ready to leave for college today Uncle Jake," Jillie said. "I would have been mad if I had missed you."

"Me too little one, but we have been quite busy getting ready for Fall as we believe it's going to be a very bad winter. Not only have we been working to secure our food, but also we have been very busy securing our village's safety. I am in fear of the white men moving closer and closer. I think we all realize that somehow my grandfather acquires this land from someone and that someone must have acquired the land from someone. So, I was wondering if you would help me find out and go look up who takes over this land back in the 1700's. Once we become independent of England, I am thinking we are forced off this land, as I read many years ago of so many American Indians moved from their lands to designated reservations."

"Will that mess up our history?" Lacey asked.

"No, it will just help me know what is coming and maybe we can avoid any unnecessary fighting and hopefully save our people," Jake explained.

"I'll go look at the public records office and research it for us. I would like to know too," Lacey answered.

"What should I do to help?" Jillie asked.

"Nothing, but go to school," Tame Tiger answered. "We will need a good animal doctor to run this farm."

Jillie smiled at Tame Tiger and nodded her head okay.

Crazy Horse came up behind Jillie, picked her up and twirled her around. Jillie laughed and waltzed around with Crazy Horse. He was like a big brother to the girls and they loved him. He was silly and always a jokester.

"We have missed you all," Jillie said, as she and Crazy Horse finally stopped dancing around and being silly.

"I saw the horses," Tame Tiger remarked. "They look good. Warrior Girl is getting plump and she will need her rest."

"Uncle Jake, you don't know about little Nadia?" Lacey asked with seriousness in her eyes.

"What?!" Jake replied, as he grabbed Lacey's shoulders.

"She's sick Uncle Jake. She has a blood cancer, called Leukemia, but she is doing well right now," Lacey explained, as she tried to tell them all that they had learned forgetting that their Uncle Jake had once been here and had gone to college. He knew enough to already know the seriousness.

"I will have our medicine man start preparing prayers and we will hold a ceremony in her honor. Mother Earth will take care of her. She has to be okay," Jake said and looked at Tame Tiger and Crazy Horse, who both stopped their joking with Jillie.

"Lacey, you come and get me if you need me. I need to know what is happening with not only Nadia, but my brother. If he should need me, I am going to be there somehow, someway," Jake said and looked at Tame Tiger. "We need to get back now. I must talk with the medicine man, Healing Heart. He is young and his senses are strong."

Tame Tiger and Crazy Horse did not question or say anything else. They hugged the girls and left Jake to have a moment with his nieces.

"Your prayers and our chants will help Nadia. Stay strong for her and for each other. We are preparing for the Fall Harvest. You and your cousins should all return so that we all come together to show Mother Earth our strength and that we are directing all of our strengths to Nadia. She will listen. Not only your doctors, but the spirits now come together," Jake said with his mind wondering. "Go to college Jillie and learn more than the average student. Remember, you have a great head start from your studies with Wise Owl. He can be your mentor in many ways."

"I am on a mission Uncle Jake and I will not fail," Jillie said with force.

"Lacey, you must stay even stronger and work to keep this land alive and moving forward for this family's survival. You have Blake and Miguel to call upon. Don't try and do it all yourself. Maybe Gregory can come home if he can take leave if we should need him," Jake said to his older niece.

Lacey was in deep thought and looked at Jillie and then at her uncle. "This is our big challenge that was foreseen. It's not true strangers, but Nadia's battle is our battle here. I know what all I have to do and that is to get more awareness and research out there and I know where to start. I need to contact my very wealthy friend, Vance Service. He knows everyone and anyone with lots of money."

"Oh Lacey, don't forget Dan, who I met. He owes me a big favor and I told him he would get something for keeping my secret. I'll give him a shout and ask him to call you," Jillie said.

Their battle was to save their little cousin and make a difference for others, not just for themselves and their family.

Jake nodded. "I think you are right, but what are you talking about a battle?"

Jillie explained about Miguel's parents' visit and their warnings for now and in his time. This made Jake realize how connected they all were even more than ever now. His descendants were feeling the pains of their past. He was worried about his little niece, but also worried about his people.

The girls said their good-byes to their uncle and watched him and Miss Virginia disappear into the barn. Jillie turned to Lacey, with tears in her eyes, and didn't say a word. Tye and Tess were circling both of them. Tess jumped up in Jillie's arms, meowed and then roared her sadness. She had already been told she had to stay here.

"Just go little cuz and study hard and fast. We need you here," Lacey said and gave her little cousin a big, bear hug. "Now go. Get in that car and drive carefully. Tell Aiken hello when you see him."

Jillie gave her cat one last kiss and then gave Tye one. She got in the car and could barely see with the tears filling her eyes. She didn't want to leave this place. It was her home and would always be her home. She whipped her car around and headed out of the driveway. Lacey was waving and blowing kisses. She didn't want her cousin see her break down. She couldn't, there was too much to do now. She also needed to get some work done around this farm. So much to do and not much help now. At least some of her parents' cousins and their children were all helping out as much as possible when they had free time. She needed to make a list of what there was to accomplish and who would be helping her. She may have to find help. She may have to finally start using her law degree and make some noise in Washington about funding for non-profits.

But before she was going to do anything, she ran inside to call and find out about Nadia. Adam answered.

"Hey Lacey, I saw your number. All okay?" Adam asked.

"Oh yeah, Jillie is off to college. How are you? Are you coming over some to help me?" Lacey asked.

"Yeah, how about tomorrow; I don't start school until next week." Adam answered.

"Great. I need help with the horses, if you would come and help me early tomorrow morning. I can come and pick you up," Lacey said.

"No, I'll get dad to drive me out and you can take me home. I may bring Luke with me, so he and mom can both take Nadia for her treatment," Adam said.

"Absolutely, we'll start him young," Lacey said. "I'll see you early for breakfast, so your dad and mom don't have to worry about it."

"Okay; see you in the morning," Adam said and hung up.

Lacey hung up the phone and ran out to the barn to check on the horses with both cats at her heels. She had promised them a walk in the pasture. She saddled up Storm Cloud and led Warrior Girl out of her stall. Lacey took a deep breath, sat back and enjoyed strolling over the land. She sat confidently atop Storm Cloud and lightly giggled, as she looked at the two magical cats riding Warrior Girl.

As they rode deeper down into the pasture, Lacey took notice of the old oak tree. She thought she saw something move around the big tree. She guided Storm Cloud in the tree's direction. Both cats sensed her caution and they stood at attention atop of Warrior Girl's back. Storm Cloud whimpered and jerked his head back and forth.

"Whoa boy; I am being cautious, but we need to see if someone is snooping around," Lacey whispered, as she rubbed the big horse's neck.

Tye let out a quiet roar and looked at his Lacey for direction. Tess made a low, growling sound too.

Lacey thought out to her Tye and his sister. "Okay, go check it out for me, but change to your kitten forms and stay out of sight."

Within a second, the protectors were out of sight and Lacey saw them further down in the pasture slowly creeping towards the tree. They were both tiny kitten and they were low to the ground. Lacey motioned for Warrior Girl to move closer to her side and she comforted the horses with quiet comments that they would be okay. Lacey could feel Storm Cloud's anxiousness to take off towards the tree, but she gently pulled back on the reigns to let him know that she wanted him to stay put. He whimpered his agreement to listen.

Warrior Girl whinnied a bit, but Lacey gave her comforting words.

***

Tye and Tess slowly crept towards the big oak tree. Lacey and the horses had veered off towards the edge of the pasture, where Lacey quietly guided them to a place she could see what was going on at the oak tree. She was in disbelief, but she was looking at someone in a uniform that looked like a soldier from the 18th century and she was quite certain it was British. She saw the cats creeping slowly closer and closer to this person and she gave Tye out a thought to capture and hold in place.

That was all it took for Tye to meow to his sister and they

both transformed to their beastly forms. In seconds they had this soldier captured with fear. Lacey told Warrior Girl to stay put and she took off in full gallop on Storm Cloud towards her captive soldier.

"Who are you?" Lacey yelled out, as she pulled up with a quick halt.

The soldier was in such shock already, he didn't speak right away.

"I said; who are you?" Lacey demanded again.

The young soldier stared into Lacey's eyes and stuttered out, "Where am I?"

"Where are you from?" Lacey demanded.

"I am from the British army in charge of a scouting party, but where are my men?" This man looked all around in total shock.

"What year do you live?" Lacey asked.

"That is a totally bizarre question," the man replied. "It's 1774 of course."

Lacey sat back in awe. "You must have fallen through the time portal. Were you near a cave?"

"Yes, how did you know and who are you?" The man questioned staring at Lacey and the beasts that stood within feet of him.

"You are now in the year of 2012," Lacey said with a smile on her face.

The man looked around and did note the oak tree looking rather large and much older. "How could this happen?"

"That does not matter, but what am I to do with you now?" Lacey said.

"What are you going to do with me? And, what about these two beasts you have guarding me? Is this something of the future?"

"You are going to have to come with me now," Lacey said, as she pulled her cell phone from her back pocket and started dialing Blake.

"What is that? Are you going to kill me?" The soldier cried with fear.

"Relax man. I am calling my boyfriend to help me with you," Lacey said.

"Calling?" What is that?"

"You have no idea, but be patient and I'll show you a few things and maybe you can be of use to me," Lacey said, as she was in deep thought how she was going to use this man to her family's advantage so many years ago.

"Blake, it's me. Where are you? I need you to come home immediately. I mean, immediately. I have a big surprise for you and we have lots to do. I think I just found a way of saving Uncle Jake and everyone," Lacey said.

"What?" Blake said from the other end of the line.

"Just get to the farm," Lacey said and hung up the phone.

"Sir, what is your name?" Lacey asked. "My name is Lacey."

"Honored Miss Lacey, I am Sir Edward Miller and I am from Her Majesties Royal Army here to secure claim to this land." Sir Miller bowed taking off his hat.

"Hate to burst your bubble, but it doesn't happen," Lacey said and laughed.

"It doesn't?" Sir Miller asked looking very puzzled.

"Nope, so just cool your jets and forget about England for now," Lacey said.

"Well, what are you going to do with me? Am I a prisoner of war?" Sir Miller asked.

"Prisoner, no, but unexpected and welcomed guest, yes," Lacey said, as she slid down from Storm Cloud and offered her hand in friendship.

The strange, young soldier accepted her hand and turned her hand over and lightly kissed the top of her hand. Lacey was taken by surprise and took her hand back feeling really weird, but she was thinking quick and realizing how this was their ticket to saving this land. This man in front of her would be her family's savior and she was the person who was going to make it all happen.

"Let me ask you something Sir Miller, what exactly do you have waiting on you in England?" Lacey asked, as she wanted to know if he had a family left behind that would be worried about him. She couldn't bear to think she would be dividing a family.

"Well my fair lady, I am a single man, who left behind a beautiful lady, who I hope to call my wife on my return to England." Sir Miller stared at Lacey in her jeans and t-shirt.

Lacey could tell he was looking at her attire and felt very self-conscious about the stare.

"I do apologize my lady, but I am not at all used to seeing a lady in such a wardrobe," Sir Miller said, as he noticed he was making Lacey feel rather uneasy.

"Well, get used to it dude, because this is our wardrobe for farming," Lacey said with irritation in her voice.

"Oh, but I do not mean to be disrespectful My Lady Lacey, but it's very different in my time. Ladies are not seen in men's trousers."

Lacey placed her hands on her hips. "These are not trousers. They are called jeans and you are way outdated in your weird 'wardrobe', but I am not making you feel uncomfortable about it."

"Very well then, I have never seen a lady in jeans," Sir Miller said and smiled to hopefully break the tension. "Now, what are you going to do with me?"

"Well, I don't really know at this very moment, but you're stuck here so get used to it for now." Lacey said. "Come on, I am taking you up to the farmhouse and we'll talk more. I'll even fix you something to eat. We women still cook in this time, but so do the men," Lacey said with sarcasm.

Sir Miller nodded and chuckled a bit, as he caught her sarcasm and even liked this very strange Lady Lacey.

Lacey looked at Tye and Tess and told them they could become her cute, adorable pets again. She watched Sir Miller's face, as the beasts became two small cats romping all around, but gave a couple of ferocious roars to make sure this man knew who they really were. Storm Cloud also moved up behind this man and gave him a forceful nudge to start walking.

Lacey smiled and said, "Come on, but don't do anything

132

you will regret."

"I would not dare be such a fool my lady. I am a man of my honor and I am also a man stricken with total fear."

Lacey laughed and so did Sir Miller, as they walked back through the pasture land towards the farmhouse. Sir Miller looked all around and Lacey acknowledged that yes, he was on the same land he had been on three hundred years before now. Destiny was working its magic.

Lacey whistled for Warrior Girl and she saw her horse quickly trot to catch up with them. As they reached the barn, Blake was pulling in and started laughing as he noticed the weirdo with his lovely Lacey. He was thinking Lacey was doing one of her fundraiser planning things she had come to do so often now.

"What's this?" Blake called out, as he got out of his car. "Are you working on a really classy fundraiser or something?"

Sir Miller was staring at the car, as if he had seen a monster.

Lacey noticed and laughed. "No, but help me get the horses taken care of and I'll fill you in on who this rather unique person is here with me," Lacey said.

Blake came up to Lacey and kissed her gently on the cheek and then turned to Sir Miller. "I am Blake and who do I have the pleasure of meeting today?"

Sir Miller took off his hat again and bowed. "May I introduce myself? I am Sir Edward Miller from Her Majesty's Royal Army and I am here to secure this land for England."

Blake broke out into laughter and hit the guy on the back. "Well, go ahead and secure her for England. Not sure what you're talking about, but what is this garb all about and really Lacey, why is he here?" Blake questioned trying to stop laughing.

"He's here to secure the land for England. I found him at the oak tree today. He fell through the time portal Blake. He's the answer to our prayers. He is going to help me save this land for my great-grandfather to buy. Get it? Destiny is working in our favor," Lacey said excitedly.

LAURA BETH

"Okay, he fell through the portal, but how is he going to save this land for your great-grandfather to buy. That is about another one hundred and fifty years in the future from his time," Blake said, as he thought out the math as quickly as Lacey was thinking.

"Yes, I know, but think about it. Uncle Jake said he didn't know how they survived or how many. This guy is with the British army trying to help win the Revolutionary War, but now he is with us and I am not letting him leave unless he agrees to leave my, our family alone. I am going to send for Uncle Jake and Tame Tiger, because I think this man is going to save our land from being taken away from our family three hundred years ago." Lacey talked so fast that Sir Miller and Blake were confused.

"Trust me," Lacey continued. "I know what I am planning will work and Sir Edward Miller, I am going to make you an offer that you will not want to refuse. Well, my ancestors are going to make you an offer that you are not going to want to refuse." Lacey rambled on, as she and Blake got the horses taken care of and Sir Miller walked around the barn inspecting all the gadgets and the tractors.

9 DESTINY HELPS FIGHT THE BATTLES

The next few days were exhausting for Lacey, because she not only had to hide Sir Edward Miller, who wanted to ask a million questions as did Tame Tiger, but she had to put her plan all down on paper. Blake and Adam kept the farm going. Thank goodness for Adam. He was Lacey's and Blake's savior with the horses. He was able to talk his parents into allowing him to stay over for the last week before his school started giving Lacey time to work with Sir Miller.

In return for Sir Miller's willingness to be apart of her plan, Lacey dressed him in modern day clothes and took him around the community. She showed him all the advances of today. Sir Miller, like Tame Tiger, said he was excited to take it all in, but he missed his own time and the slower pace of things. Lacey realized that everyone was in the time that they were destined to be living.

One of the greatest inventions that Sir Miller loved was the bathroom with all the luxuries. He was totally amazed at the plumbing system. He took everything in, but still said he was anxious to get back to his own time.

Once Lacey was sure he was on board with her plan, she decided it was time to contact her Uncle Jake and Tame Tiger to come over and meet the man who would be staking claim to this very land that they walked on together. Just in case he wasn't true to his word, she decided she didn't want to take him back across to his time. However, she felt like he was a good person. She hoped that once he met her uncle and Tame Tiger. he too would be totally won over.

"Blake, I need you to stay here with Sir Miller while I go back and get Uncle Jake and Tame Tiger," Lacey said.

"What if you stay here and hang out with Sir Miller, who I think enjoys your company, and I go get Uncle Jake and Will? I just don't know what to talk about with him. He's just a bit weird for me," Blake said, hoping Lacey would go for it. "Adam can stay here with you too and take care of the horses and do a few things we were working on around the farm. Maybe you can get 'Mr. High and Mighty' to lift a finger around here to." Blake thought this Englishman was too spoiled and didn't like real men's work. "And, how is this man going to work this land?" Blake asked. "He seems like a total wimp when it comes to hard labor. I know he is a 'brave' soldier, but he seems rather soft if you know what I mean."

"Well, I have to say you are kind of right. He does seem to like being waited on, but I have been making sure he is happy. Don't you worry; part of my plan is that my Uncle Jake helps get him started and in return, he allows our people to stay put on the land," Lacey explained. "He will get all the help he needs and when the war is over, he can send for his lovely bride and keep this land safe for my great-grandfather to purchase. However that is going to happen."

"Oh, sounds like a plan to me. I hope Uncle Jake and all go for it," Blake said.

"I don't think they will have a choice either. They know that somehow they do not survive or they do not stay here. I am hoping they are the ones that move off and somehow make it to the mountains," Lacey said. "Okay, go and take Tye with you," Lacey said. "I'll keep Tess with me."

"You think Tye will leave you?" Blake asked.

"Yes, he loves you too," Lacey said and thought out for Tye and Tess.

The cats were there in seconds. Lacey thought out what she wanted Tye to do and he roared his understanding as he walked all around Blake. Tess roared too and walked around Lacey letting her know she was here for her.

"Okay, we're good to go," Lacey said. "Blake, you will go tonight."

"Okay sweetheart," Blake said.

"Let's get some things done around here. See if Sir Miller will try his hand at getting some hoeing done in the garden. We need some weeds taken out and that isn't too hard," Blake said

Lacey laughed and hugged Blake. "You're so funny, but you're so right. He is a wimp of a man, but he's an important wimp."

They laughed together, finished having a cup of coffee together and ate a quick breakfast. Sir Miller joined them and they all talked about the plan. Sir Miller found out he was going to meet Uncle Jake and Tame Tiger.

"Do you mean that you could have taken me back to my troop when you found me? Sir Miller asked.

"Yes, but don't you see that you were destined to come here for a reason?" Lacey asked, concerned he was already going back on his word."

"I do not know about this destiny you keep talking about. It may be your destiny, but why is it mine?" Sir Miller asked.

"Because you stepped into a time portal and why would you have come here unless there was a reason?" Lacey asked. "You are apart of this land's history and destiny. I know it now."

"I do not see that I have a choice in this matter, so let us get on with our day's work," Sir Miller said and smiled giving Lacey comfort.

"Thank you Sir Miller," Lacey said.

"Oh call me Edward. Isn't that how you do it here? Nothing seems very formal here, so call me Edward," Sir Miller said.

Lacey and Blake laughed and Blake gave the Englishman a pat on his back. "Come on and I'll show you exactly what you can learn to do, since you may just need this skill very soon."

The two men went out of the house together, as Adam was walking in from taking care of the horses.

LAURA BETH

"I am starved, Lacey. Got anything great to eat this morning?" Adam asked.

"What do you want? I'll fix you a nice breakfast if you want," Lacey said.

"How about something quick and easy like French toast? Adam asked.

"You got it," Lacey said and got up to make a quick batch of French toast. She would make a few extra pieces for the men, who didn't really eat much.

"I'll make sure the cats have some food and water, while you're getting my food ready," Adam said, as he walked out onto the porch.

Adam looked out of the porch window to see Blake and Sir Miller hoeing away. Adam laughed watching this fancy man working in some overhaul jeans.

The day went by and the four of them worked hard side by side. The summer was almost over, but life was moving forward and for the best.

Adam would be leaving in a couple of days to start his sophomore year, when he would get his license. Jeremy called to remind him that he would be over to pick him up that Sunday and told him that his little sister was doing really well. Lacey talked with her uncle too and knew that little Nadia would be fine, because of their destiny to this land. With all the excitement and adventure with Edward's arrival, she had remembered to contact her good friend, Vance Service. She wanted to get him on board to make a huge donation to her 'Light The Night' team. He was actually coming down to join in on the walk. She also called Dan, Jillie's friend who promised to help Jillie out in need, and he was going to come and cover the walk with television coverage. They were constantly raising money in honor of their little cousin and her battle with leukemia.

Upon the arrival of night time, Blake and Tye made their way down to the big oak tree via the tunnels. Blake said he felt more secure away from the open air, even if he had Tye with him. He would rather not have to rely on Tye or his own muscle power. Lacey had stayed back with Adam and Edward and they reviewed her plan again. Adam was kind of tired, so he excused himself to the barn, one more time, to check on the horses and then he was up to bed.

Lacey and Edward sat up in the dining room drawing out the boundaries of her great-grandfather's land that she found out he owned.

"So Edward, you must make sure you claim all of this to keep my family's history as it was," Lacey said.

"I understand your family's history, but what about my family's history?" Edward questioned with a very puzzled look on his face. "I don't understand what is going to happen to my family?"

"Just go with it, please?" Lacey asked. "I am sure that in the next one hundred and fifty years, your family becomes whatever it is supposed to be and be wherever it is supposed to be," Lacey replied, thinking about what could happen to Edward's descendants.

"Well, I know I will not be here to know, but I hope my family is not forced off and left with nowhere to go," Edward thought out loud.

"That doesn't happen at all, Edward. My great-grandfather acquires it, so maybe you actually purchase more and your family decides to sell off part of it. I don't know either, but we could go look at the records and see if we can really see who my great-grandfather purchased his land from and see if it is your descendants. If so, then they should have your name, unless there are no male heirs and your descendants are women," Lacey stated, thinking how it would be so interesting to know.

"I think that is a splendid idea. Let's go down to the town hall for the records and just see if I really existed here. Because if I did, then I am all in for this plan of yours," Edward responded, as he scratched his head.

"Okay, first thing in the am," Lacey said.

"You have such funny ways of talking, but I am gathering that means morning," Edward replied and smiled at Lacey.

"Sorry, but yes that is another way of say 'in the morning'," Lacey said with a bit of sarcasm and chuckled out loud.

"You are laughing at me, but it does not impress me one bit," Edward said and shook his head in a bit of disgust and then smiled back at Lacey.

"You like me Edward, admit it," Lacey said.

"I think I may like you Miss Lacey, but you are a bit forward and mighty brash might I say," Edward commented back.

Lacey rolled her eyes and mumbled, as she sometimes did when she was a bit annoyed. "Well, this is my time and sorry if we do not need a man to tell us what to do or when we may talk. That is just ridiculous!"

"I apologize my dear lady if I have offended you, but please understand that I am trying to adjust to your rather manly authority." Edward tried stating it differently, but it didn't come out quite right again.

"Whatever!" Lacey said. "Time to turn in and you know your way around. Go ahead and use the bathroom and then venture on upstairs. I will be getting you up early in the AM!"

"Very well Miss Lacey. I am off to the lavatory, which is the proper word and then I shall retire to my quarters," Edward said, almost making sure to get under Lacey's skin.

Lacey just rolled her eyes and went to her room to turn on her lamp and gather her pajamas. She waited until she heard Edward tromping up the stairs and headed to the bathroom. Once she was there, she stared into the mirror and dropped into deep thought.

"This is just so far-fetched, but this is happening, right? I am not having a really long, long dream or maybe I am in a coma and this is all is playing out in my mind," Lacey thought to herself and pinched herself and flinched. "Nope, I am not dreaming," she said and shrugged her shoulders at herself.

Once Lacey was finished in the bathroom, she decided she would walk down to the barn and check on the horses too and say good night. She grabbed her robe and put it on over her pajamas. Tess was waiting for her right outside the bathroom door, as if she knew that it was her job to protect her on her way to the barn. Lacey smiled and held out her arms. Tess immediately jumped up and snuggled herself into Lacey' arms in her kitten form.

"I am so glad I have you here with me little Tess," Lacey said, as she gently hugged the beautiful, white kitten to her chest.

Tess loudly purred as Lacey opened the back door and walked across the backyard to the barn. It was extremely quiet and the horses heard her opening the barn side door and both sounded out their greetings to her. Lacey smiled and let the squirming kitten leap out of her grasp. Lacey reached for the light switch, on the wall near the door, inside of the barn. When the light came on, she saw that Tess had changed into her adult size cat form and was about to jump up to greet Warrior Girl. The horse was hanging her head over the stall waiting for Lacey. Storm Cloud was also waiting for some attention, but stood quietly waiting his turn. Lacey hugged Warrior Girl and then opened the gate to her stall. Lacey moved on to greet Storm Cloud and opened up his stall gate too. Both horses came out and circled around Lacey.

"Wow Girl, you are really starting to show," Lacey said, as she rubbed the mother horse's tight belly.

Warrior Girl moved her head up and down in agreement, which made Lacey laugh. Storm Cloud dug at the earth with his right front hoof and also moved his head up and down. Lacey laughed harder.

"I can tell you are two excited parents," Lacey replied and moved in between them to give offer gentle rubs down their sides.

Tess jumped onto Storm Cloud's back and gently clawed his mane. Storm Cloud looked back and gave Tess his approval that it felt good. Then Tess turned into the black panther and Storm Cloud bucked her off. Lacey knew she was just playing and she watched as a black panther walked up to the grey stallion and gave him a huge head butt. Then she walked over to Warrior Girl and did the same. Lacey was in awe of these three animals interacting with such love and kindness. Never in her wildest dreams could she have imagined such a sight.

Then all three animals stopped and were at full attention to the back of the barn. Lacey froze in place, but relaxed when she heard the voices of Blake, her uncle and Tame Tiger. Tess took off to greet them and her brother, Tye and her mother, Miss Virginia. Lacey stood with the horses, which both started prancing at the sight of them all coming around the corner. The celebrations of the animals uniting were always such a wonderful event to witness. The cats all meowed, roared and rubbed up against one another.

"Hey, sweetheart," Blake said with a big smile on his face. "What a wonderful greeting party. What are you doing down here this late? Everything okay?"

"Oh yeah, just couldn't go to bed just yet and decided to come down and say good night to Girl and Storm. I didn't expect you back so soon," Lacey replied, as she hugged Blake, then her uncle and then her dear friend, Tame Tiger.

"When I heard about the English soldier coming through the time portal, I couldn't even think about waiting," Uncle Jake replied.

"Me too," Tame Tiger added. "These men have been all around our area lately. We have been lucky that they have not yet made their way to our village."

Lacey immediately felt worried and looked at her Uncle Jake. "Well, I think Sir Edward Miller is a rather nice gentleman and is just serving his country and taking orders. Uncle Jake, I think this is the person who is meant to buy up the land that someday gets sold to your grandfather."

"You may just be right, but what do I do with our people?" Jake asked.

"Well, let me tell you my thought process and I have just about convinced Sir Edward Miller he was destined to this land and that he is destined to save our family. We are venturing to the Courthouse tomorrow to see the land sale records and if his name is on them, he is all in for my plan, which might not have been my plan at all, but rather destiny; his destiny, our destiny," Lacey reported.

"Sounds like a great plan and let's hope that this is destiny and we do not have to change history. Let's all get up to the farmhouse and get some rest," Jake said, as he waited for Lacey and Blake to get the horses put back into their stalls.

Tame Tiger helped Lacey with Warrior Girl and he noticed her bulging belly. He gently rubbed it. "She is showing an awful lot, Lacey. I need to check her out before I leave."

"Do you think something could be wrong?" Lacey asked with great concern.

"No, not unless you think twins could be something wrong," Tame Tiger said very nonchalantly.

"Two foals? Really? Oh my gosh, that would be so awesome. Jillie gets her own horse and Adam gets an awesome surprise. He really wants a horse of his own. He's been great helping me with them. Don't tell him. I want it to be a surprise," Lacey said, as she smiled and put her right ear to Girl's belly side.

"Well, don't get too excited. I could be wrong, but I think I am pretty confident that there are two foals in there," Tame Tiger whispered showing that he was already keeping her secret.

"You two ready in there or do I have to come and fight for my girl as always?" Blake said, as he stuck his head over the stall wall.

"No way man, I am not fighting you," Tame Tiger said, as he smiled at Lacey and winked.

"Come on people, let's get some shut eye," Jake yelled from outside of the barn.

The three young adults all scampered to catch up with Jake. The three cats followed close behind in their cat forms jumping and playing all the way back to the house. As soon as the door was opened to the porch, the three cats zipped in and disappeared. Lacey knew they had made their way to their special corner in the unfinished attic room.

Jake and Tame Tiger claimed the couches in the main room, where Lacey's great-grandparents once had slept. Blake made his way to the couch outside Lacey's room, but waited for

143

Lacey to make her way to her room waiting for a good night hug. Lacey came into the front room and joined Blake on the couch. They sat together for a moment and just snuggled on the couch.

"I'm tired Blake. I will see you in the AM," Lacey said and she gave Blake a quick kiss on his left cheek, got up and walked to her front bedroom.

Blake didn't say a word, but fell over landing his head on the pillow. He was out before he could even think. He was exhausted from a lot of excitement and traveling through time.

Lacey crawled into her bed and under the covers. She also fell into a deep, restless sleep. She tossed and turned throughout her sleep, but woke up with the five am alarm. She jumped up and hurried to the kitchen, saw that the coffee had already been made and heard people talking from the outside. She went to the porch and stopped by the bathroom, where she peered out of the window. There, she saw her Uncle Jake and Sir Edward Miller holding cups of steaming coffee and standing near the garden. They were deep in conversation and she decided to leave them to themselves. She smiled to herself, thinking how awesome it was that they had already come together. She had not even heard a sound and neither had Adam, Blake or Tame Tiger. She rushed back through the house to fetch some clothes and get dressed before anyone else got up. She would make a nice breakfast for everyone. Once she put on a pair of jeans, a tee shirt and her slippers, she immediately went to work.

As Lacey was cooking sausage patties in one pan, she started another pan and crumbled up sausage to make her favorite sausage gravy. Once she had that simmering, she mixed an entire dozen of eggs, a little milk, salt and pepper and sat that aside to scramble eggs when everyone was ready to sit and eat. She popped a dozen biscuits in the oven to bake, poured the rest of the coffee in a carafe and then made another pot of strong coffee. She sat out plates, silverware and cups for everyone to load up their plates and cups. She wanted everyone to eat in the dining room. She loved eating in the dining room as it made her feel like she was honoring her great-grandparents, since their picture adorned the wall just to the right of the big bay window.

Tame Tiger soon heard Lacey moving around in the kitchen and joined her for a second to greet her good morning and excused himself to the porch bathroom. He still loved this convenience of modern day. Not too long after Tame Tiger was already having coffee with cream and sugar, Adam came in rubbing his eyes and smiled but walked on in silence to the porch. Lacey greeted him with "good morning sunshine", as she smiled and thought about the twin horses. She didn't know if she could keep the secret, but wasn't sure just yet that there were twins.

Finally, Blake came bounding in and grabbed Lacey from behind as she stirred the sausage gravy. "Good morning my lovely little woman."

Lacey punched him gently with her elbow. "Good morning sleepy head. The traveling must have worn you out."

"Yeah, it did. Thanks for letting me sleep just a bit longer this morning," Blake replied. "Anyone in the bathroom?"

Adam walked in just after that and motioned that it was all Blake's. "I would really love some coffee Lacey. I'll take it with me and I'll go tend to the horses."

"Oh, let them sleep. I went down late last night and hung out with them, fed them a bit more and I am sure they will be okay until you have had some breakfast. Get some coffee and just sit down with all of us," Lacey said, as she handed her younger cousin a cup of steaming coffee. "Guys, Uncle Jake and Sir Edward have been outside talking and walking around now since before I got up. I am dying to know what they are talking about out there, but I haven't wanted to bother them."

"I am sure they will tell us over this awesome breakfast you're fixing," Tame Tiger said, as he leaned back and stretched before taking a big gulp of coffee.

The buzzer went off letting Lacey know the biscuits were ready. "Hey Tame Tiger, will you go let Uncle Jake and Sir Edward know breakfast will be ready in five minutes. I just need to scramble the eggs," Lacey said.

"Absolutely," Tame Tiger said. He jumped up, took his coffee and headed out onto the porch and out the door.

Blake came back into the room and Lacey had a cup of coffee waiting for him.

"Thanks Lacey. It's so nice waking up to the smell of coffee brewing and sausage cooking. Can I help you with anything?" Blake asked.

"Nope, it's on me this morning. I wanted to say thank you to all of you for helping me out. I think this is a major hurdle for our families," Lacey said, thinking about Sir Edward Miller's travel through time to find this time.

Adam and Blake both nodded in agreement.

"Hey, I am going to put some fresh food and water out for the cats, before we eat. You know they will be all down soon, once they hear all the commotion in the dining room," Blake said, as he got up and headed to the porch to get the cat bowls.

"Thanks and the mush they love is in the frig. Just add a bit of dry food too in another bowl, so they can meander back whenever they want throughout the day. You know, just in case we all get tied up," Lacey said.

"Okay. Will do, sweetie," Blake called back from the porch.

As Blake finished laying the bowls back down, the three men came inside. Sir Edward Miller stopped and shook Blake's hand.

"Well there Blake, I see you returned safely from that travel thing. So, I guess I will eventually get back to my time, I hope."

"I will make sure of it Sir Miller or should I say Sir Edward Miller. We seem to get back and forth, so far without ending up in another time or place. Don't ask how, but just call it fate, destiny, or the best luck ever," Blake said and patted the soldier on the back.

"Please," Sir Edward Miller said, "Blake, please call me Edward."

"Okay Edward; sounds like a plan to me," Blake replied and the two men smiled and nodded their heads in agreement.

"Come on guys, the food is ready. Serve up your plates and let's all go to the dining room. I have a carafe of coffee in there along with some juice and glasses on the buffet," Lacey instructed.

"Ladies first," Uncle Jake demanded and he held out his hand for Lacey to lead the way, which she did.

Once everyone was seated, Lacey asked everyone to hold hands. "I want to say a short prayer this morning. I think this marks a very important day for us all."

The men all joined hands. Lacey was between her uncle and Blake.

"Dear God, I ask that you bless this food. I ask that you bless this day in this time and in our dear family's time so many years before now. I also ask that you watch over our Jillie at school and our little cousin, Nadia, as she battles her illness. We thank you for the love you have spread over this land and all those that come upon its soil. In Jesus name I pray, Amen."

The men all nodded their heads and Blake squeezed Lacey's hand and smiled. She smiled back and also gave him a squeeze.

"Let's eat and discuss our day," Jake said, as he dug into his food.

Small talk was made for a minute or two and then Sir Edward Miller spoke up. "Please everyone, just please call me Edward. If we're going to be family, no need for such formality."

Everyone shook their heads and agreed with the request. Edward had many questions directed towards Tame Tiger. It was obvious they were becoming acquainted and the walls of being different were being torn down. Jake was in his glory watching this gift of friendship unfold. Lacey felt it too and she ate in silence listening to all the discussions. Blake and Adam just ate and listened too.

Adam finished up first and looked around to see if anyone else was done. "Do you all mind if I excuse myself and go tend to the horses?"

Lacey gave him approval and smiled. How she hoped he

was going to be the proud owner of his own horse.

Adam left with his plate and cup, dropped it off on the kitchen table and headed out onto the porch, but was startled a bit, when he saw the three cats quietly eating. They had magically made their way to the porch without disturbing anyone. Adam whispered hello and kept going. They all quietly meowed at him, but kept on enjoying their breakfast. Adam chuckled, as he headed out the door and across the backyard to the barn.

Back at the breakfast table, everyone was finishing their meal. The carafe of coffee was being passed around for one more cup.

"Great breakfast Lacey," Uncle Jake said. I forget how much I loved sausage gravy."

"Me too," Tame Tiger interjected. "We may just have to learn how to make this sausage."

"I can show you how to do it," Edward added smiling. "I have a table top meat grinder that I brought with me from my home. My mother made me pack it."

Everyone laughed.

"Your mother made you pack it?" Blake questioned.

"Oh yes, I have a mother. She is quite the cook and I grew up on a farm in England. She packed me with several items in case something happened and I needed to feed myself to survive," Edward answered.

Lacey looked at her Uncle, who was thinking the same thing. This was destiny.

"I think your mother knew that you would be finding your own home," Lacey said.

Edward looked at her and thought for a moment. "You could be right my lady and we shall see if it is I who owned this land that you now call home."

"Okay, let's help Lacey get all this cleaned up, head out and look at the gardens they have planted and then head onto the courthouse. I think we will all go," Jake said.

"Oh Jake, I think I'll hang back with Adam today and we'll get some things done here on the farm. That is if you don't mind," Blake said.

"Oh no, that is great. I just didn't want you to feel left out. You have been very dedicated to helping Lacey and her cousin from the beginning," Jake said.

"That is why I want to stay here and take care of the chores. We have lots to do and I don't think you need me to read the deeds of this land," Blake said and he winked at his Lacey.

"I can stay here too and help Blake and Adam," Tame Tiger added. "Jake, you should go, but be sure and change your clothes. I have left plenty of my really cool clothes here and be my guest."

"Yeah, but I have my own clothes I have hidden. I kind of don't care for your taste," Jake said smiling and slapped Tame Tiger on his back.

"Mine are cool," Tame Tiger said. He left the room to get his clothes he had left behind with the conveniences of modern day. He didn't want to stand out working in his leathers.

Jake excused himself and left to go upstairs and dig out his personal belongings he had hidden in the unfinished attic room.

"I'll come with you," Edward said and left the room in a hurry to follow Jake upstairs.

"Wow, they have become BFFs, huh Blake?" Lacey asked and chuckled.

"Yeah sweetie and I think it's a great thing," Blake replied, as the two of them finished carrying the breakfast dishes back to the kitchen.

"Thanks Hun," Lacey said to Blake and leaned herself into Blake for a hug.

"Everything okay Lace?" Blake asked.

"Yeah, just a bit exhausted from all the new things that keep coming upon us all." Lacey replied, as she let out a big sigh.

"Hey, don't you worry. It's all good. It will all work out here really soon and this land will be safe and life will go on as your great-grandparents had wanted," Blake reassured his petite girlfriend. "You are due a bit of doubt. No one else would have hung in there sweetheart. You and Jillie are doing something no one could have ever really believed possible. This land knew who would stay strong."

"Thanks," Lacey whispered, as tears ran down her cheeks. She was just plain tired and without Jillie around it was even harder.

"I think you need to call your cousin today and fill her in on everything. She may need to hear your voice –"Blake said, but was not able to finish as they heard a car horn outside.

Lacey went to the porch and looked out to the driveway. It was Jillie's car! She tore out of the house running and practically tore Jillie out of the car.

"I couldn't sleep last night and just knew that something was up when I got visited during the night by three tiny kittens sitting outside my dorm window!" Jillie said, as she looked around and didn't really see anything.

"OMG little cuz, you have no idea, but wait until you see who is here!" Lacey said and started pulling her cousin to the house. "Oh, did you bring anything?"

"Just my books that I need to finish up some studying. I am so glad it is Saturday. My classes are demanding and I have so much studying to do. I haven't had a moment to sit and sulk," Jillie said, as both girls skipped towards the house.

Blake was watching from the back door and laughed, as he watched these two young women skipping with joy.

"Have you had breakfast Jillie?" Blake asked, as he gave Jillie a big hug and took her off her feet.

"I smell sausage. Any sausage gravy and biscuits?" Jillie asked.

"I have one biscuit left with your name on it and there is gravy," Lacey said.

"I'll get it for her. You both need to catch up with a lot of stuff," Blake said and walked off to the kitchen humming and smiling. He had always loved fixing the girls their breakfast.

Adam came out from the barn and saw his cousin's car. He came bounding into the house. "Hey Jillie, Warrior Girl is really showing. Your foal is really growing."

"Really? I'll go see the horses in a moment. I want to gobble up some good sausage gravy. Blake, can I have a piece of toast too? I am really hungry now that I smell that gravy heating up," Jillie said smiling from ear to ear. She was so happy to be home.

Lacey was smiling too. She could not wait to really know if there were two babies instead of one. Tame Tiger would be checking it out today. Maybe she would deliver the news to Adam and Jillie while they were both here. Why not! It would just be another miracle, or unbelievable event, around here.

Lacey and Adam sat down with Jillie, while Blake waited on them all. He poured coffee and juice for Jillie.

Voices came from the front of the house and in seconds three men came into the kitchen.

"Uncle Jake, Tame Tiger and, and," Jillie said jumping up to hug her uncle and Tame Tiger.

Lacey stood up and walked in between Jillie and Edward. "Jillie, this is Sir Edward Miller or Edward to all of us now. He is from the British Army trying to help England win the Revolutionary War."

Jillie didn't say anything, but only stared at this young man, who was now out of his soldier attire, so he looked pretty normal.

"Uh, I don't really understand," Jillie said.

"He walked into the cave and traveled through time from the past," Lacey said and looked into Jillie's eyes with a huge smile.

"And, you think this is good?" Jillie asked.

"Well I think it was destiny and we'll find out soon. We're going down to the courthouse to investigate who actually owned this land before our family came upon it. Who did our great-grandfather buy it from all those years ago? I think it was descendants of Sir Miller here. I may be wrong, but he could be the answer to how our family survives. He is here for a reason and he and Uncle Jake are already BFFs," Lacey said smiling.

"BFFs?" Edward asked, with a puzzled look.

Everyone laughed, but Edward.

"Best friends forever," Lacey answered. "It's a way of communicating with these," Lacey said, as she pulled her cell phone out from her pocket.

Jillie pulled out hers and then Adam pulled out his.

"Text me something Adam," Lacey requested.

Seconds later Lacey showed Edward 'BFF' on the screen.

"Don't think about it Edward," Tame Tiger said. "It's how far this country has come since our time. Just embrace it all, but you will be ready to go back to our life. It's too much to ponder. I think our brains are just not just ready for all of this."

Edward held out his hand and held the small device. "This is a cell phone?"

Everyone nodded, as Edward handed the phone back to Adam and shook his head. Everyone laughed together. Tame Tiger put his arm around his new friend and whispered, "just think of it as great visions".

"Well, I keep pinching myself to see if I am dreaming, but I have lots of bruises now," Edward replied.

Lacey smiled and thought about just pinching herself last night. "Well, I do that too and it's not a dream. It's our destiny."

"Okay, let me finish my food," Jillie said. "I am going to run down to the barn and then I want to go to the courthouse with everyone." Jillie moved back to the kitchen table and gobbled down her food.

"Come on Lacey, let's go down and check on Warrior Girl and her condition," Tame Tiger said.

"Yes, let's do that," Lacey said, as she grabbed Tame Tiger's hand and rushed him out of the house.

Adam sat with Jillie and Blake, while Jake and Edward also went outside and headed towards the barn. They talked back and forth about the land before and now. They were totally relaxed with one another and their friendship was already established. Sir Edward Miller was about the same age of Jake's nieces and nephews and he was already feeling like he was with family.

At the barn, Lacey quietly watched as Tame Tiger gently

and carefully examined Girl.

"Come here Lacey," Tame Tiger said, smiling and holding out his hand for Lacey to take hold.

Lacey quickly came forward and gave Tame Tiger her hand. Tame Tiger pulled her close and placed her hand in one position and then took her other hand and placed it in another position.

"Feel that?" Tame Tiger said looking at Lacey

"Yes, but what am I feeling?" Lacey asked.

"Two noses. Gently push at one," Tame Tiger directed.

Lacey pushed in with her right hand and she got a push back. Then she pushed in with her left hand and she got a push back. She giggled and pushed in with both hands and she got two nudges back. Warrior Girl's belly rippled with movement. Warrior Girl moved away.

"I am sorry Girl. Did I hurt her?" Lacey asked with concern.

"No, but the twins moved around at the same time and she is moving to tell them to be still," Tame Tiger explained. "They have their ways of communicating, as us humans talk and rub the expectant belly."

Lacey nodded, got up and moved towards her horse's neck. She gently rubbed her along her side, while Tame Tiger went out of the stall and over to see Storm Cloud. He was patiently waiting his turn.

"Hey you great dad to be," Tame Tiger said and rubbed this wonderful horse from his own family's strong equine lineage. He had raised both Warrior Girl and Storm Cloud during his youth. When he met Lacey and Blake, he knew why these two had been so important to him.

Jake and Edward walked into the barn and joined the two outside of the stalls.

"Guess what Uncle Jake?" Lacey asked.

"We're having twins," Jake responded.

Lacey looked out at her uncle, who was smiling. "You knew, didn't you?"

"I have learned some really neat things in the past. Yes, I knew last night when I saw her. Adam is going to be really excited I do believe."

"Why is Adam going to be really excited," Adam said, as he, Jillie and Blake walked into the barn.

"Jillie, Adam, come here," Lacey excitedly demanded.

Jillie and Adam joined Lacey in Girl's stall. "Place your hands here and here," Lacey said, as she placed one of Jillie's hands in one place and then one of Adam's hands in another place.

The twins felt hands again and they both pushed into the hands. Jillie and Adam laughed.

"What are we feeling, hoofs or what?" Adam asked.

"Well, you are feeling one head and Jillie is feeling the other head!" Lacey said with excitement.

"What? There are two?" Jillie asked, as she stood up and was jumping up and down.

Adam got up too and went over to Lacey. "Is one of them mine?"

"Well, what do you think?" Lacey asked.

"Which one will be mine?" Adam asked and grabbed Jillie to stand still. "Which one is mine?" Adam asked very loudly, as he grinned from ear to ear.

"I don't know little cuz," Jillie said. "But, if one is a boy, he is yours and the girl is mine. If they are both the same sex, then the first one out is mine and the second one is yours," Jillie said, with quick thinking.

"You got it," Adam said and hugged Jillie and then Lacey. "I have a horse, I have a horse," he sang and everyone joined in with "Adam has a horse, Adam has a horse".

"I have to call my parents right now," Adam yelled out and ran out of the stall, but ran back and hugged Warrior Girl. Then he ran in to hug Storm Cloud and then he was gone to get better cell reception outside of the barn.

"Okay, we'll discuss the preparation of the births soon Lacey and Blake," Tame Tiger said. "I'll be sure and come back to help you. I am an expert. I help bring both the parents into this world, only many years ago," Tame Tiger said with pride.

"I am all for that," Blake said.

"Okay, let's get ready to head to town," Jake ordered.

154

"Lacey, you and Jillie get ready and we'll be off. Edward and I are ready to go."

"Give us about fifteen minutes and we'll be on our way," Lacey said, as she grabbed Jillie's left hand and they took off running to the farmhouse.

Adam came back into the barn and jumped in front of Tame Tiger. "You are going to help me with my horse, aren't you?"

"Yes, don't worry little man. I'll help you and Blake can help you too. He's learning very fast," Tame Tiger answered.

"Let's get our act together too. Lots to get done around here and you will be going home tomorrow Adam. School time is here for you now. Let me see if I can work you to the bone today," Blake said.

Adam held up his arms to show off his muscles. "You see these muscles?"

Tame Tiger put his fingers around Adam's arm muscle and smiled. "So big, my hand wraps around it."

Blake and Tame Tiger laughed. Adam crossed his arms and scowled at his teasers.

Jake and Edward left with the girls with Edward looking quite scared in the back of Lacey's car. Tame Tiger waved to him and shrugged remembering how he felt gobbled up by a monster.

After allowing the horses to go out into the pasture, the three young men all walked back up to the house. Blake, Tame Tiger and Adam went off to the garden, near the house, and walked around looking at the growth of the plants and weeds. Adam was given the chore of hoeing the weeds in this garden. Blake jumped on the tractor with the bush hog hooked up and headed to part of the pasture to start mowing for hay. They needed lots of hay, since they had added a few cows and goats to their farm. And, now they were going to add two more horses. Tame Tiger walked around the buildings and noted anything that needed further repair. Then he whistled for Storm Cloud and he took a ride around the land to check on the fencing. The farm was thriving with life.

10 HISTORY AND DESTINY

Jake pointed out things he remembered and the girls filled in the blanks for him and Edward. Edward was totally amazed at everything, as Tame Tiger had been. He asked so many of the same questions, which made Lacey realize how things appeared the same to people of the past.

As Lacey pulled into a parking space at the Courthouse, Edward took in the architecture and detail of this building.

"Very beautiful work, this building," Edward commented.

"I will have to drive him by the National Military Park and see if he recognizes a couple of people," Lacey said, looking in the rearview mirror at her uncle.

"That would be quite interesting, wouldn't it?" Jake replied.

Jillie turned around and smiled.

The four of them got out of the car and Lacey put some money in the parking meter. Edward took it all in and kept silent. It was very overwhelming.

"Okay, let's go see if we can find your name in history," Lacey said.

Lacey walked up to the information desk and asked where they could look at property deeds that would take them back to the seventeen hundreds. The lady looked at her rather funny.

"Oh, I am doing some research of our farm and we want to know who actually owned it from the beginning. I am trying to build a historical timeline for my family," Lacey said.

"How nice," the information lady replied. "We have a library dedicated to Guildford County land purchases and sales. I believe you will find what you're looking for in there." The lady handed Lacey a pass for the Land and Property Library on the main floor.

"Thank you. Have a nice day and I'll drop this pass back by on our way out," Lacey said.

The lady nodded and pointed them to go to the right for their destination. The four headed down the corridor and they all noted all the business going on in all directions.

Lacey put the card key into the slot on the door. Sir Miller intently watched her every move and was amazed at the magic of this card. He held out his hand.

"May I please examine that card?" Edward asked.

Lacey handed it over to him and smiled. "The world is full of surprises, huh?"

"It is just unfathomable," Edward answered. "I keep wondering if I am going to wake up with fever or something."

"No my friend, you are not dreaming and not with fever. You are living an experience of a lifetime that not many people will ever get to experience and all the others will not believe your stories. It's better if you just keep it to yourself and the people that you are destined to meet," Jake explained, patting Edward on the back.

"I guess," Edward answered.

"Hey Sir Edward, if I have been able to deal with all of this, so can you," Lacey commented sounding a bit irritated.

"Oh, please do not allow me to offend you my lady. I am very dedicated to this destiny, especially if my name appears on the documents that we now seek. I am just a bit overwhelmed," Edward said.

Jillie was already looking around and looking through paperwork. "I think I have already found it! I did, I did and look Sir Edward Miller, you are here and you bought some land! Uncle Jake, look. Is this our land?"

Jake, Edward and Lacey rushed over. Jake gently took the

bound book from Jillie's grasp and reviewed it. "Oh my gosh; this book is dedicated to all the lands in our community. Yes, Edward my son, you did or you are the one who buys our land and so much more. Come and look," Jake said, as he moved over to a table so that all four of them could look at it.

"See here, it is documented that you secured one thousand acres of land extending all over in the year 1780. You did say it was 1774 now, so you must have stayed here after we separated from England. Let's see how it happens that it gets divided up among so many families," Jake said, as he flipped further into the document.

"Look here! It shows that you deed some land over to your son, Walter! Congratulations Edward, you are a papa," Jake said smiling and slapped the young man on the shoulder. "It states that you deed your son, Walter, five hundred acres in the year 1810. So, he's about 25-years-old. Oh here we go; you must also have a daughter, because you leave Lady Anna Miller with the other five hundred acres upon your death in 1856. Anna must not get married, but she leaves her land to a Walter, Jr. in 1875. It appears your son, Walter, divides his land among his other children. But, it's the land that goes to Walter, Jr. that ends up being sold off in pieces and my great-grandfather buys up 100 acres in 1920 from your grandson."

Edward is taking all of this in and looks rather sad. "Who do I marry?"

"Well, let's see who may be your wife. I would think there is something with your wife's name on it," Jake said, as Lacey and Jillie quietly stood by listening and taking in all the information.

Jake and Edward both looked through the documents to search for the name of Edward's wife and then he see saw it. The woman he wanted to marry joins him in America. Edward closes his eyes and smiles.

Jake and the girls stare at him as Edward thinks of the love he left behind still becomes his wife. At this moment, he knew this is his destiny. Sir Miller opened up his eyes and looked at Jake, Lacey and Jillie.

"This is truly my destiny. Do you see that name right there?" Edward asked, as he pointed to his wife's name.

"Yes, but do you really know her?" Lacey asked.

"Oh yeah, as Lady Lacey says, this is my fiancé that I left back in England. She joins me here and now I know I was supposed to walk into that cave. I am here to save your people Jake and that I am going to do," Edward said and he grasped Jake's shoulders.

The two men hug. Lacey and Jillie joined in and the four of them share a moment of mysterious magic that no one could have ever imagined.

"Let's get out of here. Our work has just begun. We have to get you back and make sure that no one else takes charge of your troop," Jake said.

The four of them headed out of the courthouse almost skipping like little kids. The entire ride home was pure joy, especially when they drove him by the park as they had promised. Edward told them how he had actually met Cornwallis and may even again. He told them how hard it was going to be to return and be loyal to his country. But, as Lacey pointed out, something happened that you stayed here anyway.

"Maybe you fell in love with America yourself and the land which you traveled and eventually claimed as yours. Did you come from money?" Lacey asked.

"Well, actually yes," Edward replied. "My father told me he would help me establish my own estate no matter where I decided to hang my hat. Lacey, I must return to England for my dear love and then I will return to purchase my land. I mean our land," Edward said.

Once they arrived home, the four were so content. They went into the farmhouse and waited on the others to tell them the unbelievable news. Lacey called to check on their little cousin, who was doing fine with her treatments.

The house phone rang and Jillie rushed to pick it up.

"Hello?" Jillie answered.

"Is this Jillie?" A man asked.

"Dan, is that you?" Jillie answered.

"Yep; I thought you were at school. I was calling to chat with Lacey about your Light the Night team. I want to come and interview you guys in preparation for the event," Dan exclaimed. "Can I come over today?"

"Uh, let me check with Lacey. She has some friends visiting and I just came in for a brief visit to pick something up," Jillie said waving at Lacey for her attention. "Hold on for a moment."

Jillie placed her hand over the receiver. "It's Dan and he wants to come over to interview us, well you really, about the walk."

"Today?" Lacey asked with her eyes opened wide. "No way, we have too much going on with Sir Miller, Jake and Tame Tiger here."

"Ok, I'll think of something," Jillie said and took a deep breath.

"Hey Dan, Lacey has some people visiting the farm today and it's not a good time. Can she get back with you? I probably will not be able to wait either, but I hate that I am going to miss you."

"I owe you a big favor, so don't worry I will be there for you and your family. I will cover that event and I'll help spread the word how important it is to participate with organizations that are trying to raise money to make a difference," Dan said. "I'll let you go. Give me a call whenever and tell Lacey the same."

"Will do and thank you Dan. Don't worry, I am not forgetting you owe me one," Jillie said smiling, as she thought about the ski trip and how Dan got to witness the magical powers of Tess, Tye and Miss Virginia. The look on his face had been priceless. "See you Dan," Jillie said,

"Later little, powerful woman," Dan said with laughter in his voice and hung up.

When Blake, Tame Tiger and Adam returned from working on the farm, the rest of the day was pure celebration of life, family and friends like no other. They all discussed the plans of what was to happen next. The cats were all relaxed and happy. They assumed the laziness of everyday pets.

Dinner time came and they decided to order pizza, which

Tame Tiger had grown accustom to while he was here and they wanted to introduce Edward to this special pie. Jake was a bit excited too, because it had been so long since he had eaten pizza.

They all sat around the dining room table sharing the three large pizzas. The men devoured two whole pizzas themselves and helped Lacey and Jillie with the third one. They sat and enjoyed one another's company into the wee hours of the morning, only getting up to make it to the restroom or to get something else to drink. Desert came out about midnight. Another thing Jake wanted almost every time he visited was ice cream, which Lacey kept plenty of in her freezer. Tame Tiger also loved the frozen delight and tried every flavor. Lacey even kept ice cream cones handy, which became Edward's favorite.

At three in the morning, coffee was made. Jake, Tame Tiger and Edward would be leaving together just before dawn, so that it was dark in their time. Edward knew that his troops would not be looking for him at night. He wanted to make sure Jake and Tame Tiger were securely back in the village before he would find his troop. He would be working them away from the lands, which would be his for the taking as soon as the war was over.

"Your dad is going to be here early today to pick you up Adam," Lacey said. "He's going to think we worked you to death when you're totally out of it later on."

"My brother is coming here today?" Jake asked.

"Yeah Uncle Jake; you miss him don't you?" Adam asked.

"Of course, but I can be with him through you and little Nadia one day. I hope I live long enough to know Nadia when she is an adult. She is so important to this land," Jake added.

Lacey and Jillie both got up and gave their younger cousin a big hug.

"Thanks for all that you have done. When you get your license, you can come out as much as you want," Lacey said.

"Oh, I am going to be here every weekend. I have a baby on the way, remember!" Adam said, as he grinned from ear to ear.

"Me too!" Jillie said. "Let's go down and check on the proud parents Adam."

"Okay, I need something to keep me awake," Adam said and he jumped up and off they went.

Jake and Tame Tiger smiled at one another. They knew that all that they held precious was going to be okay.

"Hey Lacey, can I see that arrowhead you found?" Tame Tiger asked.

Lacey got up and pulled the arrowhead from her special box, where she kept special finds from the farm.

"You found an arrowhead that Tame Tiger made three hundred years ago?" Edward asked.

"Yes, the same day he used it. Isn't it weird how connected everything is with us?" Lacey responded.

All of a sudden, the cats all jumped up at the same time and disappeared from everyone's sight.

"What was that all about?" Tame Tiger asked, as he jumped up and took off.

Lacey was right behind him with Blake close behind her. Jake and Edward hurried to join the others. When they were all outside, the cats were totally out of sight. They all looked around, but it was still dark and they couldn't see a thing.

Jillie and Adam returned from the barn and were surprised to find out what happened.

"The horses acted a bit weird too, but we settled them down," Jillie said.

"Let's get into the truck and take a ride down into the pasture," Lacey directed. "Uncle Jake, you, Edward and Tame Tiger will need to cross back to your time soon anyway." Lacey said.

They all headed to the girls' old grey truck they had kept from their grandfather.

"I'll drive," Blake said and he grabbed the keys from under the front seat.

"I want to ride in the back, so I can look around," Lacey said, as she hopped into the back.

"Me too," Jillie said and she hopped in the back.

Jake jumped in the back with his nieces and then Adam followed. Tame Tiger decided to ride in the front with Blake. Before Blake could even back the truck out, Tame Tiger squeezed himself along the passenger side of the truck that was close to the side of the granary.

"Well, I guess I will ride in the back," Edward said and stepped up on the back fender, threw his left leg into the bed of the truck and then his right as Blake backed out the truck from under the shed that was attached to the granary.

The gates to the pasture were still open from Adam and Jillie checking in on the horses. The horses were both whinnying loud enough for the girls to hear them.

"Stop!" Jillie yelled out.

Blake stopped the truck. Both girls jumped out, ran into the barn and released the horses. Warrior Girl and Storm Cloud came out running down into the pasture. Something was happening for sure. Warrior Girl was moving quite fast for her condition.

The girls came running and both held out an arm for Jake and Edward to grab. The two men helped Lacey and Jillie into the truck bed. Once they were safely in, Lacey yelled for Blake to hit it . Blake put the truck in drive and spun dirt, as he sped into the pasture along the worn out path that led into the pasture.

As the truck passed through the narrow opening, where the second barn had stood many years ago, they could see something was happening at the oak tree. But what?!

Blake slowly drove towards the oak tree. The horses had already made it down to the tree. The cats, in their beastly forms, were circling the tree and looking up. The moon was still bright enough to allow everyone to see the darkened forms surrounding the tree.

"Stop here Blake," Tame Tiger commanded, as he held his right hand up. "Let's all get out and make our way to the tree. I think someone is up in that tree."

Blake stopped the truck and they all gathered together watching the commotion around the oak tree.

"There is something in that tree," Jake excitedly said. "Lacey, can you send out a thought to Tye and see what is going on?"

"Of course," Lacey said and immediately sent out a thought to her cat.

The cat answered back immediately by showing up within seconds in his beastly, tiger form. His eyes lit up and he told Lacey someone is up in the tree and he's talking kind of weird.

Lacey thought back and spoke out loud. "Is there only one person or more?"

Tye gently roared and thought back to her that only one person was there.

"Come on, they have someone held up in the tree. I don't think he or she can do anything to harm us," Lacey said and started towards the tree.

"Let's be cautious," Edward said. "Maybe another one of my men found the cave and walked into the time passage. I don't want someone else to know my wonderful secret."

"Come on Tye," Tame Tiger said and he took off running so fast that no one had a chance to join him.

"Come on, one person is not going to do much unless they have a gun or something else," Jake said and motioned the rest of them forward. "Lacey and Jillie, you keep behind us. I cannot allow anything to happen to you or I would never forgive myself."

The girls didn't argue. They were a bit scared. They held hands. Blake walked behind them to do his part to keep them safer. Nothing was going to harm his Lacey and Jillie.

Tame Tiger reached the base of the oak tree and looked up. "Who are you?"

"I come in peace. I do not know where I am. Please do not 'ray' me," the voice shouted from above.

"No harm will come to you, as long as you do nothing wrong," Tame Tiger answered.

"Hey Tame Tiger, who is it?" Lacey said, as they all reached the tree.

"I am not sure, but he begged me not to "ray" him," Tame

Tiger answered.

"Who are you?" Jake shouted upward.

"My name is Lope," the voice answered back.

"Lope?" Jake questioned. "Did you say 'Lope'?"

Lacey and Jillie squeezed one another's hands even tighter and Jillie pushed forward.

"Yes," answered the voice.

"Come down. No harm will come to you. We are friendly," Jake yelled upward.

"Tye, Tess and Miss Virginia will not harm you," Jillie called out. "In fact, you can turn back into cats," Jillie ordered and all three cats changed to their kitten forms and perched upon Lacey's, Jillie's and Jake's shoulders.

The young teen slowly descended down the tree and jumped from the last tree limb closest to the ground. When he landed, he scrunched down and then slowly stood up. He looked at the outlines of the people around him.

"Miss Virginia, Tye and Tess, light us up," Lacey commanded.

The eyes of the cats lit up the night and Lope stood looking at these strange people, but he held out his hand for the cats to smell.

Jake noticed his clothes and couldn't believe what he was seeing. "What year is it for you son?"

"Huh? What year do you think it is? It is 2300. Why do you ask? Where am I?" Lope asked.

Everyone was silent.

"Is there something wrong?" Lope asked.

"Were you perchance playing around a very, old, old oak tree young man?" Jake asked.

"Yes, I was climbing it and then I was here in this tree in the dark. It was still light where I was. I thought maybe I fell and hit my head," Lope replied. "We're not supposed to play in it, but it is so cool and I just wanted to climb it."

"Do you live on the land with the big tree?" Jake asked.

"No, we are visiting as we always do every year. It's our family's vacation spot and everyone comes from all over to gather once a year in celebration of something. Why do you ask?" Lope asked.

"No reason. We need to get you back. What exactly were you doing or were you in a certain part of the tree?" Tame Tiger asked.

"I was really far out on a limb that extended really far. It is so cool," Lope answered.

"Okay, I need you to get back up that tree and go back to that limb and place when you appeared here. You're with friends, but this is not a place that you should be staying for very long. Your parents will be worried," Jake said, thinking about his own ventures that started so many years ago.

"So, it's true. The tree is magic and it does take people through time," Lope said. "Why can't I stay?"

"Who are your parents?" Lacey asked.

"My mom, her name is Euzelia and my dad's name is Mason. This is my mom's family's land.

"Very unusual names, Lope and Euzelia," Jillie added.

"Oh yeah, many years ago, sometime around 2032, triplets were born and they were named: Euzelia, Exum and Etta. And ever since, those three names are handed down. I don't really know why, but anyway, that is all I know. My name is also from a great warrior, who is my, I don't know how many greats, but my great-grandfather. I was one of the lucky ones to be named, 'Lope'."

Jillie hit Lacey and leaned over. Could one of us have those triplets? Maybe Nadia? We will all be living in the year 2032 you know," Jillie said.

"Are we related?" Lope asked.

"If we tell you something, you think you can keep a secret?" Jake asked.

"Oh yes, I promise," Lope excitedly said. "No one listens to me anyway. I like roaming our family's lands and just exploring. I have found so many cool things."

The sun was starting to rise and faces were starting to come into view. Lope looked at all the strange faces, but stopped when he reached Jake's face. "Hey man, I have seen your picture in our family lodge." Then he scanned the other faces and knew now he was with the people from his family's past.

"You're Lacey and you're Jillie," Lope said pointing at each one. "Your pictures are hanging up in the dining hall. There is one other picture, her name is Nadia. She is my great, great, great, great, great, great, great grandmother –," Lope says and pauses. "OMG, you are my great, great, great, great, great, great-aunts or something like that. This is way cool."

"Lope, listen to me," Jake began. "Yes, we are your ancestors, but we need to get you back home for now

"Where is Nadia? Can I meet my great-grandmother, six times removed?" Lope asked.

"Well, she is just a little thing and right now she is battling a very bad sickness," Lacey said.

"What sickness?" Lope quickly demanded.

"Oh, it's not for you to worry," Lacey said.

"Yes it is my worry. She is my direct ancestor. How sick is she? I demand to know." Lope yelled.

"Well, she has a blood cancer, known as Leukemia," Jake said.

"Leukemia? That was wiped out over a hundred years ago. Now, we just get a nose spray for that, especially if it's in your family history. I can help her. If people get that now, it's a simple pill and they are better. I can bring one back to you. They are there for the taking. Medicines are readily available to anyone who is sick, but oh no-," Lope stopped and was in deep thought.

"What's wrong?" Jillie asked.

"Well, to get a pill, you walk through this scanner and it lets you know if you need something and if you're sick whatever you need is delivered into your hand. You just hold your hand under the dispenser," Lope said.

"Well, that is a problem, because we couldn't do that," Jake said.

"And why not?" Lacey questioned. "We know she must get better, she has all these descendants. Maybe that is why

Lope has come back in time. We cannot just discount this. Like you Uncle Jake, and you Sir Edward, it is destiny. Lope could be a part of Nadia's destiny. Lope, can you get a pill somehow?"

"Oh yeah, my dad is a scientist. I'll ask him for one to study in my lab class," Lope said without hesitation.

Lacey hugged Lope and then Jillie walked up and hugged him.

"Hey we need to get out of sight. Jake, Tame Tiger and Edward, are you guys going back or not?" Lacey questioned.

"Are you kidding me?" Jake answered. "Not in three hundred years, would I leave now."

Everyone started laughing.

"HEY!" Lope yelled out. "I want to know everyone's names and he pointed to Blake, then Adam and then he stopped on Tame Tiger. "You look like one of my cousins." Then Lope looked at Edward. "You look familiar too."

Everyone said their names and then Lacey said they should head for the house. Lope was so excited. He jumped into the truck and ran all around the inside bed of the truck.

"So, this is what a truck looks like for real?" Lope asked and everyone laughed.

"This is the coolest of cools. He took out a very funny apparatus from his shirt sleeve and touched a button. A small eye looking thing came out and scanned the area.

"What is that?" Jillie questioned.

Lope held his apparatus out for everyone to see. "Oh, I just scanned you into my database, but don't worry, it's totally safe to my eyes only. This is my personal memory cube. No one else can get in. It only recognizes my pupils, my fingerprints and my voice. Each person has their own unique set of imprints and that is how everything works now or in my time I should explain."

"This is way too much for my brain," Edward said and smiled thinking about his farm he would be working in the near future.

As Blake was driving closer to the house, Tye thought out to Lacey that Jeremy was there waiting for Adam.

"Oh no, Jeremy is at the house waiting on Adam. Do a quick u-turn and we'll drop you four displaced people back at the oak tree. You can come through the tunnels," Lacey said as she got up and tapped on the truck's cab, back window.

Blake heard her loud and clear and did the u-turn back to the oak tree. Tame Tiger, Jake, Sir Miller and Lope all jumped out. Lope was having the time of his life with these very Important strangers from the past.

11 GENERATIONS APART TOGETHER

Jake pulled up the hidden earthen trap door. Tame Tiger practically jumped down into the hole and turned on a flashlight they had left for their use. Edward looked at Jake and shook his head, smiled and descended into the earth. Lope was all grins.

"OMG, this is getting better and better," Lope said and didn't seem scared at all, as he followed behind Edward.

Jake shook his head and smiled remembering all of his own adventures and travels through time. It was like he was meeting himself reincarnated. Jake positioned himself on the top step. He grabbed the trap door and pulled it down as he descended into the earth. The other three were quietly waiting for him. Lope and Edward were looking all around this hollowed-out room.

"Come on fellows, we'll show you something special about this place," Tame Tiger said, as he shined the light towards the tunnel leading towards the barn.

"This is so way cool," Lope called out. "Do you think these tunnels still exist in my time?"

"I would think so, but I wonder why you don't know about them. Someone must have decided to keep the secret and not pass it along." Jake responded and wondered about the future.

"Well, I don't live on the farm. I'll have to ask my cousins,

Jake and Will," Lope answered.

Tame Tiger grabbed Lope's shoulder and stopped him, which caused Jake and Edward to come to a quick stop. "What names did you just say?"

"I said my cousins, Jake and Will, live on the farm now with my Aunt Luce, who is one of your descendents, and Uncle Dane. Aunt Luce and Uncle Dane live on the farm now and keep it up. It's no longer a farm, but a sanctuary for unwanted animals. Our families all take turns vacationing there and helping out. But, we all come together at this one time every year to celebrate the birth of -," Lope stopped and thought for a moment. "I better not say. I am scared I will mess something up." Lope looked at Jake with uncertainty.

"Well, you said two names that mean a lot to us and it brings peace to us. I think this land is definitely making sure it stays with our family and you are another gate keeper, I do believe," Jake said, as he smiled at Tame Tiger, also known as Will to the family here.

"Well, I am confused, but is there anyone named Edward or Anna by chance?" Edward asked, not thinking his family really stays with the farm from what little they saw on the deeds.

"Oh yeah, my sister is named Anna after somebody. Our family keeps using a lot of old names that are very out-dated, but my mom's name is Teresa and there has been along line of them too," Lope explained. "My name is really old, but it's really popular in my time, so I don't mind it. Oh, and Edward is another cousin. There are a lot of us. Trust me. The farm couldn't survive without all the families coming and helping out. The big house, as Aunt Luce says, has a revolving door. There is a family coming and going weekly. It's how it is kept alive. From what I understand, it has had lots of purposes throughout the generations."

"Wow, never in my wildest dreams would I believe we would be here all together, but Lope you are standing with people from about six hundred years before your time. I am Jake, the first gate keeper. Did you ever hear anything about me?" Jake asked.

"Yeah, yeah, I have heard your name, but the family history is enormous and it's just a bit too much for me to comprehend. But I love the farm and I have explored every inch of it. Oh, I have an Uncle Jake and there is a cousin Jake. Man, this is way weird," Lope replied.

"Well Lope, you are talking with people who actually existed on this very land around six hundred years ago. Tame Tiger here, also known as Will, is the next in line to be the leader of his people, who live on this very land. Sir Edward Miller here, well he is from England, but he will purchase all this land and it will end up being sold to my great-grandfather, Tye-," Jake said, but was cut off by Lope.

"Oh, Tye is my grandfather's name. So cool, huh?"

"It really is so cool Lope, but I don't think we have time to get into all of this now. We need to get up to the house and see if Jeremy and Adam have left yet," Jake said.

"I have a cousin named Jeremiah," Lope added.

"Let's go and see if we can join the girls," Tame Tiger said. "Jake, we do need to get back to our time you know. We cannot allow Edward's troop to find our village."

"I know. We will leave tomorrow. We need to help the girls with this little guy and also discuss what we need to do about Nadia," Jake replied.

"I am telling you, one pill and she is a new girl," Lope chimed in grinning that he could be the hero here, like he had heard about some of his ancestors.

"Okay, we have heard you. We'll discuss it all in a bit with Lacey and Jillie. Let's go up into the barn, check on the horses and see if they made it back into the barn yet," Jake said.

The four of them walked together through the tunnel to the barn, where Tame Tiger again led the way. He pushed up the hidden barn trap door and climbed up. He motioned for them to stay put and he quickly moved to peer around the corner to see if he could see Jeremy's car. He didn't see the car, so he rushed back and told them to come on up. Lope scurried up followed by Edward, who was followed by Jake bringing up the rear.

The horses were back in the barn, but they were not locked up in their stalls. Lope immediately ran up to Storm Cloud's side and gently rubbed him as he softly spoke. "Hey boy, you're a mighty awesome stallion."

The horse nickered and turned his head towards Lope. Lope walked up to the horse's head and rubbed some more. Storm Cloud moved his head up and down with approval.

"He likes you," Tame Tiger said and walked over and also rubbed the horse's side and then moved over to Warrior Girl. "Take a look over here Lope. Warrior Girl is expecting twins."

"Oh yes, she is looking very fat, but beautiful. We have lots of horses on the farm. I bet they are descendants of these two fine horses," Lope added, as he thought back to all the pictures hanging around the big dining hall. "Yep, there is a picture of these two horses, Lacey, Jillie and Adam and the two baby horses."

"Well that makes sense," Jake said and looked at Tame Tiger with a huge smile. "Was Blake in the picture?"

Lope thought for a moment, but he couldn't remember now.

"I'll take care of them and get them settled into their stalls if you want me to?" Lope asked. "I do this all the time on the farm."

"Go for it dude," Jake said. "Come on men, let's go get with the girls and redo our plans."

Jake, Edward and Tame Tiger left Lope with the horses. Lope decided to take care of Warrior Girl first. He guided her to her stall. He gently rubbed her down and lovingly talked to her, as he moved the brush top to bottom. Once he finished grooming her, he filled up her feed trough and made sure she had plenty of fresh hay and water. He shut the stall door and looked for Storm Cloud, which had meandered out of the barn and was grazing on some grass.

A great thought came to his mind. "I think I will take a nice ride with history," Lope thought and called out for Storm Cloud to come into the barn.

Storm Cloud came in and allowed Lope to saddle him up, climb aboard and the two of them left the barn as one. Once out of the barn, he gave Storm Cloud a little nudge to let him know he was ready to hit it. Storm Cloud took off and the wind blew through Lope's shoulder length hair.

Everyone was sitting around the kitchen table now sharing some more coffee and discussing Lope, what needed to happen three hundred years before now and what they should do about Nadia's sickness.

The cats all got up from their lounging positions and disappeared before everyone's eyes. Lacey jumped up and looked outside. She saw Lope and Storm Cloud racing down into the pasture lands. She smiled and told her uncle to come and look.

When Jake got to the window, he saw Storm Cloud and Lope racing through the narrow passage and the three cats racing behind them to catch up. Jake laughed. "He's got a lot of me in him I see. I don't think we can let him stay around here very much longer. I am sure his parents are going to be worried sick about him."

"I bet they are looking now and going out of their minds," Jillie said, as she got up to look out of the window.

"No, he told us he was the one that knew every inch of the farm and wandered around for hours searching for treasures," Jake said with a smile from ear to ear.

"Sounds very familiar huh Uncle Jake?" Jillie asked.

"Oh yeah," Jake replied.

"Come on, let's talk about Nadia. I wish we knew if we do get one of those pills that it doesn't harm her," Jake said. "How do we even get her to take it?"

"What if we get Lope to bring us something that we can read up on and make sure of any potential problems," Jillie said.

"We'd better do that. Hey Lacey, think out to Tye to get that boy back here," Jake requested.

Lacey immediately thought out to her cat and didn't get anything back. She thought out again and nothing. "Please, something cannot be wrong now!" Lacey said out loud. "Tye is not sending me anything back, which means something is not right. I cannot take another surprise or problem."

Blake had been sitting quietly listening, but now he got up and went over to Lacey. Blake put his hands on her shoulders and gently squeezed to help calm her down.

Jillie tried reaching out to Tess, but nothing came back. She got up and went outside and saw Tye, Tess and Storm Cloud racing back without Lope.

"Lacey, Uncle Jake, come outside," Jillie screamed.

Tye came bounding up to Lacey and magically leaped onto her shoulder. "Lope opened up the portal. He found an arrowhead and tried it out. I think he went back in time."

Lacey told them all what Tye had thought out to her. "Miss Virginia has gone back in time to stay with him. They must be connected, as you are Uncle Jake. I do think he is another gate keeper," Lacey said.

"Let's get going men," Jake said. We cannot let him go it all alone there. The war is breaking out; other tribes are out and about. This is all we need."

"Do you want us to run you down again," Blake asked.

"Yes, we need to get there as soon as possible," Tame Tiger said, as he quickly hugged Jillie and then Lacey.

"Let's hit it men," Blake said and they headed for the truck.

"Lace, I'll take care of Storm Cloud as soon as I get back," Blake yelled out of the truck window. "You and Jillie do whatever you need to do."

"I am going to call Uncle Jeremy and see if they got home yet," Lacey said. "Uncle Jeremy didn't say much, but rushed Adam to get going. I think something is wrong Jillie."

"Okay, but wouldn't Tea let us know if something was really wrong?" Jillie asked.

"Oh my gosh Jillie, so much is happening. I don't know if I can take all of this," Lacey cried out and she ran into the house.

Tye clung onto Lacey's shoulder. Jillie and Tess quickly followed. I'll send my professors a note that a family emergency has come up and I'll stay here until Monday night."

"Thank you Jillie. I am so sorry, but I am a bit

overwhelmed," Lacey said and hugged her younger cousin.

"Let's call Uncle Jeremy," Jillie said, as she grabbed one phone for herself and then got another one for Lacey. They could both talk with their Uncle Jeremy. They were anxious to hear about Nadia.

The girls talked with their uncle and aunt to find out that Nadia had taken a turn for the worse and wasn't responding like she had been. Their aunt was crying, but she mentioned how Tea didn't leave Nadia's side and she was the only thing that Nadia was responding to right now. The girls listened as their aunt and uncle expressed their worries. Lacey assured them that she and Jillie would be over next weekend to visit and allow them to have some time to themselves.

"So plan on doing something with Luke or by yourselves, okay?" Lacey said.

Everyone said their good-byes and hung up.

"Lacey, I think Lope came here for a reason. He came back through time for Nadia, who is his great-grandmother, six times removed. He wouldn't exist if she doesn't survive. I think we do what we feel is right. We'll get that little 'Jakester' to get us some reading this week and next weekend, we may be saving our cousin's life," Jillie said with authority.

"Okay, I just may let you make the call on this one. You are the medicine woman", Lacey said, with a smile and a wink.

"So I have been told, but I don't really feel like a medicine woman," Jillie said. "It's like we got thrust into this destiny and no one asked us if this is what we wanted."

"Hey, don't let me drag you down Jillie," Lacey said. I didn't mean to complain. I love what has happened and couldn't imagine life any differently. I know it's been extra hard on you having to deal with so much during high school. Are you okay with all of this?"

"Oh yeah, I just feel like getting this vet degree is going to be such a long process and I wonder if it's all worth it. I won't be back here for eight years," Jillie said. "It's just a long road ahead."

"I know, but Aiken will be back there soon and I hear

Miguel is applying to vet school there too. How many degrees with Miguel have? Are you two getting serious?" Lacey asked.

"Yeah, that will make it a little better. I don't love being away from all of this," Jillie said, as she waved her hand around the room of the farmhouse. Jillie ignored any further conversation about Miguel for now.

"Hey, you're not that far away and just come home whenever possible. Now, let's get some dinner started in case Uncle Jake and everyone return tonight starving. I cannot believe that little guy did this, but it is neat to know that all this is not for nothing," Lacey said and headed toward the kitchen.

Jillie followed behind her and the cats were right behind Jillie.

The girls fixed some fried chicken, green beans and mashed potatoes with gravy. Blake came in the house, headed to the restroom and soon came into the kitchen.

"Okay, the horses are down for the evening. It sure does smell good in here. I don't think we all ate anything today with all the excitement," Blake said. "Can we eat or are we waiting on the others?"

"Let's eat. No telling what is happening or if we will even see them," Lacey answered.

The three of them dug into the food and they stayed in the kitchen. They talked a bit, but they mainly stayed quiet in thought. Their minds were all consumed with worry about what was happening with Lope.

Night time came. The dishes had been cleared and the food was put away. Lacey got the coffee ready for the morning. She was dragging and was not going to be able to stay awake much longer. Blake and Jillie had retired to the family room. Blake had laid down on one of the couches, where he usually slept. He was out in seconds.

Jillie was sitting in a big rocker and also fell asleep.

"I am exhausted-" Lacey said, as she walked into the family room and stopped talking. She shook Jillie and guided her to lie on the other couch and covered her up. She the also covered Blake and went back to the front bedroom. Lacey crawled onto the top of the covers, pulled a blanket across herself and fell asleep too.

Tye and Tess both curled up in the family room together, but they were both on guard.

Hours went by and the clock struck midnight. Lacey woke up and checked her cell phone to see the time. She heard someone's voice and figured that Blake and Jillie were up now. So she decided to get up too.

When she reached the family room, she found Jillie and Blake still sound asleep. The door to the kitchen had been closed and she saw light shining from under the door. She opened the door and there sat Uncle Jake, Tame Tiger and Lope with plates full of food.

"Hey, we hope you don't mind we didn't want to wake you all up. We actually had a little shut-eye ourselves under the stars after we found this guy wondering around," Jake said.

"This is awesome," Lope said with his mouth full.

"Where is Edward?" Lacey asked.

"Well, he said that he didn't need to return here. He knows what he has ahead of him now and he is on his way to lead his men away from our land. We all know that we win our independence from England, so he will be back in time to make that claim to our land and bring the love of his life, Anna Tess, to start an unbelievable family. The reason my grandfather buys this land is because he wants to marry Edward's granddaughter, Tess. In the old days, a woman goes with a dowry. My grandfather loved grandmother so much, he paid for the land and he promised that he would never let the land go outside of the family and he would love my grandmother forever. Lope here is proof of that promise. The promise is kept."

"Edward knew all of this?" Lacey questioned, looking so puzzled.

"Oh no, I remembered my grandmother's heritage and her family line and the fact he came forward in time means the destiny of this land is working her magic. I still don't know how we get to the mountains, but I am not going to worry about that right now," Jake said. "It's all good and even better when we get this little guy back to his time."

"Oh Lope, I think Jillie and I want you to go back to your time and get us something to read about that medicine for Nadia. She is not doing well and we're very worried. Do you think you can get some information and whatever we need to give to her if we feel it's the best thing to do?" Lacey asked.

"No problem Lace," Lope replied and smiled big.

Lacey looked at Lope, smiled and then gently slapped his face. "Smarty pants."

"I am here, aren't I?" Lope replied and crossed his hands across his chest.

"How old are you anyway?" Jake asked.

"I am double digits. I am ten-years-old," Lope answered.

"Your parents must be worried sick. We need to get you back," Jake said.

"Oh, I go camping by myself all the time. Trust me. They don't even worry about me whenever we're on the farm. See this? It's called a cube," Lope said, as he pulled the cube from his sleeve, as he had done earlier. "It's something we get the second we're born and it stays with us always. No one else can use it. From the moment we're born, a cube is started and it holds my personal information. If you get far away from it, it starts sounding off. It knows my DNA, my voice, my finger print, my everything and it is tied to my parents. If I am not well, it sends a message to my parents. If I am hurt, it sends a message to my parents and if serious, it sends a message to the urgent care teams. And, so when one is born and the cube is synced to the baby's everything, the cube will tell what illnesses we need to be inoculated for before we are even out of the hospital."

"Wow, now that is medical advancement for sure," Tame Tiger said.

"It's the advancement equivalent to the "I have fallen and I cannot get up" thing that is available now to the older generation," Lacey commented.

"And, as long as my cube doesn't send any alarming messages to my parents, I am fine," Lope explained with excitement.

"Well, when the cats, in their beastly forms, had you caught up in the tree, did the cube not sense your fear?" Tame Tiger asked.

"I wasn't scared. We have all kinds of animals that are not wanted. And, we have some cats that turn into beastly felines too. I am pretty sure they are the same as you have here: Miss Virginia, Tye, Tess and Tea. Yep, they are still in the family forever. They were just worried about me and they sensed me here, but they know it's for a reason. I am pretty sure it's for Nadia too, now that we know how sick she really is," Lope continued on with his very intelligent discussion.

"I see what you mean Tame Tiger, when you said that you didn't mind going back to your time," Lacey said. "I cannot imagine being that advanced yet. It sounds really neat, but I like my life here." Lacey looked at her Uncle Jake. "How did you do it Uncle Jake? How did you finally leave your time?"

"I fell in love with the simple life and this land is so beautiful in our time. There is so much freedom, but I know that all changes. I fell in love with your aunt. What can I say? It was my calling and I was the gate keeper to all of this," Jake said.

"Do I have to stay back here if you think I am a gate keeper?" Lope questioned, but not looking too excited.

"I don't think so Lope. I think you're job is much simpler and that is just to help us with Nadia. I don't think you should be opening the gate to all of your cousins," Jake answered.

"Oh don't worry. We're forbidden to be around the oak tree, but I have always meandered down to the old tree and climbed it, but this is the only time I traveled through time. The others, well they are never up for an adventure and they don't really venture around the tree like me. It is so cool and the limbs are huge and spread out really far," Lope said, as he held his arms out trying to show how big the oak tree has become.

"Okay, put your cube back in place so that your parents don't get a signal to begin looking. Can you communicate with them with it?" Lacey asked.

"Yep, you're smart Lace. I can send messages to them all day and even through time. So, they have no idea I am in another time. So, stop worrying so much," Lope said and gave her a big hug. "You're kind of like a really cool, young aunt."

"Thanks little guy; I think I needed to hear that today," Lacey said and hugged Lope back.

Jake and Tame Tiger smiled and looked at one another with smiles knowing that all would be good long into the future.

"Hey, let's say we get some sleep," Jake said. "And tomorrow, we'll get you back to your time and guess what?" Jake said.

"What?!" Lope asked.

"Tame Tiger and I are going with you. We want to see the farm and the land," Jake replied with a huge, devious smile. He was getting the same itch he had as a child to look for adventure.

"Hey wait just a minute," Lacey said. "I want to go too! Tame Tiger, this won't be fair that you see the past, present and future and this little guy just got to go back to the past twice."

"Okay, let's hit the hay and we'll discuss this over breakfast in the morning. Jillie may want to go too," Jake said, as he got up and headed out to the bathroom before any more discussion could be had.

Tame Tiger and Lope waited to follow and then they took Lope up to the large attic room to hit the hay.

Jillie and Blake never woke up. Lacey used the restroom too and went back to bed, but never slept more than a few minutes at a time, because she was too excited about her next travel that would take her forward in time.

181

12 TO THE FUTURE

The next morning came too soon for Lacey, because as soon as she finally fell asleep, the alarm was sounding. She turned it off and closed her eyes. Blake was already up and had the coffee brewing. He fed the cats before heading down to take care of the horses. Jillie got up too and started fixing breakfast for everyone. She wanted biscuits and gravy. She jumped when she turned around and Tame Tiger walked into the kitchen heading out to the bathroom.

"Hey medicine woman," Tame Tiger whispered and smiled, as he walked onto the porch.

Jillie rolled her eyes and threw her hand in the air at him and then smiled to herself and thought, "I am medicine woman".

Next Uncle Jake came in and then Lope followed soon after Jake. All three came into the kitchen and sat down looking very tired.

"When did you three arrive back to our time?" Jillie asked.

"We got here around midnight, but Lacey woke up and we all sat up chatting for a while. She is probably out of it right now, so let's let her sleep-in a bit," Tame Tiger answered. "Are you going back today?"

"I am supposed to, but for some reason I don't really want to go," Jillie answered.

"Well, will you get in trouble if you skip another day or so?"

Jake asked and explained to Jillie all that they talked about last night. Lope showed her the cube again and she learned all about the advancements of medicines.

Blake came in and they told him as much as they could again. The five of them had breakfast together waiting for Lacey to wake up, which didn't happen for a couple of hours and they all tidied up and made it out to the garden to pick what was ready and hoed out the weeds.

Lope filled them in on things that would be different, so they wouldn't be in total shock. The barn is still like it is on the inside, but totally different on the outside and it was way cool. The farmhouse was huge now, but the old part was totally kept as it was at some point in history. He explained it was a bit sturdier right now. Jake asked if the smaller house, which was his parents' home, was still there and it was now, but it was used as a storage building, where all the families store their things they wanted to have whenever they visit.

Tame Tiger asked about the stream on the land and wondered if it was still flowing and it was. The stream was so important to his people's existence. He asked Lope if he had found any neat treasures, like the arrowhead that Lacey had recently found. Lope told him of some of the things he had found, which Jake's boys had made.

Back in the house, Lacey finally sat up, checked the time and jumped out of bed when she realized that it was almost noon. She ran through the house and found it totally empty. She ran into the kitchen and it was all tidied up. So, she headed for the bathroom. She washed up, brushed her teeth and ran back to her room. She grabbed some clean clothes and took a quick shower. Before going to look for anyone, she heated up some leftover coffee and also found biscuits and gravy in the fridge and smiled. She was famished. She quickly ate two biscuits covered in sausage gravy and gulped down her coffee. When she finished, she placed her dishes in the sink and headed out the door to find everyone hard at work in the garden.

"What a great sight for tired eyes," Lacey whispered to herself and headed out to greet everyone.

When Blake saw her, he walked toward her and gave her a big hug. "Hello sleepy head. I hope you're feeling rested. I guess Jillie and I bailed out on you last night."

"I sure needed that sleep. Thanks everyone for letting me sleep. I think I was going crazy yesterday."

Everyone said their hellos and kept on working.

"What is for lunch today?" Lope asked.

"I'll take care of that," Jillie said. "Here Lacey, you get to work a bit now and I'll do the housework. Come on Little Lope, you're helping your older cousin with the lunch detail."

Jillie grabbed this new Lope and pulled him along with her. Everyone laughed and patted the young boy on the back as Jillie passed by with him in tow. Lope smiled, as he waved and hammed it up for his ancestors.

Once Jillie and Lope were gone and in the house, Jake explained to Lacey that he had caught Blake and Jillie up on the plans and they were all going to the future with Lope except for Blake. He would stay here and keep an eye on the place. Lacey looked at Blake to make sure he was okay with it all.

"I am perfectly fine staying here Lace. I am comfortable traveling back in time, but going forward, I do not have any desire. It's your family, you go for it," Blake said,

"It's your family too. At least I think it is," Lacey said looking rather serious and thinking way too much. "Don't you want this to be your family?"

"Sweetie, of course, but for now, it's yours and not mine totally. Let's let it stay in the family for now. I don't want to know if I don't exist down the road," Blake answered and left it at that, as if he wasn't sure he was going to be here.

No one said anything, because it was an awkward moment.

"Okay," Lacey said. "I just don't want you to stay here if you really want to go."

Blake gave Lacey a hug. "I think I am not up for that adventure today is all. I would rather stay here, look after the horses and protect the land for you."

"That is something we need to think of Lacey," Jake added, hoping to change the subject.

"Lunch is ready!" Lope called out from the porch door.

"Saved by the lunch bell," Jake whispered to himself and took off before anymore conversation about time traveling had a chance to start.

Tame Tiger left too, leaving Blake and Lacey behind. The two stayed in the garden talking and then they came bounding in together holding hands. Jake and Tame Tiger gave one another a look of 'whew'. Jillie kind of noticed their looks, but didn't say anything.

Lunch was great. Jillie made a huge fruit salad with nuts and coconut. With direction from Jillie, Lope had made turkey and Swiss cheese and roast beef and Swiss cheese sandwiches. Jillie had him to out all kinds of sides to put on the sandwiches: lettuce, tomatoes, banana peppers, cucumbers, condiments, salt and pepper.

"This is great," Blake said, and went to town on piling up his plate.

Everyone had a great lunch and they discussed their time travel with Lope. They would go in just a bit, so they could actually get there in the dark and also stay long enough to see the land and what their home looked like. Of course, the cats would travel too. The girls were so excited and scared, but more scared for their little cousin, Nadia.

After lunch was all done and things were all cleaned up again, the travelers were ready. Lacey and Jillie each grabbed a light weight jacket, because it was always so cold when they traveled through time and they had no idea how this would feel. They hoped it would not be much different.

"Okay, everyone ready?" Jake asked.

"I'm kind of ready, but I like it here too," Lope said.

Lacey and Jillie smiled and looked at one another. They felt like they would be seeing this person throughout their lives now too, but they future so hard to predict.

"Come on you silly, very distant cousin or whatever you are to me," Lacey said.

"I'm your-," Lope started, but Jake cut him off.

"Okay Lope, enough for now; let's hit the trail forward in

time. I cannot believe I get to see the past, present and future, but life cannot be any better," Jake said and he headed onto the porch and out the back door.

Everyone followed with Lacey being last to say her good-bye to Blake.

"Okay, what will you say if my parents stop over," Lacey asked.

"I'll tell them you went to visit Jillie," Blake answered.

"Okay. If anything should happen, I want you to know that I really love you Blake," Lacey said.

"I know you do and I feel the same way Lace," Blake said, as he gave her a big, bear hug. "Now, get going and get back here really quick. I am going to keep myself busy with the garden and get that finished up. Then, I plan on hanging out with the horses. You know I will come find you like last time if I have to do that. But, try and get back here."

Lacey looked up at Blake and smiled. She flew out of his arms and out the door. Blake followed behind her and watched the five of them as they disappeared into the barn, as they were going to the oak tree through the tunnels. He turned around and went back into the house to get a big jug of water before heading out into the garden. He also wanted to allow the horses to roam the pasture land. He felt safer with Storm Cloud roaming around in case he needed him.

***

Once the five reached the oak tree, Lacey asked how they were going to make sure they traveled forward in time.

"Well, we have to crawl out on the same limb that brought Lope here," Jake said.

"Lope, which limb were you on when you appeared here?"

"I'll show you," Lope said, as he began climbing up the tree to a limb, which was rather thick and branched out toward where the time portal opened up for them.

"Wait, I want to place an arrowhead into the notch on the tree to see if a portal actually opens with you up there," Lacey said, as she took an arrowhead from her pocket and placed it in the special spot.

Once Lacey placed the arrowhead into the special spot, the branch moved as if being shook by a strong wind and they could see the portal opening. It was the same portal, as they used to travel to the past, but Lope's positioning was different than being on the ground.

"Okay, come on up everyone," Lope called. "I'll wait."

Everyone started the climb and once Lacey and Jillie were on the branch with Lope, Jake told them to go ahead, because there wasn't enough room and the weight would probably be too much. The cats, now the size of kittens, were all clinging to one of them.

Jake motioned Tame Tiger to start moving onto the branch and he was right behind him. Within seconds, they were whisked away to another time.

***

Lope, Lacey and Jillie were at the base of the tree waiting for Jake and Tame Tiger. Tye, Tess and Miss Virginia had already jumped down and were running around. Seconds later, Jake and Tame Tiger appeared upon the much larger and longer tree limb.

"No wonder why you love this tree. It is enormous and really unbelievable," Jake called down to his travel mates.

Tame Tiger quickly climbed down the tree with great expertise and grace. Jake didn't move so fast, but he did rather well.

"Oh Jake, do you think you can find the hidden trap door here somewhere," Lope asked. "That would be so cool if those tunnels still existed and I could use them."

"It's pretty dark, but let's see-," Jake said, but was cut off by Miss Virginia's loud meows and scratching.

"Ah, I should have known," Jake said, as he walked over to Miss Virginia and saw that she was scratching into the ground. "Here Miss Virginia, let me help you." Jake dug up some ground and felt what he was looking for and that was the vine handle that allowed him to pull up the trap door so many years ago. "Voila," Jake said. "After you my sweet nieces."

Lacey and Jillie went down first and found a flash light they had left centuries ago. Lacey tried it out, but it wouldn't work. So she called upon Miss Virginia and her two babies to brighten up the tunnel. The cats instantly appeared and brightened up the earthen room with their magic.

Lope didn't wait for Jake's direction and practically fell down the opening into the ground. Lacey and Jillie laughed, as he picked himself up and brushed off his pants that were pretty dirty from all of his travels. He immediately ran around the room looking at the walls and the few items that had been there for many years.

Tame Tiger motioned for Jake to go first as he held the trap door up and then lowered it down as he descended into the ground. Once they were all together, Jake led the way with Lope at his side. Jake looked down at this boy and remembered all his amazement when he first started traveling back and forth through time. This was truly an amazing moment in both of their lives.

The cats positioned themselves amongst their wonderful, human family guiding them with their shining bodies. Lacey and Jillie held hands as they walked behind their uncle and Lope. Tame Tiger was content to bring up the rear and protect these two women, who were so dear to his heart.

Once they reached the other room, Jake found an old oil lamp he had left many years ago. He searched around for his box of matches and found it hidden behind the clay jugs. He took a match out from the box and struck it. The match lit up and Lope's eyes were wide with amazement.

"Now, is that a match?" Lope asked.

"Yes," Jake answered and smiled. "I take it you have never seen a match?" Jake asked.

"No, we don't really need them or at least I have never needed one and I have never seen my mom or dad using one," Lope answered, as he came near the match and felt its warmth.

Jake lit the lantern and then moved the match towards Lope. "Blow it out."

"What?" Lope asked.

"Haven't you ever blown a candle out?" Jillie asked.

"No. Our candles do not produce such fire," Lope explained. "Our candles glow on the tip as soon as someone taps on them. We put our candles on the cake and then someone taps each candle and they glow at the top, but they never get hot. So, I just blow on this match and it goes out and then you can strike it and it comes back on?"

"No, once you blow it out, it is really useless and you throw them away. Or, you have to light it again with another match," Jake explained. "And, this is taking too long to explain, so let's not spend too much time on the subject of a match right now."

"Tame Tiger, see if you can open up the trap door for us," Jake directed.

Tame Tiger jumped up on the table and pushed on the ceiling and it opened up as easy as pie.

"Looks like it never got stuck," Tame Tiger said, as he pulled himself up and out of the tunnel room into the back area of the old barn, which was unbelievably untouched. "You have got to see this Jake. It's like we have never traveled through time. It's just like I left it."

"I gotta see this," Lacey said and moved to the table so she could jump up. She reached her hand up to Tame Tiger. "Will you give me a little help?"

Tame Tiger reached down and pulled Lacey up with one quick pull. Lacey looked all around and went straight over to the stalls, where Warrior Girl and Storm Cloud lived in her time. There were hand made name plates with their names burned into a piece of wood. "Look, I wonder who does this."

Tame Tiger looked over, but he was busy pulling up Jillie, then Lope and finally Jake. Lope ran over to Lacey and stood beside of her looking into the stall, where Warrior Girl lives 300 hundred years in the past.

"Wait 'til you see the actual place where all the horses stay now. We are not supposed to really mess around in here and it is always an adventure when my cousins and I sneak in here just to look around."

"Oh, you don't use this barn at all?" Lacey asked.

"Oh no, it is a memorial to you, Jillie and Nadia, especially Nadia. I told you, she is my very distant great-grandmother and I am named after my very distant great-grandfather, Lope."

Jillie heard him and came up and joined them. "What did you say about Lope being your great-grandfather or something like that?"

"Oh, lots of us have Lope in our names. His name wasn't really Lope, but Running Antelope or something like that-" Lope was cut off, by Jillie's gasp.

"What do you know about Running Antelope?" Jillie demanded. How come you didn't mention that to us earlier?"

"Well, you didn't really ask and I can't help if I am forgetting details that would be important to you. How would I know?" Lope asked like the kid that he was.

"I'm so sorry Lope," Jillie said. "Would you tell me more?" A tear streamed down Jillie's cheek.

Lacey saw her tear, smiled and gave her a pat on her back.

"The story is that this Running Antelope escaped from a raid by another Indian tribe and then made his way back years later after he had found another tribe and home in the mountains of North Carolina. He married their great chief's daughter, but before he became chief he returned and rescued many of his people and led them to the mountains. One of his descendants meets Nadia during college and they marry and they are my great-grandparents, I think six times removed." Lope said and smiled. "So, I do think I came back for a reason and that was to save my own great-grandmother, your cousin, Nadia."

Lacey and Jillie looked at one another and smiled. They both saw their uncle deep in thought.

Tame Tiger gazed upon this boy and tried to see their Running Antelope in his eyes. Jake thought for a moment and couldn't understand the story. Maybe Lope didn't know that they were going to survive when he fled. He hoped he would live to know what really happens. He was so confused, but now wasn't the time to try and figure it all out.

"I know that is why you came back little one," Jake said. "How about leading us out of here? I don't see an opening."

"Follow me, it's all very different," Lope said and he walked towards where the old barn gate used to be and stopped near the right side of the barn. He pressed a button, keyed in a code, and a door slid open just like you would imagine from the future.

"Wow," Tame Tiger said and he hurried to catch up with Lope. "You know, we're all related and I know now that we do not ever really die. We live on forever through our children, their children and their children. I am very proud of you Lope. You are going to be a great warrior."

Lope laughed. "We don't have warriors, but we do have soldiers and it is a great service to fight for our country."

"Okay, let's move out," Jake directed. "We have to get this medicine and get little Nadia well to live out her life." Jake was feeling like he needed to rush this expedition for his brother's daughter.

"Get ready to see some really different things," Lope said, as he headed down a long hallway that led to the new barn.

The barn was full of activity of animals of all kinds coming in and out of another large opening. Stalls were opened and animals were living in harmony. They all looked so well kept. Many walked up to Lope and he greeted them all and they seemed to know him.

Lacey finally noticed that Miss Virginia, Tye and Tess were all gone. "Where are the cats?"

Jillie looked around with worry, but tapped Lacey on the shoulder when she saw what she thought was double. "Look Lace. Our cats have multiplied."

"OMG," called out Tame Tiger, which made the girls laugh.

There were two Miss Virginias with two Tyes, two Tesses and only one Tea.

"Where is the other Tea?" Lacey asked.

"Oh, she is with little Nadia of course," Lope answered.

191

Jillie looked at Lacey and shrugged. This was still a mystery to them. "Let's not worry about this either for now. It will always be a mystery to me," Jillie said.

"I still have a hard time believing this all is happening to us, much less having magical cats, double cats or whatever," Lacey added.

"Oh, you don't know?" Lope asked.

"Know what?" Jillie asked with sarcasm.

"Miss Virginia is the second of her line. Little Tea will have the next line of kittens and in that litter will be another Miss Virginia. And well, then your cats will all live again and have another set of people to protect. I think it skips a generation or something like that," Lope said and looked at all of them as they were staring at him as if he was making up this big story.

"Lope my little man; you have to understand this is all so new to us, because it is us that start this entire family destiny. You know what, don't tell us too much about the who's who and the what's what, because I don't think we should know everything," Jake said, as he messed up Lope's hair.

"Okay, I guess you're right. No problem. I am just so excited to have you here and know I am some important person!" Lope said excitedly.

Tame Tiger grabbed him in and gave him a hug. "You are a very important person and it is because of you that this family survives."

"This is your family too," Lope said, and looked at him very weird.

"Of course we are your family Tame Tiger," Lacey said.

"Yeah, you two are family," Lope said, as he looked at them thinking they were acting so weird about it all.

Jake got it and cut into the conversation. "Hey, we are definitely all family and that is why we're here to help save you little man. Now, take us to where this medicine is and let's get it and get back. But, you are not returning with us. You have to stay here and do not bring people back to our time. I'll make a deal with you. We'll find a place and I'll send you a message in our time, which you can find and it will let you know how Nadia is doing."

"Uh, I cannot promise that now. I want to come and hang out and help. Maybe I am supposed to help do all this upgrading to the farm," Lope argued.

Jillie and Lacey both laughed and smiled at him. "It's already done Lope and you're just ten," Jillie explained.

"Jake, I think we have our hands full with this one," Tame Tiger said.

Jake, Lacey and Jillie smiled and they all nodded in agreement.

"I am going to take you to the old part of the house, so you can see how it has been kept so well preserved. No one really comes in there, except when we have our annual fall gathering. It is our biggest family reunion and everyone tries to come to this big family gathering," Lope said.

Jake, Tame Tiger, Lacey and Jillie all looked at one another and smiled. An old tradition was handed down.

The walk to the house was so different. An above ground, glass tunnel led to a glass walkway that attached the farmhouse to an enormous addition. They walked behind the old granary, the old smokehouse and the old well house. The buildings were very well maintained and very much updated. It was as if they put a protective, cement shell on all the farm buildings, except the main farmhouse. It was definitely different, but it looked just like it did hundreds of years before, but much more sturdy.

Once inside the walkway, Lope rushed them into the old farmhouse. His cube was lighting up and he answered a call from his parents.

"Hey mom."

"Yes, I am back, but I want to mess around in the old house. You know how I love to look around the old place and I won't break anything. I promise, because I don't want to tick anyone off," Lope said, and smiled looking at Lacey.

"No, I didn't wander off too far. I was just around the farm," Lope said, as he smiled at his new family with a big smirk across his face.

"Okay, I'll see you in the morning," Lope said and his cube's light went out.

"That is too cool," Lacey said.

"My mom said she has been trying to get me, so I guess the cube didn't register any calls in your time," Lope explained. "I love coming over here and I know every nook and cranny," Lope said, as he turned on a light on the porch.

It was not exactly the same, but it is because Lacey has yet to really live there and fix the place up.

"I don't think you know every nook and cranny," Jillie said. "You didn't find the hidden stairs or the tunnels?

"Huh?!" Lope said, as he got in Jillie's face.

"Oh come on, follow me and I'll show you a few things," Jillie said.

"Lope, where is this medicine?" Jake asked yelling behind them.

"Oh, just look in the medicine cabinet and you'll see bottles of things. Just pick the one that says for leukemia," Lope said, as he ran behind Jillie.

Jake went out to the bathroom medicine cabinet and got caught up looking at all the things that weren't there in his time.

"Come on Lace, let's check out the house and see what is different," Tame Tiger said.

"Okay, let's do it," Lacey said and put her hand in the crook of his elbow.

The two looked around the sitting room and looked at some of the pictures of them and saw pictures of people they didn't know. They saw little boys that looked very American Indian.

"Cute," I wander who they are," Lacey said.

"Look, there is a photo of Jillie, little Nadia and yours truly. And, it looks like Nadia is about the age she is now. Too weird," Lacey commented and noted she wanted to show this one to Jillie.

"Very adorable little fellows," Tame Tiger said.

They looked around some more and then Tame Tiger moved into the old dining room and noticed all the pictures of many generations of family hanging everywhere. Then he saw what Lope thought they already knew. He saw a wedding photo of himself and Lacey and then beside that a picture of Lacey, him and two boys. He didn't move and just stood there and stared.

Lacey came in and stopped beside him. She couldn't take her eyes off the pictures.

Jake came bounding in and stopped. "I found the medicine. It's must be like buying OTC pain medication in your time Lacey-"

Jake noticed the two standing there staring at the wall, not moving and definitely not saying a word. What he figured out earlier was true. Lacey and Tame Tiger would end up together, but how?

"Look you two. I am so sorry, but I am happy."

Tame Tiger thought about his beautiful wife to be and then looked at Lacey. He was confused.

Lacey didn't look at Tame Tiger, but walked out of the room and ran to find Jillie and Lope.

"Oh man," Jake said. "I was worried something like this was going to happen. I feel absolutely horrible."

"Me too Jake," Tame Tiger said. "I love our Lacey, but I love Beautiful Butterfly. She is supposed to be my wife and very soon. What do you think I am supposed to do?!"

"Hey, let's let destiny take its action. You have to leave this for now and go back to the plans already made. Something makes this happen. Go back to Beautiful Butterfly and let life take you where you should be," Jake said.

Then Jake saw pictures of Jillie, Miguel and their boys and girls. They have four children. And then he sees Nadia with her husband and their three children. They have two girls and a boy and he moves to see their names. Euzelia, Etta and Exum. He studied Nadia's husband and he sees his best friend. Nadia marries their own Running Antelope's descendant. The web that destiny had spun was unbelievable and so magical to the tie of this land.

***

Meanwhile back on the farm, Blake was keeping himself busy working in the garden near the house with plans to get on a tractor and head down to check on the field of corn, pumpkins, watermelons and potatoes. As he walked up and down the rows of vegetables, he hoed up any weeds that he saw and sang out loud to the music playing into his ears from his MP3 player. He didn't notice Beautiful Butterfly coming up the pasture on Storm Cloud until the horse appeared in his peripheral vision.

Blake swung around and was in shock to see Beautiful Butterfly. He grabbed Storm Cloud's reigns as she practically fell off the horse.

"Wow, don't kill yourself," Blake said, as he rushed to grab her to break her fall.

Beautiful Butterfly was sobbing and talking so fast in her native tongue that Blake took a moment to realize he wasn't understanding a thing she said. He shook her to communicate to her that she needed to slow down and help him understand. He released her and made a gesture that he didn't know what she was trying to tell him.

Beautiful Butterfly grabbed his hand and started pulling him towards the pasture, as she pointed in the direction of the big oak tree. She wanted him to go with her. Storm Cloud came up behind him and gave him a push from behind letting him know that he should go.

"Okay, okay, I get it," Blake said. "First, let's get Storm Cloud and Warrior Girl back into their stalls," he said, as he turned around looking for Warrior Girl, who was slowly walking towards the barn. She already knew what she needed to do.

Blake pointed to Warrior Girl and then Storm Cloud and motioned for Beautiful Butterfly to follow. She whimpered, but followed and slowly nodded her head. She talked non-stop trying to tell Blake something. Then, she stopped talking and thought for a moment of something to say that he would understand.

"Help," she said and looked at Blake directly in his eyes.

Blake nodded and said one of the simple words he knew in her language that meant "yes".

Beautiful Butterfly tried to smile and moved quickly ahead of him and tended to Warrior Girl to help move the process along.

Blake was so scared, but what else could he do? He couldn't say no to Tame Tiger's girl. She obviously needed him more than ever and he couldn't let him down. The two finished up with the horses and Blake led Beautiful Butterfly to the hidden, earthen trap door and lifted it up. He was at least smart enough to know that they should use as much secrecy as possible with Beautiful Butterfly looking so totally out of place. She smiled and went down so quick that Blake chuckled at how strong and athletic she was and what an awesome Chief's wife she would be in the near future. Of course he had to save this woman's life. She was going to be the wife of the Chief and practically his sister-in-law.

As soon as Blake pulled the trap door shut, he ran to keep up with Beautiful Butterfly. Neither one said a thing and he wondered how they were going to get back to her time, but she had thought of everything and went to Beautiful Light for a spare arrowhead that opened up the portal door. As soon as Blake helped her out of the tunnel, she ran to the oak tree and placed the arrowhead in the special spot and the portal opened.

Beautiful Butterfly secured the arrowhead into a special pocket on her dress, grabbed Blake's hand and pulled him into the portal and they rushed forward to the past. When they arrived in the past, it was dark. Beautiful Butterfly whistled and two horses appeared from the woods. She jumped up on her horse and motioned for Blake to get upon Tame Tiger's stallion. He was really scared, but he had to do this.

Beautiful Butterfly gave out a cry and both horses took off with Blake holding on for dear life. He knew he was not in control and just hoped that he wouldn't fall off. The horses didn't slow down until they reached the woods where the trail t was much tighter and his horse fell in behind Beautiful Butterfly's horse. Animal and bird noises could be heard from all directions and Blake was definitely scared, but a 'cat held his tongue' and he didn't say a word. What would he say anyway and all he could do was just go for it.

Once they reached the opening and he knew they were not too far from the village, he felt a little more at ease. Beautiful Butterfly screamed out another noise that reminded Blake of a screech owl or something. Sounds returned and she responded with yet another sound. She pulled up to Tame Tiger's horse and grabbed the reign and started leading them in a direction away from the village. Blake knew that something was not right and he was totally frightened. Blake started saying a silent prayer for help.

***

As Lacey showed Jillie the family photos, Miss Virginia, Tye and Tess were all meowing and circling the girls. Jake and Tame Tiger noticed how they were all three acting.

"What Tye, tell me something," Lacey said and she stooped down to look directly into this eyes and read his thoughts.

"There is trouble back on the farm. We need to get back now," Tye thought out.

Lacey called out what he was saying. "Is it Blake?"

The cats could not really know what was happening. All they could tell was something was not right. They had no way of knowing that destiny was working its magic and at this moment, six hundred years in the past, Blake and Beautiful Butterfly were being pulled to force the future at hand.

"Uncle Jake, what do we do?" Lacey cried out.

"I am so sorry little guy, but we have got to go. Something is not right back on the farm. You have no idea how important you are to us all. Now please, stay here for now and I'll leave you a sign to find and let you know when you can return. Go to the barn and in the stall that you know was Storm Cloud's, I will leave you a sign."

"Okay, Uncle Jake," Lope said and smiled. "I figured you are some distant uncle of mine."

Everyone laughed and they each hugged their little Lope.

Tame Tiger grabbed him last and tossed his dark, curly hair. "You are our hero and we will see one another again before I go to see all the relatives in the skies."

"I don't know how I am going to focus anymore, but I'll try," Lope said looking sad that he had to stay behind.

"Help us back to the barn and we'll get home from there," Lacey said and smiled at Lope.

"Okay, let's hit it," Lope said and he took off as they walked out of each room. The lights automatically went out, as if they had flipped a switch.

Lacey and Jillie both looked back and looked at one another. They knew their futures and they were both excited and confused.

13 DESTINY CALLS

Beautiful Butterfly halted the horses, as she listened to the danger signals that rang out. Blake listened in silence trying to figure out what was happening. He was totally in the dark, especially since it was dark. His horse started walking again, but in a direction away from the village. He had to trust that Beautiful Butterfly knew what she was doing. She led them away for about ten or fifteen minutes and she occasionally screeched out something so terrifying that Blake could only assume that it was a cry of distress.

Finally she stopped the horses again, hopped off of her horse and came back to Blake pulling him down to the ground. She placed her hand across his mouth alerting him to not speak. She took his hand and led him away from the horses. Blake felt helpless and all he could do was go with it.

After another few minutes, Blake could hear sounds and realized they were near the village, but coming up from the rear. He heard lots of yelling, crying and horrible sounds. Beautiful Butterfly led him to a place where they could see the activity in the village and Blake saw what he could not believe was happening. English soldiers were amongst his people. These were his people too now and all he knew was that he had to help them.

Blake grabbed Beautiful Butterfly's face and nodded his head to let her know he understood. She answered, "thank you" and dug her head into his shoulder muffling her cries. Blake wrapped his arm around her and held her tight, but watched what was going on in the village.

He saw the Chief being held by two soldiers. He saw the women and the children being herded together, as the men were being tied up. He looked for Sir Edward, but didn't see him, so he knew these were another group that Sir Edward must not have known were out scouting the area. They were in a different dress than that of Sir Edward and if memory didn't fail Blake, he remembered reading about the Dragoons of the English army and these men were evil.

Then, he saw Beautiful Light and the boys being pushed around and this made him jerk with anger. He motioned for Beautiful Butterfly not to move and she nodded she understood. Blake was about to take off into the village. He knew English and he was going to speak with these men. But, it was too late to make a move. Blake felt a sharp point in the middle of his back. He and Beautiful Light were captured by the Dragoons and hauled off as prisoners without even getting to see their people.

The twenty some Dragoon soldiers were now turning their anger towards the village men, who were tied and helpless. The women and children were frozen in fear. To explain what happened next only the eyes of the on lookers would ever believe it.

With no warning of sound, the next few minutes seemed like ghosts had arrived. A black wolf raced into the camp and within seconds wolves surrounded the soldiers and the warriors. The soldiers were taken by surprise and before they could even aim for one wolf, the wolves took each soldier down.

And then, another ghost rushed into the village. Lope and about five other warriors rushed to the aid of the men, who were bound together with their tribesmen. The women and children ran to the sides of their loved ones.

Lope's father grabbed his son and cried into his shoulder. His mother came running and held onto her son tight. Lope

201

pulled away and looked for his girl and could not find her or her family amongst the families huddled around. He asked his parents and found out that she could not bear to stay without Lope. Her family set out to find another life for their daughter. Lope was in shock and felt huge guilt. He never meant for his people to think he would never be back.

Tame Tiger's mother rushed to her husband and unbound his arms. Everyone gathered their families together and huddled to rejoice.

Chief Fierce Tiger moved from family to family assuring them they would start making plans for a safer future. He called all of his warriors together to set up extra watch from all angles of the village. Then he went with Lope for more conversation among the elders of the tribe. There would be no celebration for Lope's return. Too much needed to be discussed and planned.

Inside the teepee, where the chief and the elders gathered, Lope stood tall and proud. He shared his adventures with his people. He told them how he ran away to find help to save his people and he did. Of course, he found that out after he ran off and before he knew there would be no harm to them. But, destiny took him away for a reason.

Lope explained how he ventured to the mountains and that he had found a small tribe hidden away from everyone and everything. He had become a favorite of the chief, who was happy to hear of more people living not too far. He allowed Lope to take some of his most powerful warriors to return and rescue Lope's people and return to the mountains.

As Lope finished his tale, he looked around and finally realized that Jake and Tame Tiger were not here. "Are Jake and Tame Tiger okay?"

Lope found out more about all the exciting things that were happening and some news about this Sir Edward, little Nadia and so much more. The chief explained that he was hoping to see them soon, but things were uncertain with the English moving closer and closer to their village site.

"This is why I returned and I hope they return soon too. I

am leading you all out of here. The soldiers are all around and the war of the white man is all around. We must begin our journey soon."

***

Jake, Tame Tiger, Lacy and Jillie arrived back on the farm via the oak branch. Once they all descended down the tree, the cats immediately were in their beastly forms and pacing around the tree.

"Something is wrong," Lacey said. "I'm going to go up and find out from Blake what could be going on here."

"Okay and if you don't mind, I think I'll go back and check on the other family," Jake said. "Tame Tiger, you stay here and I'll be back soon. Oh, girls you have to get this medicine to my brother and convince him to give it to Nadia."

Miss Virginia came forward and took the bottle from Lacey's hand and thought out to them all. "I will deliver this to Tea. I will make sure Nadia gets it without anyone knowing. It has to be this way. Science is not ready for this drug and we can only allow people to see a miracle."

"OMG Miss Virginia, you are so right," Jillie quickly replied.

With that, Miss Virginia vanished from their sight. Her mission was to take care of the farm's destiny and she would as always. Everyone looked at one another in awe.

"The magic and the mystery of this land will never die," Jake said.

"Yes and we are all in this together. Okay, I'll go up with the girls, find Blake and then I'll be back home too," Tame Tiger said and hugged Jake.

Jake took out his arrowhead, touched the special spot and the portal waved for his entrance. He smiled at his nieces and quickly vanished.

"Let's go back via the tunnels, since its still daylight," Lacey said.

The three of them, Tye and Tess ran through the tunnels all the way to the barn and came up through the trap door in the back of the barn. The horses were in their stalls, but were very anxious. Tame Tiger opened up Storm Cloud's stall and he came bounding out bucking and moving his head up and down. Lacey allowed Warrior Girl to come out. She came out neighing extremely loud. The feline beasts were loudly roaring. Realizing something was very wrong, Lacey and Jillie both started crying. Lacey took off towards the house yelling out for Blake with Tye in tow to protect her. Storm Cloud took off out of the barn into the pasture. Tame Tiger rushed to follow him. Jillie stood frozen in disbelief, but Tess circled her and nudged her out of the barn and they took off towards the house to help Lacey.

"Blake, Blake!" Lacey cried out over and over.

They ran all through the farmhouse and then over to the other house, but nothing could be found of Blake. Then, as they were running back to the farmhouse and ran towards the garden where Blake said he would be working, they saw the hoe lying on the ground. They saw his water jug, on the ground, with very little water gone.

Tame Tiger returned on Storm Cloud's bare back. "I think we need to return to the village. I want you both to go with me. We do not know if it is safe here."

As they were making their way back to the barn, a jeep drove into the driveway. It was Miguel and Kai.

Jillie ran into Miguel's arms and sobbed trying to get out the words about what was happening. Miguel didn't speak, but already knew something was happening as Kai had alerted him to the danger of the past.

Tame Tiger came up and the young men embraced one another's arms at the elbows.

"What brings you here?" Tame Tiger asked.

"I know that we are in danger. Kai has seen it and we must get back to the village," Miguel answered, as he kept his hold on Jillie.

Lacey came up and hugged Miguel. "It must be bad."

"We do not know, but we must go with the pulls of the destiny that is calling," Miguel replied.

Kai, in his cat form, howled as a wolf and exchanged his

hellos with Tye and Tess, who responded with their growls and roars.

Jillie pulled away. "What about the horses?" Jillie asked.

"We take them with us," Tame Tiger said. "We cannot leave them here with no one to watch over them. Let's get their leads at least, so that they transport with us for sure through time."

Daylight was coming to an end, which meant it would be daylight in the past. They all rushed to the barn and got what they needed for the horses. Lacey thought out to Tye and Tess to become kittens, so that no one saw two feline beasts walking amongst the three and they listened immediately, but their cries were not of small cats, but roars of ferocious beasts. The kittens jumped upon Warrior Girl's back and kneaded her coat to sooth themselves and her. Kai jumped upon Storm Cloud, who bucked his head up and down letting the cat know he was okay with it.

"Are we sure we want to put Warrior Girl through this? She is getting close to her delivery date," Lacey said.

"I will take care of her," Tame Tiger answered and that was that. "Let's go."

Tame Tiger and Miguel walked with Storm Cloud in tow, while the girls walked on opposite sides of Warrior Girl. They did not rush, because they wanted to protect Warrior Girl.

"Once we reach my time, I will hide the horses in a special spot where we always leave our horses when I come across," Tame Tiger explained.

Lacey and Jillie did not say a word. They both knew to trust Tame Tiger. Once at the tree, Lacey pulled out her special arrowhead and touched the magical spot on the tree. The portal opened wide, as if it knew the horses were traveling. Tame Tiger motioned for the girls to hold onto Warrior Girl and go together. Then he, Miguel and Storm Cloud quickly fell in behind them. They were whisked back in time.

14 DESTINY'S TEARS

Jake had reached the village to find his people stricken with fear, disbelief and happiness. The invasion by the Dragoon soldiers had brought such fear to the village. The ghostly wolves had added to the uncertainty of everything. But, Lope's return had brought happiness to these people and helped them realize that maybe there was another place they could call home.

***

Tame Tiger, Miguel, Lacey, Jillie and the animals had safely arrived from their quick, cold journey through time. All three animals turned into the beastly forms. No one flinched. This was the norm for them now. Danger brought beastly protection.

Tame Tiger led the horses and all to his special hiding place where he always left his horse. There was a large trough of water and another of grains. He noticed the fresh foot prints of hoof marks and two sets of feet that appeared scattered and messy. He knew that someone had been here and that confusion was apparent. He didn't say a word to the others, but Miguel noticed it too and looked at his distant relative with a stare.

Tame Tiger spoke to the horses in his native tongue and stroked Warrior Girl's belly. Lacey watched and came forward to hug her horse and then turned her attention to Storm Cloud, who nudged her with his head. Lacey looked at Tame Tiger and their eyes locked, as they both remembered the picture they saw way into the future.

Tame Tiger broke the stare without saying a word about their future. "Let's head to the village. Girls, let me know if you need to slow down." Tame Tiger took off in a fast paced walked.

Lacey and Jillie walked fast to keep up and Miguel followed behind to keep an eye around the area. The animals ran off into the woods all around and continually circled back around their people as if checking on them and their safety. Sounds of gunfire could be heard from extreme distance. The war was moving closer to this land.

They reached the edge of the woods, where the path was narrow and they all fell in behind one another with Tame Tiger in the lead and Miguel in the rear. Jillie quietly sobbed, as she was in total fear. Lacey reached back and offered her hand, which Jillie immediately took and followed close.

Lacey could only think about Blake and where he was or what had happened? Was he here? Had something happened back on the farm?

The animals came back together with their loved ones, when they reached the village and walked close beside them. Uneasiness was sensed by them all. .

Jillie saw Lope and ran to her best friend's arms. Lope didn't quite respond as Jillie had thought and moved back from his grasp. They looked in one another's eyes, but words did not come. Lope gave Jillie a half smile, but he was mad at the white man. Jillie sensed his coldness.

"Lope, we thought something bad happened to you. Aren't you glad to see me?' Jillie asked.

"Of course Jillie, but I have things to do and so do you. We will speak later. Right now, there is much to do and to prepare," Lope said and walked away leaving Jillie standing with tears in her eyes.

Miguel watched this and left her alone for now and walked

off to find something he could do to help. Lacey saw the reunion too, but held herself together and looked around for Blake. There was no Blake here. She didn't notice that Beautiful Butterfly was nowhere to be seen. But Tame Tiger had noticed and had not acted upon it yet. He was too excited to see Lope too and ran off to catch up with him to find out where he had been all this time.

Lacey walked over to Jillie and gave her a hug. "You want to help me find out about Blake?"

"Yep; I guess I know Lope is not exactly excited to see me," Jillie said, looking around for Miguel.

First, the girls went to find their Uncle and see if he had seen Blake and found out that Beautiful Butterfly was also missing. So the girls ran to find Tame Tiger, who was walking around the outskirts of the village looking for clues.

"Hey Tame Tiger, did you ask Beautiful Butterfly's parents about her?" Lacey asked, as she and Jillie ran up beside him.

"Do you think I am an 'idiot' Lacey? Tame Tiger snapped at her.

Lacey didn't do her usual snap back, but looked at Tame Tiger with compassion. "Tame Tiger, I know you're not an idiot. I just haven't seen you talk with them."

"Well I did and now I am going to look for my stallion. He's missing and so is her horse," Tame Tiger replied, very mad.

"Do you think that is where she and Blake could be, somewhere with the horses?" Lacey asked, feeling hopeful.

"Look, how do I know?" Tame Tiger answered. "Do you want to come with me or are you going to just talk to me?"

"I want to come with you. Blake and Beautiful Butterfly may be in danger. Let me get Tye to come with us," Lacey said and thought out for her protector.

Tye came bounding out of nowhere with his sister, Tess.

"I think I'll go and find Miguel," Jillie said and she motioned for Tess to come with her.

Tame Tiger, Lacey and Tye went off in search of the two people they loved. They knew their destiny, but it wasn't supposed to happen this way. They didn't want harm to come to anyone they loved.

Jillie had totally ignored Miguel and wanted to make sure she had not hurt his feelings. She found Miguel helping some of the tribesmen and came to his side. Miguel smiled down at her and she smiled back. She was looking at her future and was happy that they would be a family one day. She thought of Lope for a moment, but knew that was something of her childhood. Lope was destined for something else and she was destined for happiness with Miguel. She knew it, because they would have four children!

"What are you smiling about Jillie?" Miguel softly asked.

"I am just happy to have you here," Jillie replied.

"Oh, so Lope isn't your choice of warrior?" Miguel asked, as he was not sure he had won Jillie's heart over Lope.

"Lope is like my brother. At one time, I thought differently, but I know that he is definitely destined for some other calling. I cannot change that destiny now, can I?"

"Absolutely not, but I am in your time and I can promise that I will always make you smile," Miguel said.

"I think you might do that," Jillie said, as she thought about the pictures of her wonderful family. She knew of her children to come, but she didn't know their names. At least that would be a surprise for her.

Jake moved around the village consoling his people that they would be fine and he finally came upon Lope standing alone looking off into the distance. He laid his hand upon Lope's shoulder. "I know what you're here to do. You came back for us, didn't you?" Jake asked, as he gazed over the land too.

"I wasn't quick enough, Jake. My one love has left me," Lope whispered back.

Jake turned Lope towards him and held him by his shoulders. "Look at me Lope," Jake demanded. "Maybe it is the way it is supposed to be. The one thing I have learned and I thought we all understood this by now, is that we cannot fight against destiny. Mother Earth has her plans and we all have our fates and it is how we use ourselves to make things better for all."

Lope's eyes filled with tears. Jake pulled Lope into his arms and hugged this young man. "I am not sure about it all either my son, but you will pull yourself up and lead our people to a new world. That is why you came, right?"

"Yes," Lope answered, as he pulled away from Jake and wiped his eyes. "I am here to save our people."

"That is my son and you are like a son to me. I know everything that has happened, and is happening, and will happen, as it is meant to be," Jake said, as he tussled Lope's hair and put his arm around him. "Don't be too hard on Jillie. Her heart broke when you went missing, but she knows what her destiny is. Your friendship is all she wants."

"I know, but I am mad at the white man, Jake. And Jillie and Lacey and their world remind me that we lost so much," Lope explained.

"Well, I am a white man Lope," Jake said.

"No, you were never a white man. You love this land as we do Uncle Jake," Lope said and threw his arm over Jake's shoulder. "Are you going to be able to leave this land Jake? You may have to say good-bye to the girls you know."

Jake threw his arm over Lope's. "You know Lope, I know we will be able to return one day. I have it on the best authority, as he thought about Sir Edward. The two men headed back to the village with smiles knowing that they would take care of their people.

***

Tame Tiger and Lacey walked and walked around the outskirts of the village. Tame Tiger led her near the creek and told Lacey to drink, as he did. Tye was out hunting on his own and brought back a catch to share with his Lacey and Tame Tiger.

"No thanks," Lacey smiled at her beast. "That will have to be yours, uncooked and raw."

Will and Lacey were hungry too, so Tame Tiger scavenged

around and found some turnip roots and shared one with her. They were both famished and eating this little piece of root made them realize just how hungry they really were now.

"We'll go back to the village if you're too hungry," Tame Tiger said to Lacey with love and kindness. How could he have been so mean to her earlier?

"No, let's keep looking while it is still daylight," Lacey said, as she looked around and found another turnip top sticking out of the ground. She pulled it up for both of them to share.

Lacey remembered she had put an energy bar in the pocket of her jacket, which now was wrapped around her waist. She pulled it out and broke it in two parts.

Tame Tiger smiled and waited for his part. They both chewed their food slowly as they both were in deep thought. They both surveyed the land. Tame Tiger pointed to the back of the village and wanted to go look there one more time. Tye roared and acknowledged something was weird over there in his thoughts to Lacey.

"Yes, Tye says there is something we need to see over there," Lacey said.

The three took off in a quick pace and found an area where Tame Tiger could tell two bodies had been lying on the ground. He also saw the prints of boots and saw the path of four people leading away from the village. He pointed all this out to Lacey.

"But where are the horses?" Lacey asked.

"They are here or they were taken too," Tame Tiger said and he moved on and found traces of foot prints leading away from the area and then he instinctively knew where to look for the horses and told Lacey to follow him.

Tye took off, as he could sense something too, but his senses were tied to Lacey, so he was not very good at helping others.

Tame Tiger found where the horses had been left, but they were no longer there. He saw boot prints here too and saw the path that they were led down. His eyes looked far ahead and no sign of anyone or anything were in sight.

"Lacey, my senses are telling me they were captured. My

mother tells me that Beautiful Butterfly left with our horses to get to the portal and come find me. I think we know where we were when she found only Blake," Tame Tiger explained, but he couldn't look at Lacey.

Lacey started crying and Tye turned into his kitten form and was up on her shoulder whispering in her ear. "It's okay Lacey. It's okay. They are okay."

Lacey grabbed Tye and held him to her eyes and thought out to him. "How do you know?"

Tye looked at his Lacey and stared back into her eyes. "Because we are here, you are here and I can feel peace, not anger."

"Huh?" Lacey asked. "What do you mean?"

"All I can tell is that they were not harmed. The horses were not harmed. I think Tame Tiger is right. They were captured, but by who?"

"What do I do Tame Tiger? How do I explain this to Blake's family?" Lacey asked.

"The truth; Blake left and you have not heard from him. The fact that it was three hundred years in the past that he left is not something people will even believe. I believe they are alive and one day we will know their fate," Tame Tiger said like a true leader. He had to put his feelings away and think of his people and Lacey, his future.

Lacey was now the one to be angry and stomped off letting Tye jump down from her grasp. He turned back into the white tiger and ran circles around his Lacey.

Tame Tiger stood looking into the fields and looked up to the skies and quietly sent a message to the heavens to watch over his love and his dear friend. He knew his fate and accepted it and moved on to catch up with Lacey. He grabbed her hand, kissed it and led her back to the village. No words were needed.

15 DESTINY'S BLESSINGS

As the day came to an end, slept took over the village except for those who would stand watch from any intruders. Jake, Tame Tiger, Lope and Miguel made sure that Lacey and Jillie were guarded and they took turns standing guard outside of the girls' teepee. Tye and Tess snuggled close to Lacey and Jillie.

Miss Virginia had returned from her visit with Tea and Nadia with assurance that the medicine had been delivered. She didn't sleep, but prowled around the village between warriors making sure each and everyone was safe. They each loved this big cat's company and love.

At the sign of first daylight, the village came to life. Today, the village would be taken down and Lope would be leading them to their new home in the mountains of North Carolina. Sadness and excitement loomed in the air.

Lacey and Jillie were both up early. For all they knew, today would be the last time they would see their special family and their Uncle Jake. They went to their uncle's tent for their ritual porridge breakfast.

Lope had invited Miguel to eat with him and his family. Lope wanted to know Miguel and felt the pull between this man and Jillie.

The mood was sad in Jake's and Beautiful Light's home. No teasing and taunting their little cousins. Instead, they cherished

213

every word they said.

"Uncle Jake, I thought we were supposed to have all those Fall Harvests together. How will we do that now? The mountains are so very far from here," Lacey said trying to hold back the tears.

"Oh, don't you even worry about that for now. Once Sir Edward claims this land, we will be back. Maybe not for good, but I believe Edward would welcome our annual visit and feast, don't you?" Uncle Jake replied, as he had thought out so many ways of not walking away from his birth family again.

Meanwhile, Tame Tiger was talking with his father, his mother and the elders of the tribe. He was embarking on a new journey. He wanted to ask Lacey to marry him today and go back with her. His mother cried tears of sadness and joy. She, above all, knew the importance of leadership and destiny. She pulled out her own wedding ceremonial robe that was hidden in the leathers of the teepee. The whitened leather wedding dress was still as beautiful as the day it had been handed to her from her husband's mother. Tame Tiger held it up and knew it would be perfect. He bounded out of the teepee and headed right for Jake's.

The mood was solemn and everyone was quiet when Tame Tiger came bounding into the tent. He startled Jake and everyone. Tame Tiger stood there in silence staring at Lacey, who became quite uncomfortable. All others' eyes were on him.

Tame Tiger cleared his throat to speak, but his words were caught with emotion and he almost spilled tears as he thought about Beautiful Butterfly. But, as quick as she had crossed his mind, she floated away and he looked at his Lacey and smiled.

"Lacey, I come to ask you to be my wife. Before the village is totally taken away from us, I want to have one last celebration here with my family, our family. We will join our families together forever today," Tame Tiger said, without looking away from Lacey.

Lacey didn't move, but stared back into Tame Tiger's eyes. No one in the tent said one word in fear they would sway the answer one way or the other. This was a moment that Jake, Jillie, Tame Tiger and Lacey knew was the future, but was this the right time to make their destiny move forward. Silence stayed there holding all sounds until Tame Tiger became impatient and he moved over to Lacey and bent down on one knee. He took her left hand with both of his.

"My beautiful, warrior sister, destiny brought us together for a reason and we know why. Yes my heart is broken for Beautiful Butterfly, but my heart also sings with joy and excitement of a future with you. I know there is much more for me to learn, but I love this land, your land and I will do everything I can to keep it safe and help you with the farm. I know we can build a wonderful life together. Well, I know we can and you do too. Let's celebrate it with the people we love today."

Jillie was holding back her tears of joy. She wanted to blurt out "yes" for Lacey, but held her tongue and grabbed her little cousins' hands. The boys too were waiting so they could jump up and yell their approvals.

Jake and Beautiful Light both smiled knowing what her answer would be and sat in silence giving her time to be able to speak.

Lacey didn't let go of Tame Tiger's hands, but took her right hand and put it upon his left shoulder and squeezed to keep from trembling. "This is so sudden Tame Tiger and it's something I didn't think we would be doing so quickly. But, I do love you so and I think I have from the moment you sat beside me the first day we met. Yes, I will marry you today if we can also mourn for the loss of Blake and Beautiful Butterfly and ask that they be safe and find a way back home to us all."

"It wouldn't be done any other way," Tame Tiger said and lifted himself up and pulled Lacey up in front of him. He gave her a great big kiss right in front of everyone.

"Hey now you 'whipper snapper', you're not married yet," Jake said laughing. "Now go, we have a wedding to plan," Jake said.

Jillie jumped up, as did the boys, and they all ran and

hugged both Tame Tiger and Lacey.

"Oh, my mom has Lacey's wedding dress all ready for her," Tame Tiger said smiling ear to ear. "And, it's beautiful. It was the dress she wore and my grandmother wore and the women before them. Only a woman worthy to marry a chief could wear it."

Beautiful Light got up, walked over and hugged Lacey and told her that she was off to get the dress.

"Come on Tame Tiger, we have a celebration to plan," Jake said, as he grabbed Tame Tiger by the shoulder and dragged him out of the teepee. Jake stopped and poked his head back into the teepee knowing this was girl time. "Come on sons, you are going to help get this festival put together too."

Jillie and Lacey looked at one another and hugged again. They cried with joy and sorrow. Their destiny, which they had both seen, was coming to life. They headed off to their own teepee to get Lacey ready.

Beautiful Light and Tame Tiger's mother, Challenging Wolf, came to the girls' teepee with the dress and special wedding moccasins. Lacey filled with emotion when Challenging Wolf held up the dress and handed her. The two women embraced and they both cried of joy and sorrow. Soon, Tame Tiger would be leaving his mother behind and Lacey could only imagine how she was feeling.

Beautiful Light and Jillie left the two women alone and headed out to help with the preparations for one last feast. As Jillie looked around, she saw Lope and Miguel working side by side chatting away and laughing. A smile came across her face and she kept on walking to help the women of the tribe. She didn't want to disturb their work or their growing friendship. She knew that Lope was still her friend and had just grown up as she had done.

Once everyone had prepared the food, a bond fire was lit for an evening of dance and celebration. The ceremony began and the drums began to beat. Tame Tiger, with his father on his right and his mother on his left, walked to the front near the Holy Man. The drums halted for a few seconds and everyone parted and an isle was made for Lacey. The drums started again and Jake walked his niece into the view of all. Together, they began their ceremonial walk to marriage.

Tame Tiger could not take his eyes off of Lacey as she smiled at all the people smiling at her and touching her arms. He noticed every detail of her face, her hair, which was braided and adorned with white leather laces intertwined into the braids. Around her head, she wore a wreath of a chief's wife. He noticed all the beadings that decorated the dress and how her petite frame was softly outlined. He noticed how the bottom of the dress gently swayed as she made her way to his side. He noticed the moccasins that covered her feet and smiled about how many women had worn them before her knowing that they were all around filling her soul with their love and strength.

Lacey glanced at Tame Tiger between her smiles and hugs to her people. She noticed his special markings across his face that made him look like a fierce tiger. His hair was pulled back and his head piece was that of a chief. He was in a ceremonial leather outfit, which she had never seen. It was well worn and had been worn by his father and many other first born sons. Tame Tiger would take this to hand down to his first born too.

Jillie, Miguel and Lope were all with Beautiful Light and her sons watching in joy for Lacey. Jillie didn't notice, but her special necklace, which she hid most of the time, was out adorning her dress made by Beautiful Butterfly. One of the three gems was sparkling as if lit up by a light bulb. Miguel looked over and saw the necklace's gem shining bright. He smiled, as he knew where she had received this necklace. Destiny's magic was working.

Lacey finally made her destination to the side of Tame Tiger. Jake took Lacey's hand and placed it in Tame Tiger's and he walked to take his place with his wife and sons.

As promised, the first words were those of mourning the loss of Beautiful Butterfly and Blake and everyone cried and prayed for their safety and for wishes that they would find their way back home.

As soon as the Holy Man said his last words to honor Beautiful Butterfly and Blake, he raised his hands and made a loud clap. "Now, we celebrate this match, destined by Mother Earth, and we bless their union. For today, this land we all call home will be our families' home forever.

This day marked a day in this great family's history. The events which would be written down and sealed in a time capsule by Lacey and Will in hopes that one day their descendants would find this unbelievable information and cherish the magic of it all.

16 DESTINY'S MAGIC

As the celebrating ended, the village fell silent one last time. Warriors took turns guarding the village until first sight of light and then they turned in for a few hours of rest, while the village was being taken apart one teepee at a time and securely placed upon sleds that the horses would be pulling along. Of course, Jake and Tame Tiger had helped design some pretty fancy sleds to help with maneuvering over different terrains which now they would need.

Everyone knew what needed to be done and no one stood by and watched. Even Jillie and Lacey had their jobs and worked right alongside all the other women.

"You're awful happy this morning big cuz," Jillie said, as she noticed Lacey humming along.

"Oh well, it's what marriage does to a woman," Lacey replied and smiled at her younger cousin.

But the smile quickly left and Jillie noticed.

"Are you okay Lace?" Jillie asked. "Are you thinking about Blake?"

"No, not this time; I'll think of him for the rest of my life. What do I tell my family? Mom and dad will be so mad," Lacey said, looking off in the distance.

"Don't tell them Lacey," Jillie said.

"How do I not tell them?" Lacey asked, looking at her

219

cousin like she was not so smart.

"You and Tame Tiger have to do it all over again in our time," Jillie said with a big smile on her face.

"OMG," Lacey said. "You are smart. Why didn't I think of that?'

"Because I am —" Jillie said, but was cut off by Tame Tiger who had walked up to grab his new bride in surprise.

"We were just talking about you," Jillie said, as she smiled at Lacey.

"Oh yeah, what could my beautiful wife and her charming cousin be saying about me?" Tame Tiger asked, as he flexed his arm muscles.

The girls laughed and shook their heads.

"You tell him Lacey," Jillie said.

"Husband," Lacey started off, "you know my family doesn't know we are married and I think they may be totally confused. So, do you think we can fake it and pretend we're not married yet? You know they don't know a thing and I think they might be really upset," Lacey said.

Tame Tiger listened, but he didn't speak right away. He looked away in deep thought, which was making Lacey and Jillie nervous that he would be very angry. But, he turned back to Lacey and smiled. "I think you are right Lacey, my wife. This way, I can 'court' you the proper way and ask you to marry me all over again," Tame Tiger said smiling from ear to ear.

Lacey relaxed and jumped into Tame Tiger's arms and looked at Jillie, as she mouthed "thank goodness" and rolled her eyes. Jillie joined the two of them and hugged them both.

"Okay, that is settled," Tame Tiger said. "Let's get back to work women. We will have to head back very soon and prepare what we have to do about Blake's disappearance. Lacey, you will have to do something to start a search for Blake as soon as we get back."

Lacey and Jillie nodded their heads in agreement and turned back to their work. Neither one of them wanted to have to deal with Blake's situation, but Lacey knew it was something that could not be delayed. Tame Tiger squeezed his new bride from behind again and left to go help the men get everything ready for their long journey to their new home. He found Jake, Son of Running Deer, Lope, Miguel, the other chief and his father talking very seriously. He walked up, but didn't dare interrupt. He stood quietly and listened to their plans.

"Okay, let's send out some scouts to see what is around the area where we want to begin our movement," Jake said.

"I think we should move out in groups, so that if there are any surprises along the way, our entire village is not wiped out at once," Fierce Tiger stated.

Everyone all nodded with solemn looks of agreement.

"We will all split up and take charge of our own family and others," Fierce Tiger added. "Lope and Tame Tiger, begin grouping our people so that there are four clans with plenty of warriors for each group. Miguel, will you be in charge of gathering all the horses for us?"

"No problem Chief. I have helpers, so we can make quick work of it," Miguel said and off he went to call out for Kai and his friends to come and help herd the horses, who were all scattered around the fields. He would also use Kai to scout around for any possible intruders.

Jillie saw Miguel running through the village and wondered what he was doing. She thought out to Tess and her protector appeared as quick as ever with Tye following close behind. Miss Virginia even showed up after being out of sight for many hours.

Jillie thought out to Tess to go find out what Miguel was up to and the three beasts were off in a flash. They were on a hunt, but for some fun, so they spread out and came upon Miguel in the woods calling out for his friends. Soon, Kai appeared with many other wolves and the feline beasts joined in on the herding of the horses. Tess thought out to Jillie, who told Lacey what Miguel was doing.

"Impressive little cuz," Lacey said. "Well, we're not marrying dull men are we?"

"I am not married and how do we; I mean I know that Miguel and I are exclusive. Maybe we both see others before we want to be together," Jillie said with her hands on her hips trying to make a point.

"Okay, okay, I just thought you really liked him. Your eyes sparkle whenever you see him," Lacey added.

"OMG, I cannot believe I forgot to tell you this," Jillie said, as she pulled her necklace out from beneath her shirt. "See this stone? It was shining like a flash light yesterday during your wedding!"

"Really?" Lacey asked. "Can I see the necklace? I never really thought much about it, but didn't the Holy Man in the NC Mountains give you this?"

"Yes and I showed it to you when I came back and he said you would understand it. So, do you understand it?" Jillie asked, as she took the necklace off of her neck and gently placed it in Lacey's palm.

Once the necklace touched Lacey's palm, the gem to the right of the middle stone immediately began shining bright. Lacey jumped and Jillie came closer.

"OMG Lace; it's magical," Jillie said.

"I think because I am on the right track of my destiny, it is happy. Now, let's see what it does whenever you and Miguel are together or you and Lope are together. OMG little cuz, it knows our destiny. Come on, let's have some fun. Put that back on and let's go find Lope while Miguel is out chasing horses."

"Okay," Jillie said, as she put the necklace back over her head and placed it behind her t-shirt.

The girls took off giggling and chatting all the way until they came upon Lope, who was not in the most happy of moods. The girls came to a halt and waited for Lope to notice them standing there.

"Hey you two, 'what is up?' as you both say," Lope said showing a little smile.

Jillie pulled the necklace out, as if she was just fidgeting. She looked at Lacey and walked over to Lope and gave him a big a hug. Lacey kept her eyes on the necklace and nothing happened.

"I am sorry Jillie, I know I promised we would spend some

time together, but I have to get things ready to move soon," Lope explained, as he held Jillie at a distance.

"I know, I know. I, we just wanted to come and give you our love and best wishes," Jillie said and she motioned Lacey to join in on the hugs.

Lacey rushed in and they all gave one another a big bear hug. Lope actually laughed and chatted for a few moments, but stopped as quickly as he had started.

"We will see one another again, don't you worry, okay?" Lope said and waited for the girls to agree.

They smiled at Lope and went on their way. Now, they were out to find Miguel, which was going to be easy since they only had to send out their thoughts to their protectors and in minutes they were headed in Miguel's direction.

There he was riding bare back upon a black stallion guiding the other horses towards the pasture nearest the village. He saw the girls waving and came galloping their way. As he rode up, he slid off the horse's rear and the girls both laughed.

"That is good Miguel," Lacey said not even noticing it was Tame Tiger's black stallion Miguel had just been riding.

"Thank you Lacey," Miguel said. "What brings you two girls out this way? Do I need to get to the village?"

"Oh no," Jillie said. "We were just roaming around, since it might be a while before we come back."

Lacey looked at her little cuz and smiled thinking, "good one little cuz".

"Okay, well I better keep getting these horses rounded up," Miguel said.

"Wait," Jillie said and she ran to hug Miguel.

When she did, Lacey saw the necklace light up like it did for her. Lacey's eyes were wide and fixated on the necklace.

Jillie saw the look in Lacey's eyes and quickly put the necklace under her shirt again. "Okay, you better get that done."

Miguel leaned over and hugged Jillie one more time and Lacey could see the light showing through Jillie's t-shirt. It truly was a necklace of destiny.

***

By day's end, the village was baron of any trace of life, other than the center village fire pit and the markings left by the many teepee homes. The clans were all grouped together and ready to head out. Night time was the best time to move out and the route had already been mapped out by the scouting team, who had traveled over half the day to make sure they were not in harm's way.

Now the good-byes would have to be quickly done, because Fierce Tiger, Son of Running Deer, Chief Charging Bull and Jake and Lope were the leaders of each clan.

Tame Tiger, who would soon only be known as Will, would have to say good-bye to his father and mother. Lacey and Jillie would have to say good-bye to their uncle, aunt and cousins and Jillie would have to say good-bye to her dear friend, Lope.

The tears were shed and many hugs were given. Finally, Jake looked at Tame Tiger and Miguel letting them know it was their responsibility to take the girls back home. The young men took the lead and grabbed hold of the girls' hands and pulled them back, as the clans moved out. The girls sobbed and their beasts were right by their sides circling them for comfort.

Jake ran back to the girls and held them close. "We will return as soon as Sir Edward claims this land. We know the destiny of our farm is in good hands. Remember, we will be seeing one another again. Now, both of you have your work cut out for you. Stay strong and be there for little Nadia. Her life is just beginning. She will have more to endure than either of you, because she will have Tea to contend with all of her life and many other obstacles with growing up. Help and guide her. She will need it, I am sure."

The girls sobbed out their 'okays', as their uncle pulled away and ran back to his group.

Miss Virginia loudly roared at her two offspring and left on the journey with Jake. She would make sure they reached their destination.

Kai appeared in front of Miguel, in his wolf form, and

howled telling him that he would also be making the journey with his friends to the mountains. Miguel knew that he would see his friend again in another time and would know that these people, his people had made it safely home.

Tame Tiger, Lacey, Miguel and Jillie stood frozen until they could not see or hear anything of the clans. Tame Tiger looked all around one last time and turned to Lacey.

"It is time to go home my dear wife and follow the destiny set out before us," Tame Tiger said and also called out into the night for Storm Cloud and Warrior Girl to come find them.

In moments, the horses appeared with a surprise. Tame Tiger's black stallion, Shadow of the Night, was also with them. Tame Tiger ran to greet his beloved horse. The horse neighed and ferociously bucked his head all around. He was trying to tell his tale of capture and escape. Tame Tiger knew this fearless animal had fought to be free. The day was almost gone and the darkness would not allow any further search for Blake, Beautiful Butterfly and her horse. Tame Tiger knew he would return to search the land again. But for now, he had to get his wife, Jillie and Miguel back to their time. So much needed to be done for Blake's family. Lacey did not speak one word. She knew exactly what Tame Tiger, her Will, was thinking.

Tye and Tess changed to their kitten forms and jumped upon Storm Cloud's back.

Miguel gave Jillie a hug and quietly whispered. "It's time to get back to our lives too."

The stone lit up, but no one noticed this time.

The four of them led the horses back to the time portal in total silence.

17 A FARM, A FAMILY, FOREVER STRONG

Lacey began the search for Blake, Jillie returned to school and Will left to the mountains with Miguel so that Lacey had time to mourn with not only her own family, but also Blake's. The authorities were called in and many days were spent walking the farm for clays. Finally, Blake's disappearance was added to unsolved mysteries. Lacey and Blake's family held a memorial ceremony in his honor.

Jillie, Miguel, Will, Adam, all the cousins, Lacey's parents, Jillie's parents and many others came together for the memorial on the farm. Jeremy, Stacey, Luke and little Nadia were there too. Everyone also found out that Nadia had a miraculous turn of health and the doctors had pronounced her free of cancer. Now the family was very involved with the annual Light the Night Walk to not only celebrate Nadia's great fortune, but to help other's battling a blood cancer.

Even Tea came with Nadia, who the family had come to love. Jeremy even shared the funny stories of Tea being so protective of his daughter and told everyone he thought the cat might be possessed. Lacey and Jillie chuckled to themselves.

The day did not end with sadness, but with excitement. Warrior Girl went into labor and the twins were born. Jillie and Adam were the most excited with birth of foal and a colt. Jillie got her girl and Adam got his boy.

A feast was prepared, as the girls' had seen done many years ago to celebrate Blake's eternal journey.

Jillie and Adam huddled together to discuss the names of their new arrivals.

"We have decided on their names," Jillie said. My foal will be named Blake's Little Girl and we'll call her Little Girl. Adam will call his colt, Blake's Baby Boy."

Lacey's eyes filled with tears again and sobbed, but couldn't run into Will's arms. Will watched as his wife cried into her father's arms. He wanted to walk over and grab her, but he didn't. He just stood there hurting for his love.

Miguel put his arm on Will's shoulder. "In time Will, in time."

As the day came to an end, Will and Miguel stuck around to mingle with Lacey's and Jillie's families.

Finally Will made his move and walked over to Lacey's parents. "I would like to remain on the farm and help Lacey get things going. I really enjoyed my time here and I know how hard it will be without Blake to help her." Will stood proud and he spoke with confidence.

Wayne and Ginger looked at one another and then looked at Lacey.

"Well, it's not really up to us, but why don't you ask Lacey," Wayne said.

"I agree," Ginger said. "Lacey is a big girl now. She doesn't need us making decisions for her."

Will smiled, because this is what he needed to hear. He was free to court his wife now. And court her, he would do.

Miguel did the same thing and tried to warm up to Jillie's dad, but he was a tough one to break. Finally Miguel started talking about hunting and fishing in the mountains and Kent actually cracked a smile. The man actually let his guard down a bit. He wasn't too happy when he learned Miguel was also going to State for a vet degree. Aiken and Miguel were already buddies and he had given Miguel his okay to date his sister. Karla adored Miguel and really liked his parents too, especially since they were good friends with her sister.

Tye, Tess and Tea ran around like happy cats and all three of them returned to circle Nadia throughout the day. Nadia would hug them all and whatever she said the cats seemed to react to her request. Of course, this totally freaked out Jeremy.

"Do you think our daughter is the one possessed?" Jeremy asked his wife.

Lacey overheard her uncle and wanted to burst out laughing. She ran and grabbed Jillie to tell her what their uncle had said. The girls ran over to their little cousin and picked her up and gave her a big hug. The cats all ran over and joined in with the girls.

"Let me get a picture of that," Jeremy said and grabbed his camera.

The girls stooped down with the three cats sitting in front of them.

Lacey and Jillie looked at one another and remembered seeing this picture in the house three hundred years in the future. Cold chills ran down their spines, as they posed for the picture that would adorn this family farm forever. The magic and the mystery never end.

THE MAGIC AND THE MYSTERY NEVER END!

The Magical Cats

Written by-

GK (Laura Beth's sister-in-law)

There once were two girls that found a cat.
The cat had two kittens that they found in a house.
The girls loved the cats and name them Tess and Tye.
They seemed to disappear, but where and why?

Chorus:
But, the cats came back. They would not stay away.
They came right back to the house everyday.
The cats came back; they just wanted to play.
They lead the girls to a land far away.

The girls found tunnels under the house.
The mother cat led them as quiet as a mouse.
The tunnels lead them back to a land long ago.
They found a lost uncle they didn't even know.

(Chorus)

The house and the cats are very magical.
Come join the two girls for adventure and fun.
The cats will lead you to a different time and place.
So hurry and come follow them before it's too late.

(Chorus)

Made in the USA
Charleston, SC
26 August 2016